The Chronicles Of

Dia & Spora

Néomi Ngera

THE CHRONICLES OF DIA & SPORA

Cover design by Amoni Green Agbenoo

ISBN: 978-1-7399000-0-7

Contact: neomingera@gmail.com

Printed in the United Kingdom

Dedication

To My Sylva, Lubu, Wutor & Dzi
If laughter is the best medicine,
then you have been my physicians,
with your inimitable brand of wit and quirkiness.
It's actually quite scary imagining what I would be without
your inspiration, encouragement, guidance, humility and love.

The God I serve has been beside me unfailingly...
It's even scarier to imagine what everything would be like,
if this were not the case.

"You keep complaining; you say that you are last...
But who do you think is going to willingly move out of the way,
or exchange places with you, so that they can now become last?"
KoSyAg

Contents *(1)*

The year is 1995

The year is 2019

Contents *(2)*

Contents *(3)*

The Writer

I'm just an ordinary woman and proud to be an African one. There's nothing much more to say about myself; but somehow, I think that's enough.

Once upon a time I thought: perhaps I could've been a media professional... a reporter or correspondent... I think I would've enjoyed the ad hoc life of being here, there and everywhere; yesterday, today and tomorrow. Well that's how I imagined it would be like anyway. I would think of what I could've probably written, reported on, edited, made up... excuse me... made up headlines for, and all that. I would think about stories and events that I could've covered, but never did. Then I would think some more, and console myself somewhat... maybe I wouldn't have been that good a reporter anyway... And the ad hoc life... would that really have suited me? Hmmm? But I'll never really know, will I, because that ship has sailed right on by.

I gave up hoping and dreaming and all that, as one must at some point.

And then, seemingly from nowhere... slowly but surely, into sharp focus, came Morowa and Kira... I don't think I'll ever really get over the shock... and delight... of meeting them. I have had the unique opportunity and the privilege of 'listening to'... OK, 'eavesdropping on' them and a few of their acquaintances' phone calls, over a year or so... At last! By cataloguing some of their calls, I got the chance, albeit a brief and mini one, to sort of live my media dream, because it was just like doing some reporting.

Apart from the first time when Morowa and Kira meet in person, all the other conversations are three way calls... *you, My Dear Reader,* being the third party... And that's why some of the dialogues may appear a bit lengthy, because you see, it would've been too much...

a bit boring in fact... to record every 'yes', 'no', 'hmmm'...'are you serious?', 'what?' and so on... so, I'll leave you to fill in some of those, OK? I'm sure you won't mind.

Have I got any regrets? Of course; there were some 'juicy' calls I *really* wanted to include... but after careful consideration and taking well-meaning advice, I had to leave them out... for your wellbeing and safety... and mine too, if you know what I mean.

We all know that life can get quite serious and intense sometimes, so I hope the characters you meet as you turn the pages will help you relax a little, and make you smile now and again. Well, that's the plan anyway.

Néomi Ngera

Acknowledgements

I would like to acknowledge all the people you may be reminded of, in one way or the other, as you read The Chronicles of Dia & Spora; they are the real stars in all this.

There just wouldn't be enough space to thank all the people I really need to, so for the sake of brevity, I'll narrow things down thus:

I would sincerely like to thank those who've read The Chronicles and left many uplifting comments, such as those below, thereby sort of validating my effort, helping me to overcome my doubts and believe in myself, and just generally making this my hesitant venture into writing, feel so very worthwhile.

*"Néomi Ngera, high spirited and whip smart, has brought to life
a set of amazing and rich cast of "Diasporan" characters.
Enjoy and get engrossed in the antics of Moro, Kira, their
family and friends, in this witty, quirky page-turner..."*
Gloria B

*"Hilariously funny with a delicious verve and energy to relax
and enjoy. A number one read..."*
Lily G

*"So relatable. It's like the writer's somehow been spying
and eavesdropping on me, my friends and family, but in such
a refreshing way. It's very cleverly written and something that
people from diverse backgrounds will definitely appreciate
and enjoy..."*
Florence A

*"I read the C of D&S in a day, no exaggeration. I could not
put it down. It's so smooth, it just flows. I've read lots of
books... this one is going to go down as one of my favourites..."*
Janet M

*"For some reason I thought this was something that would
appeal mainly to women. I was wrong. This is an insightful
narrative for everyone..."*
Ernest O

The year is 1995

Tuesday 25 July

THERE ARE SOME PEOPLE IN THIS WORLD

**It's about 5.30 pm at a bus stop at the Elephant & Castle, London.
Very few people had personal mobile phones then.
Morowa and Kira have just got off the same bus.**

**Kira realises her bag feels a bit different; and a quick rummage
through it, has left her with a look, and not just on her face...
a look all round, that Morowa cannot ignore.**

They have never met one another before.

Morowa walks up to Kira.

Morowa
Are you OK?

Kira
Hmmm... I can't find my pouch... I don't know if I dropped it on
the bus or what... my purse, pager... everything's in there...

Morowa
Oh no... Was it in *this* bag?

(Morowa points to the bag Kira's holding.)

Kira
Yes...

Morowa
I don't think it would be that easy for something to just fall out
of this bag... just like that...

Kira
Well exactly...

Morowa
Hmmm... hmmm...

Kira
What? What is it?

Morowa
Well, I'm just putting two and two together here... I don't know
if you noticed a girl standing right next to you on the bus... she
was wearing like a jeans jacket...

Kira
Which girl? The bus was so crowded... everyone was wriggling
for space... I didn't really notice anybody or anything...

Morowa
Well, where I was sitting, I noticed her... and one or two other
dodgy looking ones too...

Kira
Oh my God... don't tell me you saw her take...

Morowa
To be honest, I didn't actually see anybody take anything... but
she looked *very* suspicious... that much I can tell you... you
could tell she was up to no good... And if I'm not mistaken, I
think she jumped off after just one stop... so...

Kira
Oh, what is this now? It must've been her... she's taken my
purse, my pager, my bank card... only God knows what else...
She took the *whole pouch*... just like that...

Morowa
When the buses are so full, it's a paradise for thieves... and some of them are so damn smart... you can't beat them... they know all the tricks... and when they see the slightest opportunity, they will not miss it... She's probably on another bus doing exactly the same thing to somebody else as we speak...

Kira
So what kind of bad luck is this now, eh?

Morowa
Well, what can you do? These things happen...

Kira
All I wanted to do was get to the hospital... Guy's... and my husband will pick me up from there... What do I do now? I don't think I had much in my purse... but my bank card... my cheque book... What kind of trouble is this now?

Morowa
You need to contact your bank so they can stop them...

Kira
My bank will be fed up with me... they replaced that card just two weeks ago, because I misplaced the last one...

Morowa
And you probably need to go to the police as well...

Kira
I didn't even think of that, you know... thank you...

Morowa
Actually, you could even contact the bus people as well... it's possible someone could hand it in... but to be honest, I wouldn't hold my breath...

Kira
Look, I didn't bargain for this at all today... And I was in such
high spirits before all this... my sister's just had a baby boy...
early this morning... that's why I'm heading to the hospital...

Morowa
Oh... congratulations...

Kira
Thank you...

Morowa
Anyway, what do you want to do now? Police, or bank, or...?

Kira
You know what, I think I'd better call my husband first...

Morowa
Oh, OK...

Kira
But you know something... hmmm... you have to help me oh,
my sister... As I am now, I haven't got a penny on me...

Morowa
Oh, don't worry, I've got some coins... hang on a minute... here...

(Morowa hands some coins over to Kira.)

Kira
Thank you *so* much... I really appreciate this...

Morowa
You're welcome...

Kira
I just hope to God my husband hasn't left work yet, because if he

has... then I really don't know what I'm going to do...

Morowa
Well, I hope you get him... Ah, let me rush... I need that C244 coming, so I need to get to that other bus stop over there...

Kira
OK... mind how you go... thank you *so* much...

Morowa
You're very welcome... all the best...

(As Morowa rushes off, Kira walks a few yards to a phone booth. About five minutes later, she walks back towards the bus stop Morowa had rushed off to and is now waiting at.)

Kira
Ah... you're still here? You didn't get on that bus?

Morowa
It was packed... in fact it's like they're all packed today... the last one didn't even stop... just drove straight past... Anyway, did you get your husband?

Kira
No... I think he's already left work... he must be driving to the hospital now... I wanted to call one or two other people... but of course my address book was in the pouch... so that's gone too...

Morowa
Oh no...

Kira
And I'm just too confused to remember anybody's number off head now... You know what, I'm just going to walk to the hospital... when I get there, I'll be fine... Thank you so much for all your help...

Morowa

Oh don't mention... but...

Kira

Oh, I didn't use all the coins, so here... thank you...

(Kira attempts to hand the coins back to Morowa.)

Morowa

Oh come on... it's just a few pence... But you say you want to *walk*... from here to Guy's?

Kira

It's not that far...

Morowa

You can't do that... it's not just round the corner... Wait... let me see how much I have...

(Morowa looks for her purse.)

Kira

Oh no, no... Please, don't worry... you've done enough already... I'll be OK... honestly...

Morowa

I don't think so, you know... It's quite a long walk... And look, you're shaking... you're a bit stressed... Look, I've got my bus pass, so I'm OK... Here... take this... it's just a pound and a few more coins... It's not much, but at least it'll get you to Guy's... Then you say your husband will be meeting you there, right?

Kira

Yes... Look, I don't know what to say... I don't even know how I'm feeling at the moment...

Morowa

Let me tell you, I was on a train once... I had my bag on the seat next to me... I put my hand in my bag to get something, and someone else's hand was in it...

Kira
What?

Morowa
Can you imagine? I don't think I've ever been so shocked... So I think I have a rough idea how you're feeling at the moment...

Kira
There are some people in this world...

Morowa
Oh most definitely... they say 'it takes all sorts'... But anyway... let me see if I can fight my way onto this one coming now... But look oh... this one looks just as full... What's going on? Will I get home today?

(Morowa is determined to get on this bus. Kira starts to make her way to the next bus stop where she'll get a bus to the hospital. When the bus Morowa is meant to be on goes past her, Kira can't believe it when she turns back and Morowa is still standing at the bus stop. Kira walks back towards Morowa... again.)

Kira
You mean you couldn't get on this one too?

Morowa
I think there's probably a strike or something... this is too much... something's *definitely* going on...

Kira
Oh sorry... You know what, I don't want to hold you up any more, but before the next bus comes, *please* can I have your details?

Morowa
You want my details? You chatting me up now?

(They laugh)

Kira
I *have* to pay you back... somehow...

Morowa
Oh, don't be silly...

Kira
Well, I must have 'silly' or *something* written all over me...
Otherwise why would that so-and-so rob me... just like that?

Morowa
Well... we're not hundred percent sure it was her... but I'd bet
good money it was... she definitely looked somehow... You
know what, just leave that unwashed whatever she is to her
karma... You can see she's the type that causes misery anywhere
she goes... If she actually nicked your stuff, she'll get what's
coming to her, don't worry...

(Morowa writes her details down and hands over to Kira.)

Morowa
I hope you can read my handwriting...

Kira
Morowa?

Morowa
That's right... Morowa Owusu...

Kira
From Ghana, right?

Morowa

Mm-hmm... And I'm guessing from your accent that you're from... Sierra Leone?

Kira

Yes... you're right...

Morowa

Aha... I thought as much... I've actually met quite a few Sierra Leoneans... I met some when I was studying... there's a few in my church... nice people... And it was nice meeting *you* too... in spite of *everything*...

Kira

Ah... same here...

Morowa

And congratulations again for your nephew... I bet you, he'll be very troublesome... just like the day he was born...

(They laugh)

And that was how Morowa and Kira met... in person, of course.

Kira called Morowa to thank her again; they chatted and Kira invited her to the baby, Omar's christening. Kira was delighted when Morowa attended, and told everyone there about the unusual circumstances in which they had met a few months earlier. And the rest, as they say, is history... or, in this case, 'herstory'...

All the following conversations in this novelogue, are over the phone.

About Morowa & Kira

Morowa, a teacher, was born and raised in Ghana. She came to the UK in the mid-1980s to study, where she met **Sonny**, also a Ghanaian. They got married and have a daughter, **Debbie**. Morowa adopted her niece, **Kukua**, daughter of her older brother **Yaa**, and brought her to the UK to live with her. Debbie and Kukua are very close in age, and even though they are first cousins by birth, technically the adoption made them sisters, and they've always seen each other as such; in fact they share a flat together. Morowa also has a younger sister, **Wusi**, who like Yaa, lives in Ghana.

Kira is of a similar age to Morowa; she came to the UK from Sierra Leone with her husband Quincy (**QC**) in the early 1990s. QC worked for an oil company in Sierra Leone, before being offered a scholarship by the parent company to study in the UK. Kira accompanied QC to the UK, and she embarked on a course in social work. They both finished their studies successfully and were planning to return to Sierra Leone, but by then civil war had broken out there; so they ended up staying in the UK. They have two grown up sons, **Ralston** and **Richie**, but their marriage failed and they legally separated. Kira has an older sister **Salma,** who lives in America, and a younger one **Nish** (Nausha), who lives in London with her husband **Bolu**, and **Omar**, 'the baby', is their son.

A list of the characters and some miscellaneous African words are on pages 412-413.

The year is 2019

1   Wednesday 16 January

Earlier in the day

WHAT'S WRONG NOW?

Kukua is on a break in Ghana, visiting her birth parents, Afia, who she calls 'Sissy', and Yaa (Morowa's brother), who she calls 'Papa'. Afia and Yaa are married, but Yaa has a second wife who he lives with in Accra, whilst Afia lives in the village. Having lived with her Aunty Morowa and her husband, Sonny, in the UK for most of her life, Kukua calls them 'Mummy', and 'Daddy'.

Featuring Mrs Osei, Morowa's friend from church, Lisa, Kukua's friend, Wusi, Morowa's sister and Efa, Sonny's sister.

Morowa in the UK calls Kukua in Ghana.

Morowa
So if I die now, you and Debbie will have the nerve to stand in front of people, shedding crocodile tears left and right, about how you can't believe I'm gone... how you miss me... how you would've done anything for me to have stayed longer... and this and that... when in reality both of you would've been *solely* responsible for killing me...

Kukua
(Laughs)
So we're murderers now? Hi Mum...

Morowa
Don't 'hi' me... don't 'hi' me at all... You mean you haven't seen my missed calls?

Kukua
Mum, is this really the way to start a conversation?

Morowa
Oh... show me how to start a conversation then, Kukua... show me...

Kukua
Mum... Sissy and I have been trying to get you... but it's just crazy out here sometimes... If you'd called about an hour ago, you wouldn't have got me, because my phone was stone dead... I've just started charging it because the light's just come back on... it's been off since last night... The light's one thing... the network's always playing up as well... it's just too much sometimes... To be honest, I just can't wait to get back... I've had enough...

Morowa
But Debbie says the two of you spoke just a couple of days ago...

Kukua
It was about two o'clock in the morning... I was sending her a message when she came online, so we talked... but I couldn't have called *you* then... But I've sent you a couple of messages though... check your phone...

Morowa
Really? I didn't see any message... But first things first... Have you been taking your anti-malarial tablets?

Kukua
They make me feel sick...

Morowa
That's not what I asked you? Listen, taking them is not an option oh, Kukua... you just *have* to take them... I don't have to remind you; you know very well what malaria can do... you know where we ended up the last time...

Kukua

I've been taking them...

Morowa

You answered too quickly... too sharp... I don't believe you...

Kukua

Mum, I *have*... and on top of that, Sissy has been forcing me to drink those herbs and leaves... they taste like outright poison... According to her, they cured me the last time...

Morowa

What do you mean 'according to her'? Those herbs actually work better than the tablets, I'm telling you... no side effects... because they're pure... organic... no fancy chemicals... What do you think they gave us when we were growing up?

Kukua

Well that explains a whole lot... if they made you drink stuff like that all the time... urgh... oh my God... No wonder you and your mates have so many problems...

Morowa

Which mates and which problems are those?

(They laugh)

Morowa

Actually, you know what... tell Afia to give you some of those herbs for me... they're very good... and not just for malaria...

Kukua

So it's an all cure...

Morowa

It is oh.... But you know what Kukua, I have a problem...

Kukua
Oh... What's wrong now, Mum?

Morowa
It's Mrs Osei...

Kukua
Oh, her?

Morowa
Look, she called me almost in tears yesterday... She says you refused to take the stuff from her nephew in Accra, to bring back for her...

Kukua
That's right...

Morowa
What do you mean 'that's right'?

Kukua
I agreed to take a few things Mum, not a suitcase...

Morowa
But she said it was just one small bag...

Kukua
No it wasn't... it was about the same size as that red bag, the one you've got those duvets in... and I'm not exaggerating... It was definitely a suitcase... Oh, I should've taken a picture...

Morowa
OK... So you mean you're not going to bring her things?

Kukua
I actually took some of the stuff from her nephew... but I'm sorry... I couldn't take everything...

Morowa

But she needs those things for her business...

Kukua

So hang on Mum... is that how she runs her business? Looking for people... just anybody who can bring things over for her?

Morowa

Kukua... please... she's relying on you... and you did agree... She's such a nice lady, she'll be so disappointed...

Kukua

She should be disappointed alright... in herself... And I'm afraid she's just going to have to rely on somebody else... What kind of liberty is that? Asking someone to take *all* that... So where am I supposed to put *my* stuff?

Morowa

OK, you know what... for *my* sake, bring all her stuff, whatever the cost... If you get excess, pay it, I'll reimburse you...

Kukua

No Mum... I won't let you do that... that's just taking advantage, plain and simple... In any case, it's too late now, I've already taken what I can squeeze in... I just haven't got any more space...

Morowa

You should've spoken to me first before sending her nephew away...

Kukua

How did I send him away? *I* actually went to meet him in Accra to collect the things... and it was sheer hell with the traffic and all that... You know what, I shouldn't have got involved in this whole thing with Mrs Osei... I was just trying to be helpful... But what have I got out of it all? Stress, that's what...

Morowa
OK... So what do you want me to say to her now?

Kukua
I don't know... tell her the truth... Apart from *my* stuff, I've got stuff for you... and I've got Lisa's favours... they're actually quite bulky... I didn't realise how much space they would take...

Morowa
Which Lisa?

Kukua
Huh? Which other Lisa, Mum? Our Lisa...

Morowa
Oh... So you actually want me to remember Lisa? Lisa who pushed me in your kitchen?

Kukua
Mum, she didn't push you... please let's not go over all that again...

Morowa
No, let's go over it... So are you saying she didn't push me... or what? So I'm lying... is that it? So you mean you're going to leave my stuff behind so you can take *hers*? Prioritise her over me? Why wouldn't she push me? She may even punch or kick me next time she sees me... Because if *you* can treat me like this, what should stop her? So I'm at the very bottom of the pecking order here? I see...

Kukua
You're twisting things now, Mum... it's not *your* stuff... and you

know Debs and I decided ages ago that we'd get favours done over here for Lisa's wedding... way before Mrs Osei even got wind of me travelling... And I wonder how she even got that wind...

Morowa
Look, you know we all help each other out at church if we're travelling... take money, medicines, little parcels...

Kukua
It wasn't a little parcel... at all...
(Hisses)

Morowa
Kukua, did you just hiss?

Kukua
No...

Morowa
I sincerely hope not... And let me tell you something else... make sure I don't see Lisa's favours oh... make sure... because if I do, I'll destroy every last one... She will not enjoy them...

Kukua
Mum, I think the line's going... it's fading in and out... I can barely hear you... I've got to go now...

Morowa
Well *I* can hear you clearly... don't go yet oh... this network thing... If we're not careful, we may not be able to talk again before you leave... You're arriving on Saturday, right?

Kukua
No, I'm *leaving* on Saturday night, arriving Sunday morning... I've already sent Dad the details anyway...

Morowa
I hope you've collected the ashoebis?

Kukua
I saw the seamstress yesterday... she says all that's left are the zips... she says she'll drop them off *herself* when she closes today...

Morowa
Ah... Kukua... you mean you haven't actually collected them yet?

Kukua
Mum, I've told you, they're ready... I would have had them by now if you and Aunty Kira had made up your minds earlier about the styles you wanted... Look, don't get yourself worked up... they're done... Will there be anything else, Madam?

Morowa
Who are you calling 'Madam'? Are you crazy? Apart from the ashoebis and one or two other things, what else did I ask you for?

(SILENCE)

Morowa
No tell me... So just some dried fish, palm oil... a little bit of gari and some pepper... is that the problem? You know something Kukua, you are just *so*...

Kukua
Don't stress yourself looking for a word, Mum... I know I'm *'so'*... Seriously Mum... why can't your generation just wish someone 'safe journey' and leave it at that? But no... it's 'can you take this, can you bring that'... Papa and Aunty Wusi have told me to leave space for the stuff they've got for you as well...

As for Aunty Efa... she's actually going to meet me at the airport... she says she's got some slippers for you and Daddy... and you know there's no way Aunty will turn up with just slippers... Now you've just added those poisonous malaria herbs to the shopping cart...

Morowa
So, what are you saying? I can't ask you to do anything for me without getting a mouthful from you every time? So just bringing these few things for me now is such a big deal? Is that it? It's OK... don't worry... this is the last time I'm going to ask you for anything, you hear? The very last time... Anyway, is Afia there? Let me say 'hi' to her before I go...

Kukua
She's in a meeting with some of her clients... she'll call you as soon as she's done... In fact, just this morning she was asking me if there was anything else I could think of that you would like from over here... Do you need anything else, Mum?

Morowa
I thought you said you don't have any more space? Isn't that what you've just told me?

Kukua
Mum, just calm down...

Morowa
I say I don't need anything else... I'm fine... thank you...

2   Wednesday 16 January

Later in the day

THE USUAL COCK AND BULL STORY

Featuring Morowa's elderly friend, Mama Abena, and Tarina, Ralston's on-off girlfriend.

Morowa
When I do what I have to do, people will say, 'Moro always takes things too far... Moro is a bad person, etc, etc'...

Kira
(Laughs)
What's happened now?

Morowa
It's not a laughing matter, oh... If you hear the way Kukua spoke to me just now...

Kira
Is she back?

Morowa
She's back on Sunday...

Kira
So how long did she go for?

Morowa
About three weeks...

Kira
So what's her problem?

Morowa
Just after a few days in the village, she's turning like the people back home... *they* always reach you when they want something, but *you* can't reach them... I've been trying to get her for how many days now... She was telling me the usual cock and bull story of no network, no electricity... no this and that... Instead of going to stay with her father in Accra, where she could've relaxed like a human being, with all possible comfort, she had to go and stay with her mother and her miserable people in the village... people who are still figuring out what sunlight is, never mind electricity...

Kira
They can't be that bad...
(Laughs)

Morowa
They're worse...

Kira
So you mean she didn't spend any time at her father's place?

Morowa
If I want to be honest, I can't really blame her; the last time she stayed there, she and Yaa's second wife actually came to blows... They're almost the same age... in fact, Kukua's actually older...

Kira
Oh... So that his wife is *younger* than Kukua? So how will there be peace?

Morowa
I don't know... Anyway, my problem now is, Kukua promised to

bring some stuff back for one of my church members... now she says she's going to leave some of the things behind... I don't know what I'm going to tell the woman...

Kira
You and your church people... please... Look, as long as she brings our ashoebi... tell me she's got those...

Morowa
She hasn't oh... she was telling me something about the zips...

Kira
Ah... Kukua had better not disappoint us oh...

Morowa
Well this is the thing... we have to be in top form at Mama Abena's 90th...

Kira
That her last bash was a showstopper... ten good years ago, and we still talk about it... I can imagine what they'll do this time...

Morowa
Oh no, as for that family... they don't do things by halves... We're in for a very good time... no two ways about that...

Kira
The invitation alone tells you they mean business...

Morowa
Oh yes... And the ashoebi's not for everybody, you know... they handpicked the people they gave it to... only very close people to Mama will be wearing it... I told you they made it especially in Gabon for this birthday... It's not over the counter stuff that anybody can just go and buy anywhere...

Kira

Oh you can tell it's not the usual stuff at all... it's unique... You said her mother was from there... Gabon, right?

Morowa

No... her *father*... he was from there... he went to work in Ghana and that's where he met her mother...

Kira

No wonder, you can tell... she looks somehow 'foreign', that Mama Abena...

Morowa

She does actually...

Kira

You know what... we could've saved ourselves a whole lot of stress if we'd just sewn the ashoebi here...

Morowa

What's the big deal? Give fabric to the seamstress... collect the sewn dresses... put in your suitcase and bring back... Tell me, where's the stress in that? And it's so much cheaper to get these things made up back home... And that seamstress, she may be a villager, but she's really good... she really knows her stuff...

Kira

I know, but... OK, if for whatever reason Kukua doesn't bring them now, someone else can bring them for us later on... We've got plenty time anyway...

Morowa

If she leaves them behind, you think it'll be that easy to find someone else to bring them? You know our people... it will be back and forth, here and there... give it to this person, give it to the other... before we know what's happening the ashoebi will go missing... We'll end up with nothing if we're not careful...

Kira
Look, worst case scenario... we'll go and look for something else... something to match the colours...

Morowa
You and who? So we'll look like we weren't properly invited... like slaves who just couldn't afford it?

Kira
(Laughs)
How will not wearing the ashoebi make us look like uninvited slaves? Come on, it'll be annoying and disappointing and all that... but it's not the end of the world if we don't wear it...

Morowa
Whether beginning or end of this world or the next... no world will be able to contain me and Kukua if she comes back minus those ashoebis... By the time I'm through with her, my God...

Kira
(Laughs)

Morowa
It's not funny at all... you needed to hear her on the phone just now... her whole manner... just wrong... And the final insult... I didn't want to talk to Afia as such, but out of politeness, I asked for her so I could say 'hello'... What did I hear next? 'She's in a meeting, with clients...'

Kira
(Laughs)

Morowa
Help me laugh... that illiterate pest... now she's in meetings...

Hey-hey... she's completely forgotten the days when she was selling palm kernels virtually on the roadside with her mother... before my brother picked and brushed her up... Now she's graduated to labelled palm oil... on shelves...

Kira
So she didn't talk to you?

Morowa
That's what I'm trying to tell you... I distinctly heard her voice in the background... Are you telling me she couldn't have just stepped aside for a moment to talk to me? Now she's a big girl, she doesn't need me any more... I don't blame her... In days gone by when she was desperate for money and things, she would've actually driven everybody away, just to clear the way to be able talk to me... Now she's got 'clients'... OK...
(Hisses)

Kira
Don't worry... I'm sure she'll call back...

Morowa
Worried? I'm not worried oh... that's her business... I don't care... I used to take her side over my brother... openly... *you* know that... But as time has gone by, I've been getting a clearer picture of what my brother must have suffered with her, before he finally decided to go and stay with this his second wife...

Kira
Calm down... Whatever the case, you've always had a pretty good relationship with that your sister-in-law...

Morowa
If I didn't have time for her, would I have taken her daughter... at the age of six? Kukua was just six when I brought her to this

country... One time when I was having problems with the immigration people over here, and I told Afia, the way things were going, I may have to send Kukua back to her... I'll never forget the way she screamed... that did I want people to laugh at her? Did I want people to say that her daughter must be the youngest person to ever be deported from Europe?

(They laugh)

Kira
I remember at one point they even wanted your grandfather's birth certificate...

Morowa
And marriage certificate as well... I'll never forget the look on the immigration woman's face when I said to her: 'Look here, my grandfather himself didn't know when he was born, and he had five wives... So where do I start?'

(They laugh)

Morowa
Look, as a Christian, I try to watch myself... but I have put up with so much nonsense from Kukua and Afia, you just can't imagine... So this is the thanks I get for rescuing Kukua and giving her such a good life... my own kindness is strangling me now... that's what's happening here... As for Afia, if I tell you her story... You know I told you Yaa had a terrible car accident...

Kira
Yes, but funnily enough, you've never really gone into much detail about that...

Morowa
March 1988... I will never forget... I was in my little flat studying

for a re-sit, so I was already well stressed out... Next thing I get a call from home... people were screaming in the background... Cut a very long story short, Yaa was in hospital... someone had offered him a lift home after some drinking session or something like that... next thing accident... driver dead...

Kira
Oh... The driver actually died?

Morowa
Oh yes... Luckily they'd dropped off a few people beforehand, otherwise things could've been much worse... You know our people: they'd packed about ten people into a four or five-seater...

Kira
Oh, that's just normal for us...

Morowa
But anyway, when the accident actually happened, it was just Yaa and the driver... We're not too sure whether the driver was drunk, dozed off or what... But as for Yaa... by the time they got him to hospital, they were talking amputation... of both legs...

Kira
What?

Morowa
Only God helped him... But you've seen him now... he walks a bit funny...

Kira
Well... just a bit of a limp...

Morowa
You call that a *limp*? He was critical for months... He had to

learn to walk again... he couldn't talk properly for a good while...
He's never been quite right since then... any time I even think
about it, I get very upset... that's why I think I've never really
explained... Yaa's always been a wheeler dealer kind of person...
so before the accident he always seemed to have money, he was
looking after the folks back home... so I wasn't under too much
pressure to send anything back regularly... But when he ended
up in a coma... couldn't do anything... I had to step up to support
all of them back home... including this Afia... she'd had the
twins by then... Overnight I became more or less the sole
breadwinner for everybody... And apart from food, school fees
and normal, regular things, there were medical bills to pay now
as well... It was not easy...

Kira
Wow...

Morowa
At one time I was doing *two* jobs... and studying... When I look
back, honestly, I don't how I managed... exams... work... And
then of course back then, we didn't have all these plenty money
transfer places like now... so you had to look for someone going
home to take money and stuff for you to your people...

Kira
And you had three options: the person could deliver all, some or
nothing to your people... you just had to take the chance...

Morowa
Of course you know that's how I met Sonny... I was looking for
someone to take some money for me, and one of my course
mates knew that Sonny was going home... so he introduced us...

Kira
Sonny made us all laugh at your party when he said in his

speech, that he worries to this day about you taking lifts from strangers... the way you apparently jumped into his car the first day you met him... according to him...

Morowa
Don't mind him... if you see the rusty death-trap he was calling a car... nobody in their right senses would've entered that thing willingly... He more or less abducted me... in broad daylight... and he knows it...

(They laugh)

Morowa
But seriously, when he saw how much trouble I was in... financially, emotionally, in fact all round... he began to help me out... Without him... honestly... I don't know what would've happened to me... I think I would've just gone under...

Kira
Awww...

Morowa
And it's not as if he didn't have his own problems... far from it... He was feeding and clothing his own people back home too... and of course that's never stopped...

Kira
No, that doesn't stop... once you get on that treadmill of supporting our people, that's it... you just can't get off... It's like you've signed some lifelong contract with them...

Morowa
Exactly... with a never, ever get-out clause...

(They laugh)

Morowa
But seriously, back then in those days, we weren't so scared of people... particularly our black brothers... they weren't really a problem... We took lifts from them anyhow, even though some of them were complete strangers... They were quite frisky alright, but they were harmless...

Kira
They couldn't afford to be harmful... they weren't that many, so they were very easy for police and immigration to track down...

(They laugh)

Morowa
Oh, I miss those, carefree days...

Kira
Very much... I think life was safer and simpler then... Don't know whether that was just down to the fact that there was less drama, or the fact that the media was different... no internet and all that... so we just weren't being bombarded with news and information like nowadays... Who knows? But anyway, you were telling me about Afia... and the accident...

Morowa
Oh yes... So with her husband... my brother... drifting between life and death... with two children already... the twins... in that desperate situation... Afia had the raw nerve to announce that she was pregnant... again...

Kira
What do you mean, 'she had the nerve'?

Morowa
Are you listening to me? Yaa was in a coma... couldn't stand up, couldn't open his eyes... totally lifeless and helpless... Tell me

where the pregnancy came from in that situation? No, tell me...

Kira
So what are you saying now?

Morowa
Look, I know what I'm talking about... When Kukua was born, the dates just didn't add up... Even before the accident, I was getting reports of Afia running around... with different men...

Kira
Reports? From who?

Morowa
Look, apparently the first thing my grandmother said when she saw Kukua was: "This is not our child..." And you know old people, they can see these things...

Kira
Of course they can... through the cataracts... Please... Look, our people... old and young... they can be very mischievous... come up with anything, anyhow... OK, you know what, let's put the pregnancy down to juju, OK?
(Laughs)

Morowa
So, how did you guess?

Kira
Look, I was just kidding...

Morowa
Well I'm not... Afia's family are well known juju people... It's one of the main reasons she and Yaa broke up: she would drag my brother to fetish priests and shrines here, there and everywhere... day and night... At a point, he just couldn't cope...

Kira
But the few times I've met her... she struck me as quite sweet...

Morowa
Afia? Sweet? She's as sly as... Who do you think is putting Kukua up to cheek and defy me like this? Today's rudeness from Kukua is not a one-off... at all... She's like this all the time now... I was practically begging her on the phone... but she was telling me point blank that she can't bring stuff for me, but she can bring for some stupid friend... But we shall see...

Kira
That's how they all are, these our children... selfish, awkward... The last time I went to the US for that wedding with Ralston... you know then we were entitled to two suitcases each... he was hell-bent on taking just *one*...

Morowa
I don't understand... So he wanted to let free baggage allowance go just like that?

Kira
Can you imagine? And I had so much stuff to take there... not to mention what I had to bring back after shopping like mad over there... He was telling me: "Mum, there's no rule that says you have to use *all* your baggage allowance all the time..."

Morowa
This oyibo way they think sometimes, it's beyond annoying... Was he crazy or what? But what's all this nonsense from these children?

Kira
The thing is, they're not even children any more... but the nonsense just doesn't seem to stop...

Morowa
Anyway, how is he? I haven't seen him for ages...

Kira
Ralston? He's all over the place with work...

Morowa
How's Tarina?

Kira
Those two... hmmm... Things haven't been too right since the sickle cell issue...

Morowa
I know you liked her...

Kira
I did... I do... But they absolutely did the right thing to get tested... particularly as they want children... Ralston already knew his status, but Tarina didn't... Anyway, now they know they're both AS, like me and QC... with the possibility of having a sickle cell child... it's a bit of an issue...

Morowa
But they could still have children without sickle cell, right?

Kira
Oh yes... and they could have children with traits like them, or one with no traits at all, completely sickle cell free... But worst case scenario... it could be a complete sickle cell case outright... and that's no joke...

Morowa
Hmmm... I guess that's the sickle cell game... it's about how much risk you're willing to take...

Kira
Personally, I think it's irresponsible to take *any* kind of risk with sickle cell... there's too much suffering involved...

Morowa
But you and QC risked it?

Kira
'I and I', as my friend would say... ignorantly and innocently... we didn't know that much about sickle cell, full stop... never mind the risks... Back then there just wasn't as much awareness as there is nowadays... But in this day and age, there's no excuse not to get tested and know your status...

Morowa
I agree...

Kira
Anyway all is not lost... there's lots of ongoing research and new techniques to help people like them if they want to have children... The thing is, I think this sickle cell issue was in the background to start with, then they've had a bust up about something else... so things are not too good at the moment between the two of them... there's a few things going on...

Morowa
Hmmm... And what about Sir Richie? Do you know I haven't seen him for at about two or three years now?

Kira
Really? Surely it can't be that long?

Morowa
OK... well maybe a year, but it feels like three... tell him his Aunty Moro is not necessarily kicking, but still alive...

(They laugh)

Kira
He's fine... him and his creatures... He's just got dog number three now... and he's got two other small animals... can't remember exactly which ones now... The only reason he hasn't got cats is because he's allergic...

Morowa
So he's running a proper animal farm...

Kira
He says when he's made money, he's going to open a zoo...

Morowa
He should've been a vet...

Kira
I'm sure he can teach some vets a thing or two... honestly... he knows *everything*... what temperature the animals should be... if they lift their left hand it means one thing... if they close the right eye it means something else...

(They laugh)

Kira
And the amount of money he spends on them... food, medical... The last time he went on holiday, he took them all to a hotel...

Morowa
Hotel? I've heard about those places... but for God's sake...

Kira
I think he paid about seventy pounds a night... for each dog...

Morowa
Are you serious?

Kira
I wish I wasn't... The dogs had spa treatment and all...

Morowa
No... Instead of treating *us* to some spa treatment...

Kira
Well exactly... When last did I go for a spa or anything like that?

Morowa
So you mean those dogs had the nerve to go and enjoy that spa?
Look, if I see them, I'll secretly pinch or even kick them out of
pure jealousy and spite on my part...

(They laugh)

Kira
You need to see the way he's made his conservatory where he
keeps them at home... His animals are actually living in
luxury... better than he is, if you ask me...

Morowa
So you say it was his nanny who got him interested in animals...
cos I know you and animals just don't mix...

Kira
From the age of four, five... she taught him all sorts about
animals and plants and stuff like that... He would sit for hours
just watching nature programmes... he had no fear of handling
the animals; he would talk to them and all...

Morowa
I distinctly remember one Christmas, he said to me: "Aunty
Moro, tell Mummy to get me a tortoise"... and I thought to
myself, 'I don't think I'll get far with that particular request oh'...

(They laugh)

Kira
Look, that's the main reason he actually moved out and got his
own place... just so he could be free to have all these creatures

around him all the time...

Morowa
And as for Ralston, he just wanted anything he could pull to pieces...

Kira
The beating that one got from me for tampering with things... Anything he set his eyes on, he wouldn't rest until he saw inside it... The people over here would say he's just inquisitive... it's healthy for him to do all that... more or less encouraging him to tamper and break more things...

Morowa
Because *they* could afford to replace things anyhow... We were battling to save up for furniture, fridges, TVs and stuff... precious items to us... so we didn't see a child tampering with such things as 'healthy' on any level... at all...

(They laugh)

Morowa
So Richie... instead of looking for a wife to look after him, he's spending all his time and money on pets...

Kira
Well, he's told me that when he's ready to take the plunge, it'll be at very short notice, so I should be ready to go at any time... So I'm on permanent standby... So, you're now on notice too...

(They laugh)

(Morowa's other phone rings)

Morowa
Ah, it's my tormentors... Kukua and Afia... Let me hear what else they have to say, just to upset me some more now...

(They laugh)

3 *Sunday 20 January*

HOW LONG HAVE YOU KNOWN ME?

Featuring Caspar Danso, a childhood acquaintance of Morowa's.

Morowa
How come you took so long to answer?

Kira
I told you my phones are playing up... so I had to run upstairs to get this one... it's the only one working now...

Morowa
(Laughs)
I'm not surprised... they're almost as old as you are...

Kira
What do you mean? I found the receipt for them... they're only about five years old...

Morowa
I rest my case... in phone years they're elderly...

(They laugh)

Kira
Look, *I* can hear you, but *you* can't hear me too well, right?

Morowa
Yes, it's definitely a bit faint...

Kira
One or two other people have complained too... I just have to

get a new set, whether I like it or not...

Morowa
I'll send you a link... check them... they've always got deals on electrical things... So do you want me to call the mobile instead?

Kira
The mobile's in the kitchen... so I'd have to go downstairs again... no... let me manage this one...

Morowa
Look, I'm so annoyed...

Kira
What's happened now?

Morowa
Sonny left the house before 6 this morning to go pick Kukua up at the airport... by the time he got there, she'd left...

Kira
I don't understand...

Morowa
You know he has this arrangement with the girls: most times when they travel, he insists on picking them up and then dropping them off at their place... I keep telling him they can sort themselves out now, they're old enough... but no... Well, after today, maybe he'll listen and learn... There was an accident on the motorway, so he was held up a bit... so of course he told Kukua to just stay put and wait for him... In fact he was blaming *me*... as usual... saying I delayed him... how he could've left home earlier, but I insisted on him having some coffee...

Kira
You were right... it's really cold out there...

Morowa

Exactly... If he falls sick, will Kukua come and look after him? Anyway, he got to the airport and started calling her... no joy... went into the terminal to look for her... no Kukua... So of course, he was getting worried, so he called me... and he never calls me when I'm in church, unless he really has to... We called and called... we just couldn't reach her...

Kira

So what happened? Where is she?

Morowa

Eventually she called Sonny back... long story... her phone had died... she was in a taxi... in fact she was using the driver's phone... She said she just had to leave the airport, because she had a bad headache... in fact the headache had started before she left Accra... this and that... Bottom line she left the airport without seeing Sonny... Sonny didn't even sleep properly last night, because he had to be up so early to go and pick her up...

Kira

Oh... That's a bit much...

Morowa

I've been telling you about this Kukua... you think I'm just going on and on about her... it's getting too much... Sonny, of course, he's not seeing it as a big deal... even trying to make excuses for her... But *I* have had it up to here with her... Look, I've put up with her nonsense for too long... enough is enough... She really needs some home truths and she's going to get them...

Kira

Which home truths are those now?

Morowa

It's high time I tell her who her real father is... When I eventually see her, it's going to be a case of 'Happy New Year, Happy New Father'...

Kira
(Laughs)
Oh, of course, you haven't seen her yet this year...

Morowa
No... she travelled on New Year's Eve...

Kira
So where is this supposed 'new' father, then?

Morowa
Where? Wouldn't we be happy if we were sure *who?* There were quite a few candidates, but the frontrunner is one serious loser called Caspar Danso...

Kira
Moro...

Morowa
Remember that FFF walk we did last year?

Kira
FFF?

Morowa
Fundraise For Fibroids... in North London...

Kira
Oh yes... that was a brilliant event...

Morowa
And they say they raised quite a lot of money... I think they're doing it again this year... If they do, we'll go, right?

Kira
Why not? It's for a good cause... this fibroid thing is no joke for us women of colour, as they call us... But you said yours were shrinking?

Morowa
Well according to the last scan I did... but they always seem to come back... Anyway, moving swiftly on... I don't know if you remember one loud-mouthed fellow... made sure everybody saw and heard him... he had some unique kind of walking stick...

Kira
Oh yes... I can't forget that walking stick...

Morowa
Well that's him... proper show off... That's Caspar... he's Kukua's father... everybody said it...

Kira
Who's 'everybody?' Whatever...

Morowa
I know what I'm saying... I've got no time for him... real black sheep, from the beginning of time...

Kira
So he's a loud-mouthed loser, black sheep... What else?

Morowa
Don't get me started oh... All the above and more... But you saw and heard him yourself... just full of big talk... They say he spent a fortune campaigning at the last election back home... he thought he was in line for some big government position... but of course when the time came, they just kicked him to one side... they ignored him completely... he got nothing... So now he's penniless... owing people all over the place... If you look at him

closely, you'll see that Kukua looks like him...

Kira
Whatever, Moro...

Morowa
OK... Well, she may not look too much like *him*, but if you see his last sister, you won't argue... Kukua is a carbon copy of her... face, complexion, height... I say carbon copy...

Kira
Hmmm...

Morowa
Kira, how long have you known me? Well over twenty years now... I try to do the right thing... try to be fair... You know I don't judge people... I don't gossip... I don't like mentioning, never mind spreading bad news, or anything like that... that's just not me...

Kira
I know...

Morowa
So what's that supposed to mean now?

Kira
Ah... What did I say now?

Morowa
No, it's the way you said it: *'I know'*...

Kira
Whatever Moro...

Morowa
Anyway, when I say bad luck people, those Dansos... Caspar's

grandmother was a full blown leper... lost all her fingers and toes... So all this nonsense from Kukua is probably hereditary... before she eventually loses her fingers and toes like her great-grandmother, she's losing her senses first...

Kira
(Laughs)

Morowa
Look... I'm not laughing... I must deal with Kukua once and for all... A girl I've looked after her whole life... literally from the day she was born... If I'd treated her the way most people treat outcasts like her, would I be going through all this pain now? I don't think so...

Kira
How is she an 'outcast' now? You know why you and Kukua have so many issues?

Morowa
Tell me, oh Wise One...

Kira
She's just like you... To start with she actually looks more like you than even Debbie does...

Morowa
Oh please... go on the internet you'll see wonders... so many cases like that... people look almost identical to other people they have no relationship to whatsoever...

Kira
Look, she doesn't just look like you... her mannerisms, the way she walks... she's as feisty as you are... in a nutshell, she's just you... So I think it's a case of when you're dealing with her, it's like you're dealing with yourself... she's your Mini-Me...

Morowa
Is that all you have to say? Are you done?

Kira
Actually no, I'm not... I've just let you rant on a bit about, what's
his name... Caspar, and this and that... we all need to let off
steam from time to time... So do you think I've actually
forgotten the time the immigration people made you and Kukua
do a DNA test to prove her blood relationship to you?

Morowa
And your point is? You think those tests are foolproof? I'm
telling you she's not my brother's daughter, and you are telling
me about some white man's test...

Kira
(Laughs)
Well, maybe the white people needed a test, but *I* don't need
anything to prove that you and Kukua are from the very same
stock, same gene pool... there's no doubt about that.... Look, you
go and have some Campari... how you drink that stuff I don't
know... but it seems to calm you down, so off you go...

Morowa
I can't hear you... this your phone... it went off completely just
now... You say what?

Kira
I say go drink some Campari...

Morowa
I don't want to drink... but I suppose I'll have to have a hefty
glass... or two... Look at me now... turning to alcohol for
God's sake... all thanks to Kukua...

Kira

No... you can't blame her for that oh... I'm sorry, but if I'm forced to give evidence under oath in court, I'll have to state categorically, that you'd already *turned*... way, way before now...

(They laugh)

Kira

Look, I better go order these handsets... and I could do with a few pillows as well...

Morowa

OK... Well make sure you order different sizes...

Kira

Of what?

Morowa

The dildos... Isn't that what you just said you were ordering?

Kira

Dildos? Where did that come from? I said *pillows*...

Morowa

Ah... you definitely need to change those handsets... ASAP... I did wonder a bit just now... I thought, 'dildos'... well...

Kira

Well you thought wrong... just shows the state of your mind...

(They laugh)

Morowa

But come to think of it... same difference... dildos... pillows... all comfort givers...

(They laugh)

4   *Friday 8 February*

THAT'S WHAT I HEARD

Featuring Lola, a fashion agent, who has supplied Morowa and Kira with cosmetics, accessories, etc, for years. She attends the same church as Morowa and lives close to Kira. Also featuring Brianna.

Kira
Guess who just left here now?

Morowa
Let me see... your ex? You know he calls me now and again... begging me to beg you...

Kira
If QC knows he's a man, let him bring those his dry, bow legs here... I'll straighten them for him, once and for all...

Morowa
(Laughs)
You see, QC really knows his dear wife: he tells me he misses you untangling his legs when he used to wrap them round your neck...

Kira
OK, you know what, I'm not going to answer you... Lola came by... she just came to drop off the stuff we ordered last week... she gave me yours off as well to give you...

Morowa
She left *my* stuff with you? Why? She usually takes mine to church, so... hmmm...

Kira

She did say she might not be able to attend service this Sunday...

Morowa

Oh... she never misses church... I hope she's OK...

Kira

Between me and you, I don't think so... You should've seen her today... she was a really pathetic sight... She's lost so much weight... at one point I thought she was going to just pass out... I think she needs some kind of psychiatric assessment... she definitely needs *something*... She always used to look so good and put together...

Morowa

If she didn't look put together would we be getting our stuff from her... fashion stuff for that matter? She was *always* on point... I haven't had a chat with her after church for a while now... she just seems to rush off straight after service these days... I'll call her...

Kira

I felt sorry for her, I really did... Her clothes were literally just hanging off her... In fact I don't even know what she was wearing... it looked like a jumpsuit from one angle, then from another angle it was like a wrapper... Everything was held up with some sort of rope, because I can't even call that a belt... As for her weave... you know the part that looks like a scalp? Her own had some dandruff...

Morowa

Ah... that bad?

Kira

Even when she hugged me it was like she actually had some small stubble on her face...

Morowa
No... Oh Sister Lola...

Kira
I'm not kidding... something's not right...

Morowa
Actually, on the church grapevine, I heard her husband had a minor stroke... But surely that can't be the reason for her to look like what you're telling me now...

Kira
You know, it's probably a build up of things...

Morowa
It must be... For starters, I understand that her husband has about three or four other kids...

Kira
Other kids? You mean apart from Lola's four and the albino, there's more?

Morowa
Apparently, even before he met Lola he'd had at least two children with a Zambian or Zimbabwean... one of those places... So there's those two as well... possibly more...

Kira
Are you serious? So how come you've never told me any of this before?

Morowa
I just heard most of this very recently myself... in the last fortnight or so... seriously... I wouldn't be surprised if Lola herself doesn't know the full extent of things...

Kira
Hmmm... By the way, that his albino son is doing well oh...

he's always in films and adverts and stuff...

Morowa
Oh yes... taking full advantage of his uniqueness...

Kira
Good for him... it's not a disability as such...

Morowa
At all... But in some parts of Africa, albinos get a very rough ride... they get attacked all the time... In fact, I think this chap did a documentary on what some of them go through...

Kira
He did... I saw it... very sad... Our people tend to make an issue out of anything they don't understand, or that's a little different...

Morowa
Oh yes... ancestrally... anything that baffles or scares Africans... either they worship it or attack it... that's it... Anyway... so how many children have we counted so far for Lola's husband?

Kira
About six or seven already...

Morowa
And apparently he has at least one still in school... primary school for that matter, if I'm not mistaken...

Kira
What? *That man?*

Morowa
That's what I heard... With his face like a pig's bum...

Kira
True... that's exactly what he looks like... and obviously with the behaviour to match as well... I can't stand him...

Morowa

I don't think even *he* can stand himself...

Kira

How won't he have a stroke, for God's sake? So poor Lola is having to put up with all this, and only God knows what else... How will she look right? I just kept looking at her today and thinking to myself: this is how I could've ended up looking if I hadn't gotten away from QC...

Morowa

Oh how? So in what way is *your* story like Lola's? Did you end up growing a beard?

Kira

I didn't say she had a beard, Moro...

Morowa

OK... what did you say... stubble? What's the big difference? The thing is, it's all down to stress anyway... When you're stressed, the body starts to malfunction... your hormones start going haywire... So some people lose their hair... others start growing hair, lumps and other things in the wrong places...

Kira

So are you saying because I didn't grow a beard or whatever else, I wasn't really stressed, or what?

Morowa

No, of course you were... And that's why, even though you kept telling me to mind my own business... I have no regrets in more or less forcing you to see that counsellor...

Kira

The thing is, you're still not minding your business...

Morowa
Look here... we met as a result of me not minding my business, so what's your point? And look, just in case you haven't figured this out: you will *always* be my business... OK?

(They laugh)

Morowa
I had to step in that time with QC... I couldn't just stand by and watch... You were becoming a shadow of yourself...

Kira
Hmmm... There was I working all the hours God sent so we could pay the deposit on that house in Hertfordshire... only for QC to go and give that skinny bitch of a Brianna, or whatever she calls herself... give her virtually all our savings... for some stupid, no head no tail business venture... Missing out on that house for me was just the final straw... Well, that was of course until I heard she was pregnant...

Morowa
But thank God for DNA... it wasn't even his child...

Kira
But the idiot... paid child support for years for a child that wasn't even his... money that me and my boys could've used...

Morowa
As for that sorry specimen of a Brianna... How anyone could've preferred that withered whip to you, I'll never know...

Kira
QC just wanted to make me look bad, that's all... So people would say, 'Poor QC... poor man... he must've been desperate... going through sheer hell... Otherwise why would he leave his wife and run into such dry, haggard arms?'

Morowa
(Laughs)
But seriously, we've been over Brianna and all these things many times... and you know what, you have to forgive QC... After all, he's forgiven you...

Kira
Forgiven me? For what? All I did was beat him at his own game... that's all... And was it just Brianna? What about that...

Morowa
Let's not go into all that... that's all in the past now... Let's all move on... Please...

Kira
Look, I don't know what bit of we're *legally separated* you're not getting... When I look back... the time and resources I wasted on QC... I don't know why you're even encouraging him... honestly...

Morowa
The counsellor told you to take some time apart... it was never meant to be anything long term... Next thing you start getting all official and legal... you went too far and you know it...

Kira
Really? The thing is, I didn't go far enough... I should've gone all the way and just divorced him outright...

Morowa
Don't say that... You know that would've been a mistake... a big one... QC wouldn't have agreed anyway...

Kira
Look, I keep telling you, I don't have to have a man...

Morowa
I know... I understand...

Kira
No you don't...

Morowa
I do... I know some people don't want or need a man... But QC
is not just *any* man... particularly to you... and you know that...
Come on now... you have to give him a chance... Please...

Kira
Who made you his godmother anyway? Always fighting his
corner... Why don't you check *my* corner out for a change?

Morowa
He's regretted *everything*... But you know that already...

Kira
Look, that's his business...

Morowa
The last time you promised me you'd at least take his calls...

Kira
Well I've changed my mind, OK?

Morowa
You can't tell me you don't miss him...

Kira
I can't lie, I do sometimes... but I don't think I'm quite ready to
start anything up again with him... not any time soon anyway...

Morowa
He's not a bad person, so you're not the only one who misses

him... we all do... He's such a good laugh... But I guess, as Nigerians would say: 'Nah laugh you go chop?'

(They laugh)

Kira
Talking of Nigerians: how far with your Debbie and the fellow you say she's seeing now?

Morowa
Ah... don't remind me... just help me pray, please...

Kira
Why? What's the problem? You haven't met him yet, have you?

Morowa
No... but the way she's going on about him... She says she's bringing him round next weekend... I'm not looking forward to that... at all...

Kira
Well, just keep an open mind... you never know...

Morowa
What do you mean 'you never know'... with *those* people? Look I've already lost all hope in advance...

Kira
(Laughs)

5   *Sunday 17 February*

WHAT DO YOU WANT ME TO SAY?

Sonny has travelled to Newcastle for a work meeting; he's just checked into a hotel. The day before, Debbie had brought her boyfriend, Rotimi, home to introduce him to her parents.

Featuring Liam.

Sonny calls Morowa.

Sonny
Just telling you I'm indoors...

Morowa
Oh good... It's almost midnight, so I guess it's straight to bed...

Sonny
Straight to bed? Are you kidding? No chance... I've still got quite a bit left to do for this presentation tomorrow... And I didn't get any rest on the train... I was on the laptop throughout...

Morowa
Anyway, how's the hotel?

Sonny
It's the usual place... 'same old, same old' as the youngsters would say... And guess what? I'm in room 142... again...

Morowa
Really? Isn't this the third or fourth time they've put you in that room?

Sonny
Something like that... but it's nice and comfortable, so nothing to

complain about... But you know something... I think I'm getting too old for all this... travelling for work and this and that... I've been seeing it in your eyes lately... I know you're desperate to give me the go-ahead to retire early, so you can look after me full time... pamper me and rub my head from morning till night, that kind of thing...

(They laugh)

Morowa
You know me too well... of course all I want to do is move back to Accra... *right now*... so we can stay in the unfinished house... no windows, no doors, no bathroom... I guess we'll be just fine...

Sonny
Of course we'll be fine... As long as we're together, who needs a bathroom, windows... all those unnecessary things?

(They laugh)

Morowa
Look Sonny, I'm not even joking with you... I'm not happy with you... at all...

Sonny
I know, I know... but let it wait till after my meeting tomorrow... please... I beg...

Morowa
No, this can't wait... I won't be able to sleep... I think I'm feeling a bit funny... I'm sure my blood pressure's up...

Sonny
Here we go... calm down...

Morowa
Were you really supposed to receive and welcome that boy like that?

Sonny
Which boy?

Morowa
Stop it, Sonny... just stop it...

Sonny
(Laughs)
You mean Rotimi? What did I do now?

Morowa
How could you be so familiar with him... on a first visit? That's
not the way to do things... at all...

Sonny
What are you talking about?

Morowa
All the years Liam visited Debbie, you never relaxed and
interacted with him the way you did with this one... When Liam
came round, you would just grunt something and walk off...

(SILENCE)

Morowa
Hello?

Sonny
I'm here...

Morowa
Well say something then...

Sonny
What do you want me to say?

Morowa
Our daughter brings a very strange fellow home to meet us, and

you're so casual about the whole thing?

Sonny
How is he strange?

Morowa
He couldn't even comport himself... Didn't you see... he even got soup on his shirt and beard at one point?

Sonny
I'm not surprised... the poor chap was nervous... the way you were looking at him... it actually reminded me of the first time I met *your* mother...

Morowa
Oh, how is that the same thing? Even when they said they met online, Sonny, you just carried on as normal...

Sonny
What's your problem?

Morowa
Oh... so I'm the one with the problem now?

Sonny
This is how they do things these days... Our Debbie is a sensible girl... you know this... she knows what she's doing...

Morowa
It doesn't come by sense, Sonny, I'm telling you...

Sonny
Look, I know you... Be honest, your issue is that he's a Nigerian... That's the problem, right?

Morowa
No, no... It's just that he doesn't look quite right for our

Debbie... I didn't get a good vibe about him... at all... You know what I mean?

Sonny
No, I don't know what you mean... You see you women... only God knows how you judge people... or what you're looking for... All I saw was a young chap... polite, hard working, trying to set up his own business... He looks and sounds decent enough; let's give him a chance...

Morowa
I should give that one a chance... to finish Debbie off, or what? I know we're all God's children, so I don't mind Nigerians per se... But let's face it Sonny, have you ever heard of a success story with them... particularly when they marry foreigners? The thing is, even when they marry their own people it's a problem...

Sonny
So how do you know this? Did you carry out a survey... or were you married to one or two Nigerians before me? And who said anything about marriage, anyway? They've just met...

Morowa
That could be the next step... then what do we do then?

Sonny
I don't understand... So what would you want to do?

Morowa
Look, if anything happens to Debbie I'll hold you responsible oh... In fact you know what, I'm just going to have to take matters into my own hands... with or without your help...

Sonny
Behave yourself now... I can't believe you're going on like this... The simple fact is this: Nigerians, like us Ghanaians,

Chinese, Italians... some marry their country people, some marry foreigners; some marriages work and some don't... that's just life... there's no formula or guarantee of success...

Morowa
You're not getting this whole thing...

Sonny
What is there to get? Look... not just me... *we both* know so many people from different backgrounds that are happily married... including Nigerians... Then look at that couple we met on the cruise... Egyptian and Samoan... look at that combination... I think they said they were celebrating their 45th anniversary or something like that... Look at me and you... we're not from the same part of our country, but that's never been an issue for us... But then look at your brother... Yaa and Afia... they're from the very same village, if not the same street... Didn't they almost kill each other?

Morowa
It was mainly that Afia anyway... messing around... with men and juju... *She* caused most of their problems...

Sonny
According to you and your family... All the allegations were unfounded, if you ask me...

Morowa
Nobody is asking you about that... What I *am* asking you to do, is to protect your daughter from imminent danger...

Sonny
'Imminent danger'... listen to yourself... So you want to go and find husbands for Debbie and Kukua, or what? Maybe there are some eligible chaps in your church? Go and pair them up then... Honestly, I don't know what you want...

Morowa
Sonny, you never support me in matters like this...

Sonny
How can you say that? OK, but if that's what you think, I'm
sorry... I apologise... But this is not really a matter of supporting
you or not...

Morowa
So what is it about then?

Sonny
Look, you're upset and tired... you need to calm down... You've
made me talk too much this evening...

Morowa
See... I'm making you talk too much... is that fair?

Sonny
You just want to fight me now... Look, it's been a long day... try
and get a good night's sleep... you'll feel better by tomorrow...

Morowa
I doubt it...

Sonny
You will... If I were home I would've given you a nice, long,
professional massage...

Morowa
With those your bony fingers? Thanks, but no thanks... I still
haven't fully recovered from the last one you gave me...

Sonny
(Laughs)
See, I'm trying, but I can't win... Look... I know you're worried
about Debbie and Kukua... I may not voice it often, but as their

father, you think I don't have my concerns too? I do... But I know they'll be OK... We've done our best for them... so we have to trust that our best was good enough, and that we've equipped them to find their way in life... And I'm sure they will... and they'll do us proud... just you wait and see...

Morowa
OK... I don't know... but if you say so...

Sonny
I do... they're not bad girls... Come on... they're not like *you*...

Morowa
What?

Sonny
(Laughs)
Look, seriously... Again, I don't say this all the time, but you've done an excellent job with them... you really have... I'm so proud of you too... and I really mean that... You couldn't have done more or better... honestly... And you're very prayerful, so just continue to pray for them, OK? That's about all you can do...

Morowa
OK...

Sonny
Look, I've got to go now... let me try and finish off this stuff... I'll call you straight after my meeting tomorrow, OK?

Morowa
OK... don't forget to take your medicines... they're in that side pocket with your snacks...

Sonny
Thanks... Night-night me ole darling...

6   *Monday 18 February*

NOTHING BUT MISCHIEF AND WAHALA

Featuring Rotimi and Salma, Kira's older sister.

Kira
Your line was engaged for ages yesterday evening...

Morowa
I had a bit of a hotline...

Kira
Anyway, before I forget, Salma called... she sends her love and says to remind you about next February...

Morowa
Valentine's weekend... date already saved... You know what, she could be trying to tell us something... maybe she's got a secret Valentine somewhere?

Kira
You have her number... call and ask her yourself...

(They laugh)

Kira
You need to leave teaching... go and set up a dating agency... there's no way you won't make it...

Morowa
Love makes the world go round... maybe not in a circle, but...

(They laugh)

Kira
So how did the 'royal visit' go? They came on Saturday, right?

Morowa
No, it was *yesterday*... and everyone is very happy... everyone apart from me...

Kira
(Laughs)
So what happened?

Morowa
Where do I start? Before they came, Debbie deliberately refused to tell me much about the fellow... You know them, as if I was prying too much: 'Oh Mum, you'll meet him eventually'... that's about all I got before yesterday... For starters, guess where they actually met?

Kira
Where?

Morowa
Look... when they told us they met online... for a few moments, everything around me just sort of went a bit cloudy... dark...

Kira
Online? Nigerian? Oh God... What is Debbie's problem now? This doesn't sound too good oh... I can't lie...

Morowa
Can you imagine? This is the beginning of the end for her, I'm telling you... It's over for her... completely...

Kira
So where has this one come from now? Debbie... such a pretty girl... Can't she get a nice young man the normal way, for God's sake?

Morowa
Ask her for me oh... ask her...

Kira
So what does he do?

Morowa
He says he's an accountant, and he's setting up some transport...
haulage business or something or the other... you know them
with their big, big talk and things...

Kira
Ah... 419, right there...

Morowa
Of course... What else? What do I see for Debbie if she settles
for this one? A minimum of forty long, bleak years in the
wilderness... What am I even saying? She won't even last forty
days, never mind forty years... Oh... where did I go wrong?

Kira
Calm down; she'll be OK...

Morowa
How? You could see nothing but mischief and wahala scribbled
all over him... from head to toe... Every time he called me
'mummy', it was as if I was having some minor heart attack... It
took me all my restraint not to say to him: 'Look here... a
character like you... on what planet would I be your 'mummy'?'

Kira
(Laughs)

Morowa
Don't laugh... Why is my own story always different? Why?
Other people's children get involved with Nigerians... we know

they can be a bit forward and troublesome and all that, fair enough... But in spite of that, you can usually see the high life and some good times on the horizon with them...

Kira
Oh yes...

Morowa
But not me... not Morowa... my own encounter with Nigerians must be the opposite... With *this* fellow... pain and misery are dancing directly towards me now... all thanks to Debbie... Why? How come?

Kira
It can't be that bad now...

Morowa
It is... Why would Debbie do this? Look, I couldn't sleep...

Kira
So what is Sonny saying?

Morowa
You won't believe it: he's in full support of them... You need to see the warm welcome he gave this boy... laughing and joking with him, like old friends... Even when they mentioned that they met online, Sonny didn't flinch... And instead of talking some sense to his daughter, *I* was the one he ended up lecturing... All the time Liam used to come to see Debbie before she left home, I never saw Sonny relax with him the way he was doing with this one yesterday... never... I just couldn't believe it...

Kira
Why are men always like this? He's just not seeing the danger here...

Morowa
At all... I don't understand him... And I don't understand these our children either... We want them to settle down and sort themselves out, but it's like that's not a priority at all for them... Look at Kukua as well... she's had some nice chaps show interest in her... but it's complaint after complaint: one had fat fingers... another one, she said he blinks too often... I'm just fed up...

Kira
Hmmm... So are you telling me Debbie's totally finished with Liam?

Morowa
She doesn't want to hear *anything* about him...

Kira
Oh no... they fit so nicely those two... So what happened?

Morowa
She said Liam slapped her...

Kira
Ehn?

Morowa
The poor boy actually came to see me, trying to explain... According to him: they had an argument alright, but he said it was Debbie who rather started punching *him*... So he said he held her wrists to steady her... Next thing, he says she was screaming that he was trying to kill her... I've tried to talk to her about the whole thing, but she says she's done with him... You know these oyibo children... you should've heard her... her mouth was going twenty to the dozen... how Liam should count his lucky stars she didn't call the police, because she could've pressed charges and that could've affected his CRB or DBS, or whatever rating... and you know the kind of job he does...

Kira

I liked Liam oh; I really did...

Morowa

Who wouldn't like him?

Kira

You can clearly see he's destined for good things...

Morowa

Just good? Better things... in fact the very best of things... Who said, 'When they go low, we go high'? But, of course in my case, again it's the opposite: we start high and then sink so low... Who in their right senses leaves someone like Liam for this so-and-so? I say, if you see him...

Kira

I can imagine... What is all this?

Morowa

Look, I was so relieved that the visit was sort of cut short, because Sonny had to go and catch the train... he's gone to Newcastle... So Debbie and this fellow... I think they say his name is Rotimi... they dropped him off at the station... But of course before that, I had to entertain him... reluctantly, of course... Do you know by the time they were leaving, there was soup on his shirt and beard?

Kira

He has a beard and all?

Morowa

And of course you know: there are beards, and there are *beards*... if you see his own... all bushy...knotted... joined to some sort of moustache and all... like some kind of werewolf... I couldn't even see his teeth properly... Coming to think of it, maybe he doesn't even have any...

Kira
(Laughs)

Morowa
Don't laugh, Kira... I'm telling you everything that comes to me is different... And there were some other little, little things I noticed... I made some nice, spicy meatballs... you know the way you showed me... Do you know he had about five or six at a blow? Just gobbling one after the other...

Kira
(Laughs)
Well because he probably doesn't have any teeth, he can't chew... so he just swallows...

Morowa
Look, it's not funny... He claims he doesn't really drink alcohol, but if you see the way he was guzzling the juice... I couldn't believe my eyes... Sonny says he was just nervous... Look, he was a bit too relaxed for my liking, I'm telling you...

Kira
But seriously... How could he be meeting you people for the first time, and behave like that? Couldn't he at least just *try* to make a good impression? Make an effort... Does someone have to tell him that? This is quite disappointing oh...

Morowa
Well... you can just imagine what I went through... I'm telling you, everything was just wrong, from start to finish...

Kira
So I take it, this is not a happily ever after story...

Morowa
Ah... there's no happiness here oh... Why would Debbie do this to me? Then Kukua was telling me, he's really quite nice...

Kira
OK... well maybe...

Morowa
Maybe what? Does Kukua know what a nice person is? Please...
Sonny says I should leave them alone, they'll sort themselves
out... I shouldn't interfere... So, I should just fold my arms and
allow this so-and-so to come and wreak havoc in my life? How
can I? No way... I can't...

Kira
And the thing is, if anything goes wrong, then *you*'ll be left to
pick up the pieces... In fact, we'll *all* be picking up the pieces...
including Sonny, who seems to be blind to what you seem to be
seeing so clearly... Anyway calm down... they've just met... I'm
sure it's not too serious yet... With a bit of luck, he'll soon go
back to wherever he came from...

Morowa
Would I be this worked up if he looked like the type that will just
clear off? The way I see him, he won't just go quietly... he's a
problem, I'm telling you... I don't want to see him again...
honestly...

Kira
Hmmm... Look, we don't want any trouble... This fellow should
just go back to sender...

Morowa
Oh, as for that... he will go... one way or the other... he must...
right back to wherever he and his wahala are coming from...
First class, recorded, special delivery, track and trace... whatever
it takes...

7   *Thursday 28 February*

IN THE MIDDLE OF A THICK FOREST

Featuring Pastor Joel, who runs the church Morowa, Lola and Pearlette attend.

Lola calls Pastor Joel.

Lola
Pastor, I'm really sorry for calling this late, but I just couldn't wait till morning... I'm completely finished...
(Sobs)

Pastor
Calm down, Sister Lola... a child of God is *never* finished... We are grounded firm and deep in the Saviour's love... secure in the knowledge that with Christ in the vessel, what storm can we not smile at? So tell me... what's going on?

Lola
First thing, let me thank you for your prayers, Pastor... they always work... you are really anointed...

Pastor
I am just a servant... a tool being used by the Most High...

Lola
As I told you the other day, my husband's stroke has been improving day by day... It's taken a while, but he's getting his strength back in his fingers... it's like a miracle...

Pastor
Well, I deal with a miracle-working God...

Lola

But there's more trouble again oh, Pastor... more trouble... Now they say his lungs are failing, and they're very worried about a lump in his neck... it's too much for me... it's too much...

Pastor

Calm down... The thing is, I knew there was more trouble before you even spoke... the Holy Spirit always reveals things to me...

Lola

(Sobs)

So are we the only people sickness can see? Are we the only people, Pastor? From stroke... to lungs... to neck... So what next? It's like we manage to get over one thing, then even more serious problems come to take their place... My enemies... they have got me where they want me... they have succeeded at last...

Pastor

How can they succeed when the Lord is in control? Don't talk like an unbeliever... Wait, wait... the Lord is speaking to me...
(Speaks in tongues)
Speak to me Lord, Your servant's ears are wide open... Show me how to deliver Sister Lola and her husband from all these calamities on the horizon of their lives... They are full of woe now, but You Lord, can easily remove disease, death, in fact any disaster from their path... Step in, Oh Lord... Show the devil the exit door, and may he stumble and fall for ever on his way out...

Lola

Amen...

Pastor

Sister Lola, this is a spiritual attack... I see you in the middle of a thick forest... and like Absalom, you are hanging from a tree by your hair...

Lola
Jesus!

Pastor
The forest trees are closing in and preventing the light... the light of the Almighty, from getting to you... The devil wants to play with you... but believe me, he can never win this game...

Lola
I'm in trouble... My husband's mixed-up life has finally caught up with him... Girlfriends and children all over the place... Tell me why I shouldn't just walk away, and leave all these other people to look after him now... The thing is, I just haven't got the energy any more... I'm really tired now...

Pastor
You cannot be tired... by the Holy Spirit you are strengthened... I rebuke and bind all weakness and doubt from you... How can you be tired when you have been chosen to be a prophetess?

Lola
What?

Pastor
Oh yes... It has been revealed to me that you are a disciple in waiting... your destiny is to go far and wide to spread the gospel... Before the end of this year, you will be operating on a different spiritual level... And mark my words: one day you will be famous for this work... Thank you Lord for favouring and choosing this our special sister for such an assignment...

Lola
Amen... As long as that's what the Lord wants, I'm ready...

Pastor
Believe me, all that's happening now is that your faith is being

tested, in readiness for your spiritual duties to come... The Lord has tested me many times, so I know what I'm talking about... And you must prepare for more tests... To abandon your husband in this his hour of weakness and need, would mean you have failed... You must have pure faith... Did Daniel not come out of a lion's den? Did Jonah not emerge from inside a whale? Answer me...

Lola
Yes...

Pastor
So if the Lord could do those impossible things... and so much more that we as believers know of... why can't He help you? His crown has *never* slipped off His head, and He has *never* slipped off His throne... so I assure you, He can *never* fail you...

Lola
Amen...

Pastor
I've been telling you to bring your husband to church... for years... maybe he will come now, at last... so we can pray for him and lay our anointed hands on him...

Lola
They admitted him... I'm just coming back from hospital...

Pastor
Oh... I wish you'd spoken to me before his admission...

Lola
Everything happened so quickly... This morning he couldn't breathe properly, so we rushed down to our GP... next thing they sent us to A&E... Before we knew what was happening, they were telling us he had to be admitted... immediately...

Pastor
Oh, don't get me wrong, the doctors are very hardworking and
some are very good... but no medicine works better than what
Our Heavenly Father prescribes... He is the master physician and
healer... So we must try and get your husband out of hospital as
soon as possible, so we can perform back to back laying on of
hands... offer special prayers and fasting for his speedy and total
healing... But in the meantime, if I know the visiting times, I
will accompany you and go and pray for him in hospital...

Lola
Oh, thank you Pastor... I would appreciate that very much...

Pastor
I will send you passages that you need to read as often as you
can... When we visit your husband in hospital, we will need holy
water and anointing oils... I will take some, but you will need
plenty for your personal devotion and prayer programme that I
will draw up for you...

Lola
Well, I have some oils...

Pastor
Just to be on the safe side, why don't you get the holy hamper?

Lola
Hmmm... It's a bit expensive though...

Pastor
You think so? It's on discount now... for just £250 you get
several bottles of the Wrath, Cherub and Rapture oils and water...
you also get the soaps and candles... Most of our church brothers
and sisters are saying it's very reasonable, because the hamper
lasts a good six to eight weeks if you use everything as

instructed... But if you can't afford it, don't worry... we can always sort something out... particularly for nice looking sisters like you...

Lola
Ehn?

Pastor
People think just because I'm a man of God, I can't appreciate nice, good people and good things... I can and I do...

(SILENCE)

Pastor
You're not saying anything, Sister Lola... Are you shy? Don't be shy or offended... What is wrong with me appreciating you? We're all God's children... each and every one of us, fearfully and wonderfully made to appreciate one another... Anyway, whatever the case, you need your oils and stuff... you can never have too much of them... and they will never go to waste because we're in a constant battle with the devil... So as I always say, forget the cost... God will always provide and replenish...

Lola
OK...

Pastor
It has been revealed to me that you must fast for twelve hours daily; so I suggest 6 to 6... until I get further spiritual instructions...

Lola
Hmmm... OK...

Pastor
You sound very worried, Sister Lola, but you don't have to be...

you have come to the right place at the right time... The Lord says, 'Be still'... so there's no need to panic... At the end of this episode in your life, you will stand in front of all and give testimony... like Sister Pearlette did last month... You heard her with your own ears listing all the challenges she has overcome... So if *she*, with all her problems, could be delivered, then tell me, what is too much for our Lord?

Lola
Nothing... nothing at all... I apologise again for calling so late...

Pastor
That is what I am here for... to guide God's children... be it night or day, it doesn't matter... The devil doesn't sleep... and he never gets tired of causing pain and trouble... so some anointed ones like us can't sleep either... we always have to be on the lookout... on the alert for him... ever ready to confront and tackle him...

Lola
Hmmm...

Pastor
Anyway, we'll speak in the next couple of days to confirm the hospital visiting arrangements... and of course, to sort out your oils and stuff...

Lola
OK... thank you, Pastor... Good night...

Pastor
Don't rush off, Sister Lola... and don't thank me; thank The Lord... and continue to thank Him... for He is ever faithful, ever sure... I will ask Sister Morowa to put you on the Prayer Warrior List... But before you go, if you can kneel where you are, do so and let us pray...

8 Friday 1 March

ARE OUR STORIES EVER STRAIGHT?

Featuring James, an acquaintance of Kira's.

Morowa
Kira... Do you know you were absolutely right about Lola?
Pastor Joel just called me... he wants me to add her to my prayer
list...

Kira
What did I tell you? I told you something was wrong... I'm sure
you thought I was exaggerating... So what's actually going on?

Morowa
Just as we suspected... it's to do with that her husband... Between
me and you, I think he's on his last legs...

Kira
No... With the stroke?

Morowa
Not just that... Apparently kidney, liver, heart, neck... I think
everything has packed up...

Kira
Oh no... Cancer?

Morowa
He didn't say, but... it doesn't sound good... at all... Look at it
this way... what are your chances if all those vital organs have
packed up? She'll tell me more when we talk to arrange our
prayer times...

Kira
There's plenty trouble in the world, you know...

Morowa
Tell me about it...

Kira
Remember James, who laid my floor?

Morowa
Oh no... Please don't tell me... what's happened to him now?

Kira
Oh no, he's OK... sort of... he called me last night... But they've taken him back home...

Morowa
Back home?

Kira
Deported... about two or three weeks ago... The immigration people went to his workplace and bundled him from there... after twenty-seven years in this country...

Morowa
You're joking... Another Windrush victim...

Kira
More or less... He called me... in desperation...

Morowa
From where?

Kira
I say he's in Freetown as we speak...

Morowa
Ah-ah... So what about his wife... and kids?

Kira
I asked him about them, but he didn't give me a straight answer...

Morowa
Are our stories *ever* straight?

(They laugh)

Kira
Obviously, there's some issues going on there... he said he couldn't reach them... or something like that....

Morowa
So what does he want *you* to do now?

Kira
I think he could do with all the help... and cash he can get... He was detained for a couple of weeks before they took him back... He sounded so confused...

Morowa
How wouldn't he be? To be taken back like that... after *twenty-seven years*... Oh my God...

Kira
He said they wouldn't let him go home to collect anything... not a thing... So he left this country with virtually the clothes on his back, and just a few pounds he happened to have on him... So from work, to detention, to the airport...

Morowa
Sometimes you don't want to believe some of these stories... that they actually *do* treat people like that...

Kira

Well, believe... because they do... Now I think he's more or less in hiding with one of his sisters back home now... You know our people: they see being deported as a disgrace...

Morowa

Disgrace? You think that's their problem? I don't think so... The main problem for those hardened folk back home now, is that he's not the cash cow any more...

Kira

You're right... He said his sister was telling him he needs to hurry up and find a job... and he's only been back a few weeks... He was explaining to me, that this is someone he's been feeding and supporting for years... I think she's now treating him like a nuisance... an extra mouth to feed... talking to him anyhow...

Morowa

I've heard of a few sad cases of people who've landed back home like that... If he's not careful, he's in line for some serious hardship... serious maltreatment and humiliation...

Kira

I say, that has already started... he was virtually crying... I think what finished him was when he overheard this sister saying that other people come back from overseas with cars and fancy things, after building houses for their families... but look at him... empty handed, nothing to offer... Apparently she's come to the conclusion that he must've committed a serious crime, that's why he must've been sent back... with no money...

Morowa

But do you think he committed some offence? But to be honest, he doesn't look like the type that would go causing any trouble... particularly when he knew his papers weren't quite right...

Kira

But even if he committed an offence... surely after *twenty-seven years* he should have some rights...

Morowa

True... Even the right to commit an offence or two, if you ask me...

Kira

You didn't say that...

(They laugh)

Morowa

No it's true...

Kira

But seriously... he had to leave his job, house, everything... just like that... no time to arrange *anything*... How can you bundle someone away just like that... after he's lived here all this time?

Morowa

But wait... how come he didn't get his papers all these years?

Kira

I don't know... Look, everybody has their own story... Remember the time I had to report to Home Office virtually every week?

Morowa

How can I forget? Look, one has been through one or two things in this country oh...

Kira

Just one or two?

(They laugh)

Morowa
So what is he going to do now?

Kira
He said he has an interview with someone in the British Embassy
or Consulate, in a few weeks time... Apparently they've asked
him to produce some plenty documents and paperwork...

Morowa
But all his papers and stuff are all likely to be over here... So
how is he supposed to access them, for God's sake?

Kira
He said his lawyers are doing what they can...

Morowa
Well obviously not enough, or they wouldn't have taken him
back in the first place...

Kira
I don't think it's that easy, Moro... The immigration people...
they've deliberately made the whole deportation process so
awkward... even for the lawyers... It's obstacles all the way...

Morowa
This is serious oh...

Kira
Very... And as if that's not enough, he says just before he left,
they diagnosed him with lupus or something like that... so he's so
worried about how he's going to sort that out over there... he
needs specialist drugs and treatment...

Morowa
Oh my God... What about money? I bet he can't access his bank
account from over there...

Kira

I don't think so ... he asked me to send what I could for him... I'll send something, but of course, I can't make it a regular thing...

Morowa

Africans in particular... both legal and illegal immigrants... we should always have one or two solid people in our lives, who we can trust with some confidential things like bank details, GP information, mortgage, stuff like that... so just in case something like this happens... suddenly, unexpectedly... there's a starting point to help sort things out...

Kira

You're right... The thing is, culturally, we black people can be quite secretive... we don't want people to know our business...

Morowa

No-one is saying you should go broadcast your story all over the world... but you need someone who knows one or two vital things about you... Some of our people actually *die* with no-one having a clue where to start... no will, no instructions, nothing...

Kira

Let's face it, what do our people usually leave behind anyway, apart from some hereditary sickness, or some family problems that had probably started even before you were born? Please...

Morowa

And some serious debt, of course, to round everything up...

(They laugh)

Morowa

Oh yes... Remember that funeral we went to in East London... where those three daughters nobody seemed to know about, turned up from Italy?

Kira
No, that was a real classic...

Morowa
We say our people don't make wills... Well, I don't know how true, but I understand that man left *two*... two different wills...

Kira
Two *different* wills?

Morowa
Something like that... Apparently he gave one to the wife and children here, and the other to the Italian family...

Kira
What's all that about?

Morowa
My friend who was telling me about the whole thing, is a cousin to the ones here... they're saying *their* will is the up-to-date, revised one... but of course the Italian ones are saying that that's a forgery, and that *they* have the original... It's a mess...

Kira
Why would a father do that to his family... to his children?

Morowa
Apparently they've been in court, back and forth, since the funeral... that's a good two or three years now...

Kira
And he will be expecting to rest in peace after leaving such drama behind...

Morowa
You know what, I've come to the sad conclusion that that's what

some of our folks want... it's all calculated... Leave things as messy as possible for their survivors to tear each other's eyes out after they're gone... I think that's their own sick way of making sure they'll never be forgotten... Otherwise, what kind of nonsense is this?

Kira
The thing is, if people take the energy and time they use to fight wills and stuff like that, into making their *own* money and way in life, they'd be better off...

Morowa
True... Sometimes being left property and stuff is almost a curse... If you're not careful, it can make you lazy... Because if you're like me... nobody left me anything... you realise you've got nothing to fall back on... you have to fight to get whatever you want for yourself...

Kira
And the thing is, you appreciate and enjoy your own hard earned stuff better...

Morowa
Exactly... The thing is, with these kind of property disputes... by the time they've paid the lawyers and fees here and there, there's usually nothing much left to share anyway...

Kira
And most times things could be shared amicably... but there's always one or two greedy, bitter ones who will make sure things don't go smoothly... every family has them... the ones who just can't help themselves... they're prepared to go to any length to grab property and stuff... Some are even prepared to *kill* their own flesh and blood, for God's sake... just to grab, grab, grab...

Morowa
Unfortunately, some people were just born that way... Even
from childhood people would've noticed that grabby trait in
them... they're just never satisfied... Anyway, coming back to
James, I've just had a thought: I'm sure he must've had his bank
cards on him when he was arrested... Suppose he found a way to
send them to you? Maybe you could help him withdraw some of
his money and send to him? That would be a big help...

Kira
No-oh... I know we've just said we should have a confidante or
whatever... but I'm not *that* close to him... I'll help where I can,
but I have to be careful... especially when it comes to money...

Morowa
You're probably right...

Kira
Think about it... If the bank or authorities get wind of someone
here in the UK operating an account of someone who's been
deported... How will that look?

Morowa
True... Before you know it, you'll be headline news...

Kira
The bank and the press are one thing... The next thing I'll hear,
will be *James himself* talking nonsense: about how he never
actually gave me permission as such to withdraw his money...
that he's not too sure what I was trying to do with his bank
account and cards... Before I know it, one or two may even go as
far as to say I was probably having an affair with him... please...

Morowa
That's the thing about our people... they must make you regret

trying to help them... it's really sad...

Kira
Even his wife and children, the ones he says he can't reach
now... see the way they'll jump out of the woodwork the
moment they hear the word 'money'...

Morowa
Well, I guess as things stand now, his money will just remain in
the bank...

Kira
How do you think these oyibo countries make some of their
money? They would claim, probably rightfully, that they don't
have a legal next-of-kin or whatever to give the money to...

Morowa
And there must be loads of situations like his... So we're back to
what we were saying about having a confidante, or somebody
who can say or do something on your behalf... officially...

Kira
Then again... our high commissions or embassies... surely they
should be able to say something about people who are just sent
back home like that? It's like they don't say, or do, or challenge
anything... Aren't they supposed to take care of their nationals...
their welfare... look out for them?

Morowa
Not some of the African ones oh... their attitude to their nationals
is: if you get arrested, deported... in fact if you get into any
trouble whatsoever... that's *your* own business and problem...
you'd better sort yourself out... It's like most of our embassies
are more concerned about making life as easy and as smooth as
possible for foreigners to go and exploit us...

Kira

Crazy as it sounds, that's exactly what it seems like... And we Africans, do we even deport anybody from *our* countries?

Morowa

If we do, it's bound to be fellow Africans... We welcome and treat everybody else like royalty, but when it comes to our *own* people, it's a different story... Look, let's just face it: as black people, our image is very poor... we can be treated any damn how... nobody cares, nobody wants to know... nobody respects us, because a lot of the time it's like we don't seem to respect ourselves...

Kira

And as they say, you can't demand respect, it has to be earned... Look at the way we treat each other... just look at the miserable setup in most of our countries... how can we command any respect from anyone or anywhere else?

Morowa

But seriously, whatever the case... whichever way you look at it, some of these deportations are just wrong you know...

Kira

You think the authorities don't know that? They do... but they keep doing it with impunity, because they can, and they know they can get away with it... no questions asked... It's so unfair... Do you know, if care is not taken, James may never be able to come back to sort himself out... probably never be able to get his life back on track again... People have actually died in these kind of circumstances...

Morowa

Of course people are going to die... you'll just lose the will to live... I'm pretty sure I would... Is it a joke to be removed from everybody and everything you know... just like that? Overnight you find yourself in a place you probably haven't been to for decades... Look at poor James now... you say apart from money issues, his health is playing up as well... OK, he may be back in his country of birth and origin alright, but he's been away so long... he's more or less in a foreign land now...

Kira
He told me he doesn't understand how anything works there any more...

Morowa
How can he? But what did he do *so* wrong to be treated like that? If you look at things on balance, he's probably contributed more to this country than he could've ever subtracted from it...

Kira
Not 'probably'... he *has*... People like him usually stay quietly under the radar, doing the jobs their own people feel too good to do... Yet they're treated like second or third class citizens all the time... they get passed over for *everything*... health, housing, education... you name it... they always draw the short straw....

Morowa
They don't draw anything... they're given it...

Kira
Well exactly... Then after *all* that... something like *this*... it's so unfair... These are all the things that have to make us make Africa better, at whatever cost.... We can't go on being treated like this when we have a *whole* continent that should be working for us... But instead of it being a place for us to live happily, it's like we're trying to escape from there all the time... like we're being chased away... It shouldn't be like that... When I think about it... it makes me so sad...

9 Monday 25 March

ONE THING AFTER THE OTHER

Featuring Celine, Morowa's friend, and a few children.

Kira
You're scarce these days oh...

Morowa
My dear, I'm completely snowed under with work... My bed's covered with papers and books... I'm doing some marking... One of our really good teachers is off sick with stress... and I don't think he's in any hurry to come back... A couple of weeks ago, a parent came and head-butted him in front of his class...

Kira
What do you mean, 'head-butt'?

Morowa
Proper head to head banging stuff...

Kira
No...

Morowa
Oh yes... of course, the children thought it was *so* funny... but of course it wasn't... Left to me, I was going to call the police, but the Deputy Head stopped me...

Kira
Was it *that* serious?

Morowa
Very... the teacher was bleeding from his nose... I couldn't
believe it... Then we got a supply teacher in to help with his
classes, but she's not too hot... She's supposed to be an English
teacher, but the kids say they can't understand what she's saying
most of the time... and to be honest, neither can I... but we're
just going to have to manage her till the end of term... She can't
control the kids... so I spend half of my time trying to calm her
classes down... Mind you, I'm Head of Year, but I've got to
teach as well... so it's like double, triple work... I'm exhausted...

Kira
You sound it... Take it easy oh...

Morowa
When they say you don't know what you have till you lose it...
The teacher they head-butted... he knows his stuff and he's so
pleasant... I'm so missing him...

Kira
But what would make a parent do such a thing? Head-butt their
child's teacher?

Morowa
Well, if you saw the so-called parent, most of your questions
would be answered on the spot... just wrong... all round...

Kira
Oh yes... when you see some of the parents, you know their kids
have no chance...

Morowa
By the time we rushed to the class when he heard the
commotion, this 'parent' was bare-chested... he'd taken off his
T-shirt... just wanting to fight... right in front of the children...
Imagine...

Kira
That's bad oh...

Morowa
And as for the son that he came to fight for, Travis Gulliver or whatever he calls himself... he's been a proper nuisance since day one... the type that can disrupt anything, anywhere... and he does... all the time...

Kira
Well, just as we're saying: what do you expect with a father like that? Funnily enough, I have a Gulliver story too... Gulliver and Goliath...

Morowa
Sounds like the name of a pub or something...

Kira
No... twins... identical... Some years ago when I was in the foster care section, they brought the two of them in for placement... Gulliver and Goliath... they couldn't have been more than five or six at the time...

Morowa
What kind of names are those now?

Kira
Well... those were the names they gave those two mites... If I remember right, they were the last of about seven or eight siblings, or something like that... Anyway, I think the mother just couldn't cope... so the school had contacted us... They were turning up wretched and hungry and all that, so of course we had to step in...

Morowa
Awww...

Kira

Look, when we'd tidied them up, if you saw them, you'd fall in love with them... really lovely... They were mixed race, so we decided to place them with this nice couple: English man and the wife was Jamaican... she was born here, that kind of thing... They were looking to start a family, so we thought this is a match made in Heaven... The lady came to take them home on a Friday... filled in the paperwork and left... I remember their placement was to be indefinite... we'd review as we went along... and the couple had said that if all went well, they could see themselves adopting them... So we all had smiles on our faces...

(Morowa's other phone rings)

Morowa

It's Celine... if I answer her, we won't finish just now... we'll be on till the weekend...

(They laugh)

Morowa

I'll call her back later... But remind me, I need to talk to you about something concerning her...

Kira

About Celine? Is she OK?

Morowa

Oh yeah... nothing serious... I beg, tell me about the twins... their names alone tell me that they must be characters...

Kira

Where was I? Yes... they took them home on the Friday... by the following Monday morning, the lady was there with the two of them, waiting for us to open the office...

Morowa

Oh...

Kira

As soon as we opened the main door, she just pushed the two of them into the reception area, and she was more or less running away, before we chased after her and begged her to come back in and at least talk to us...

Morowa

No...

Kira

She broke down completely... She said she and her husband had never experienced anything like what they went through with those twins... Apparently, they wouldn't eat anything apart from McDonald's... She said she prepared proper, healthy meals... different things to tempt and coax them... But no... it had to be McDonald's... they wouldn't eat anything else....

Morowa

You're kidding...

Kira

So they got them the McDonald's... reluctantly... but they wanted beer as well... McDonald's washed down with beer... and there was a particular brand and all that they wanted...

Morowa

Oh stop...

(They laugh)

Kira

As I say, they gave them the McDonald's, but apparently, when they refused to give them the beer, it was out and out war... they

went out of control... they started screaming, throwing things...
She said she and her husband just didn't know what to do... It
was the weekend... they had an emergency number... but the
husband in particular... he was reluctant to call... he was saying if
they called for help it would seem as if they'd failed... as if they
hadn't tried hard enough with them... you know oyibo man...
But at one point she said it got too much for him, he actually
started crying...

Morowa
The husband?

Kira
Yes... She said, if she'd had handcuffs, she would've used them
on those twins...

(They laugh)

Kira
She said they put them to bed one night, then they heard sounds
coming from their room... When she went in, one was holding
the bed sheets up... the other one had scissors... cutting away...

Morowa
Ah... they had scissors?

Kira
She said she didn't know where they got them from... they
weren't hers... they must have smuggled them in... By the time
she got there, they'd already cut up several pillowcases and
stuff... She said she ran a bath for them... put them both in and
wanted to give them a hand... they were just tiny little things...
Next thing, one of them bit her... she showed me the mark... they
told her to get out of the bathroom... they didn't need her help,
they could bathe themselves...

Morowa

No...

Kira

Apparently it was one thing after the other... There were a few
other things, but it's been a while ago, so I can't remember some
of them... But as I said, in spite of all this, the husband was
apparently saying they shouldn't give up on them... But she said
she told him *he* could stay with them if he wanted, but *she* would
rather go into exile than stay under the same roof as those two
again...

(They laugh)

Morowa

All this over one weekend... from two five-year-olds...

Kira

If I hadn't been a sort of eyewitness, I wouldn't have believed
this story myself... Anyway, after we'd calmed her down, we
had a bit of a laugh before she left... She said one time, this her
husband had wanted to get a pet snake...

Morowa

Oh these people... pet snake, for God's sake... Show me which
part of a snake looks like it wants to be petted? We were born
more or less alongside these creatures, but we don't keep them as
pets... never...

Kira

Even Richie and his animals... he draws the line at snakes...
Anyway, she said she had been *totally* against it... but she said
she was reconsidering, because she didn't think any snake on
earth could've traumatised them like those twins...

(They laugh)

Morowa
So what happened to them eventually?

Kira
Good question... They must've gone back into the system... foster care... Actually, if I remember when I get to work, I'll check the database... maybe there's some follow-up information on them... They'll be big men now... at least early twenties... Gulliver and Goliath... I don't think any of us who were involved with that case will ever forget those two...

(They laugh)

Kira
Talking about twins... what about your nephews... Yaa's sons?

Morowa
They're doing OK... I hear from them pretty regularly actually... Kukua saw them when she went home...

Kira
Oh good... So what's up with Celine?

Morowa
Oh... her daughter's got this placement... she's going to Sierra Leone and Liberia for about three months or so... so she just wanted some general info and stuff from you... She said she lost your number when she changed her phone, so I gave it to her... so I'm sure she'll call you...

Kira
Oh... she shouldn't worry at all... she'll be okay... I'll give her a couple of numbers and contacts as well...

Morowa
She's part of a charity... and I think they're encouraging young people of African origin and descent to go to Africa, to offer

their skills for free... Let's face it, it's non-Africans who tend to be more interested in things like that... so it sounds like a good initiative...

Kira

It does... and well overdue actually... Do you know when she'll be going?

Morowa

Hmmm... soon... sometime next month, I think...

Kira

If I know when she's going, maybe I could beg her to take something for James... just one envelope with some documents for his case...

Morowa

(Laughs)

If Kukua and Debbie hear this, they'll say, 'Here we go again... Why can't your generation just wish people 'safe journey' without giving them something to deliver or collect?'

Kira

Look, it's part of our culture now... Tell them it's an old African tradition... that once upon a time, in the Land of MoroKira: as long as you delivered or collected something when you were travelling, you were assured of a safe and fruitful journey...

(They laugh)

10 *Thursday 11 April*

JUST DO THE RIGHT THING

Featuring Justice Otto Dighton.

Morowa
(Sings)
Say your prayers... never cease... your enemies will know no peace...

Kira
I don't think your future lies in singing...

Morowa
Remember that judge who sentenced me... for not doing jury service?

Kira
He didn't 'sentence' you... you didn't go to jail... though I think you should have... even if just for a few hours...

(They laugh)

Morowa
Whatever... Anyway, the gods of my forefathers have spoken and the tables have turned...

Kira
What happened?

Morowa
The Right Honourable Justice Otto Dighton... with his stuck up

chicken face... as if his wee and poo are made of gold dust...

(They laugh)

Morowa
'Right' and 'honourable' my foot... He was on the news this
evening... and it's all over the internet as well, anyway...
Apparently he had some issue with a cleaning company over a
bill... I don't know whether he was owing them or vice versa....
or whatever... Anyway, instead of just paying up or letting go...
emails back and forth... I guess he wanted to show them that he's
a judge and would have the final say... Next thing my gods
confused his miserable fingers... he sends an email to the
cleaning people... with a video attached... by mistake...

Kira
Oh...

Morowa
As soon as the cleaning people opened the attachment, they
called the police... so they seized his computers and stuff... In a
nutshell, there he was in frilly pants and bra, dancing about with
some very dodgy looking people... and some kids as well, if I'm
not mistaken... high on cocaine and God knows what else...

Kira
Oh my dear God! How do you wriggle out of that?

Morowa
Apparently there were hundreds of videos and pictures... Imagine
him sitting in judgment on others... He was probably wearing
that same underwear under his gown when he sentenced me...
okay *fined* me... £350... I was crying my eyes out in front of
him in court that day, but he just didn't want to hear my
explanation... I wish they could make me a juror on his case...

I won't rest until they bring back hard labour for him...

(They laugh)

Morowa
But, of course, he's likely to go scot-free... He'll have an army of your colleagues, psychology people, etc... they'll be making every excuse they can find for him now...

Kira
So they're my colleagues now?

Morowa
So are you trying to say they're not? Next thing we'll hear in his defence, is that something happened to him in childhood, when he was in nursery during the First World War... they gave him juice one day instead of milk... and that affected his relationship with fluids... for life... and only frilly underwear and underage company help him to put things in perspective... or some crap like that... You know what your people can come up with...

(They laugh)

Morowa
He's just a sicko... These so-called top people carry on as if they're upright and all that... as if they know it all and everybody should listen to them... The reality is, a good lot of them are always up to some real mischief or the other...

Kira
The name of the game is 'Don't Get Caught'... If you're slack, or unfortunate, or whatever, and *do* get caught... well...

Morowa
Like our brother somewhere in the north... with his mother's disabled disc...

Kira

As for him... What was his problem, for God's sake?

Morowa

I don't know... You know you shouldn't be using the disc if your mother isn't in the car... you're an MP... surely you must know this... Then when they caught him, instead of owning up, he starts lying that it wasn't him driving, it was his researcher...

Kira

Every thicko knows that there's CCTVs all over the place... you're going to get caught... For God's sake, if you're going to get into trouble, let it be for something worthwhile, not something like this...

Morowa

Now look at what he's lost...

Kira

Oh, he's lost everything... they tagged him and all...

Morowa

Look at that...

Kira

Where could he have wanted to park that he just couldn't afford to, so he just *had* to use that disabled disc? Where? Why? Or for what? This type of thing just plays right into the hands of our plenty detractors...

Morowa

Of course... And that's my personal beef with him... As a black person, when you're elevated to a high station, it's not just about *you*... you have a responsibility to *all* black people... whether you like it or not... you just do...

Kira
Well this is it...

Morowa
Wait... let me see if I can find something someone sent me...
here, let me read it... *'The whole system is set up, in fact almost
rigged for us to trip, fall and fail'*... 'us' of course, meaning
black people... *'It's a hard climb to the middle, never mind to the
top; but wherever you are as you ascend, try to clear at least
some of the debris out of the way, so you can make things just
that little bit easier for others trying to come up behind you'*...

Kira
In short, if you can't do anything, don't go adding more debris...

Morowa
That's all we ask... is that too much? And don't be selfish... just
do the right thing, for God's sake...

Kira
But I tell you what, it's all about *who* you encounter when you're
in a spot of bother... I've told you about the time the police
stopped me when I had my first car... and they breathalysed me...

Morowa
You've been breathalysed before? I never knew that...

Kira
Oh yes... I blew into the machine and all... next thing they're
saying I'm 'borderline'...

Morowa
What did or does that mean?

Kira
Till this day I'm not too sure... Anyway, he asked me my name

and date of birth... I told him, then he sort of chuckled...

Morowa
Police... chuckled?

Kira
Well you can imagine... I thought to myself: I'm finished... I'd had a glass or two of wine, but I didn't feel drunk at all... but I thought I must be... otherwise why would it appear as if the police are actually cracking jokes with me now?

(They laugh)

Kira
Anyway, next thing, he says something like: "Our mothers must've been in labour at the same time..." Again, I'm thinking: For God's sake, what am I hearing now? What is he saying? You won't believe this, but it turns out; he and I were born on exactly the *same day, same year*...

Morowa
You're joking...

Kira
Are you sure I haven't told you this story before?

Morowa
No... there's no way I would forget something like this...

Kira
It happened to me oh... But cut a long story short, he cautioned me... and he stressed to me that you don't necessarily have to be drunk to fail a breath test... or something like that... And I think it was up or down to him... he could've pushed things further... but he didn't...

Morowa
Push things further... like how?

Kira
I don't now... maybe they could've given me points on my
licence, for starters... Anyway... that's my all time feel-good
police story... I met my police 'twin'... and he was so nice...

(Kira's other phone rings)

Morowa
Isn't that your phone?

Kira
It's my aunty back home... she can keep ringing... I'm not
answering her today... she can stew there for a couple of days...
Yesterday, I was trying to console myself after spending nearly
£500 on my new glasses... when she rang...

Morowa
Don't remind me... I almost had to take out a loan for mine last
year... for just a basic lens prescription...

Kira
I thought she just wanted to thank me for some extra money I
sent her... on top of what I regularly send her... But before I
knew what was happening, she put her grandson on... Then
she's whispering to him in the background, 'Ask your Aunty
Kira... talk to her quickly... she will help you...' Next thing I'm
hearing, 'Aunty Kira, I need a laptop, I'll send you a picture of
the one I like... but if you can't send it immediately, don't
worry... I can manage a tablet for now... There was no 'Aunty
Kira, how are you?'... nothing... just went straight to business...

Morowa
Imagine... You shouldn't worry... he can *'manage* a tablet... *for*

now'? If you don't laugh, you'll cry...

Kira

Look eh... I just told him to put Aunty back on the phone...
immediately... and I warned her that if she tries that nonsense
with me again, that would be the end for me and her... *the end...*
And she knows that would not be good news for her... at all...
I'm the one she has some rapport with... my sisters don't talk to
her as such, because she's so demanding... they just send her
what they can, when they can... no regular arrangement like me...
She knows I'm mad with her, so she's been phoning almost
non-stop to try to make the peace... but I don't want to hear
anything from her now...

Morowa

What's wrong with our people?

Kira

Don't mind her... trying to be greedy and clever...

Morowa

And training the grandchildren to follow in her footsteps...

Kira

Exactly... I've been sending money to her every single month...
for years... I pay school fees for three of her grandchildren,
including this one who opened his beak to ask for a laptop...
Apart from what I send her regularly, there's always something
extra that she needs money for... weddings, funerals... As for
doctors... there's no sickness on earth Aunty hasn't made me pay
medical bills for... It's a miracle she's still standing, because
she's had everything going... from TB to typhoid... guinea worm,
tapeworm, snake bite... just name it... even ebola... She's staying
in our family house rent-free... We even send money for utilities
and all... Now it has come to this nonsense...

Morowa

Just calm down... Our people... they just don't know when to stop... you never end a conversation with them on a high note... where you feel good and refreshed...

Kira

Refreshed? Some of them are just toxic... you put the phone down after talking to some of them... and for the next hour or so, you feel dizzy... anaemic... Whatever juice you have, they make sure they suck it out of you... you get no benefit whatsoever...

Morowa

Most of the time, Sonny doesn't answer calls from back home... Sometimes I beg him to at least listen to what they have to say... He's told me I can answer his phone if I like, but he's warned me that if I do, I have to sort out the finances that come with the call... because there's always a problem when they call... and it's always about money... So in short it's a case of, if I answer, I have to pay... simple...

(They laugh)

Morowa

One time I went to see one of my elderly aunties in the village... I don't know what video or film they'd shown her... so when I told her we actually work very hard over here for our money, in all sorts of weather, and that things can get really hard and tight for us too; you know what she said to me? I shouldn't try to fool her... she may not have travelled abroad, but she knows exactly what's happening... She was telling me she knows that all we have to do in oyibo-land, is just put a card in a machine in a wall, and we can draw out any amount we like... anywhere, any time...

Kira

Well, there you go...

11   *Sunday 21 April*

Earlier in the day

YOU MUST NOT MENTION ANY OF THIS

Pastor Joel calls Morowa.

Pastor
Happy Easter, Sister Morowa... You were not at worship today... We had a wonderful service... we missed you... Is everything alright?

Morowa
Happy Easter to you too, Pastor Joel... I'm fine... a friend of mine invited me to her church out of London, so that's where I went... I put a message on the forum saying I wouldn't be around...

Pastor
OK... I must've missed that... I've been so busy...

Morowa
Is everything OK?

Pastor
Well... Is your husband around?

Morowa
Yes... What's going on?

Pastor
To be honest I don't want him to hear our conversation...

Morowa
Why? What's wrong?

Pastor
The Holy Spirit is my guide, Sister Morowa... When I'm
finished talking to you, you will understand...

Morowa
Oh... OK...

Pastor
You told me a while ago that a few things were bothering you...
particularly about your building back home... Now my visions
about you are making sense... because nothing is hidden from
those of us who dwell in and with the Holy Spirit... You see,
even before you came to me, I was divinely directed to put your
name in prayer for special deliverance... Since then the Holy
Spirit has revealed so many things to me...

Morowa
Revealed things... about *me?*

Pastor
Oh yes... I was hoping to see you after church today so we could
talk...
(Speaks in tongues)
*Matthew 12 vs 30 says 'Whoever is not with me is against me,
and whoever does not gather with me scatters.'* Do you believe
that when someone stands firm and trusts and obeys the Lord,
no-one can go against such a person... no weapon fashioned
against them can prosper?

Morowa
Amen...

Pastor
As for me, I stand answerable only to God and not man... so
therefore I'm duty bound to deliver messages to you, as told and
instructed by the Holy Spirit... no matter what those messages
may be... good or bad...
(Speaks in tongues)
The devil comes in different forms and disguises, and if you are
not covered by the blood of Jesus, you may never recognise or
realise what is happening... or by the time you do, it may be too
late for divine rescue...

Morowa
Too late?

Pastor
That's why people like me are here... to deliver children of God
from all evil... in a timely fashion... indeed before it is too late...
(Speaks in tongues)
As they say, only those close to you, those with access to you,
can hurt you... I tell you now, the aim of the enemy is to finish
you... all round... completely drain you of the luck, prosperity
and blessings that have been set aside for you from above...

Morowa
Ehn?

Pastor
And you are so favoured, Sister Morowa... your star is so
bright... but the enemy is making every effort to cover your
glow, your shine... in fact erase it... You are going to have to fast
and pray for protection over everything, every aspect of your
life... your children... your home... your career... your marriage...
otherwise your bright future will be shattered... your destiny will
be suffocated... hijacked...

Morowa
What is all this?

Pastor
Before you even told me about the building in Ghana, in one of my visions, I could see that the enemy was removing a pillow from under your head... not a good sign or symbol at all...

Morowa
What?

Pastor
Now the meaning is clear... the enemy is determined that you will not sleep in peace in that house... in fact you will not sleep in peace anywhere...

Morowa
I don't understand...

Pastor
I can't lie to you, you are in trouble... but you know that nothing, absolutely nothing, is beyond our God... It really pains me to tell you, Sister Moro... but to cut a long story short, the source of your problems are that you have been living with the devil...

Morowa
Living with the devil... How?

Pastor
And for a long time... And tell me, whose story will end well if they're living with the devil?

Morowa
What are you saying, Pastor Joel? What do you mean? Are you sure?

Pastor
Am I sure? I don't deal with a god who makes mistakes, so I can
never be given the wrong message... I know what I am about to
tell you will hit you hard, but I have to say it as it is revealed to
me... The things is, now we know what we are up against... and
as long as we are using the Lord as our weapon, we can defend
ourselves and fight back... Say Amen...

Morowa
Amen...

Pastor
And we will win if you follow the divine instructions that I will
surely be given for you... You do have a choice though, Sister
Moro... you can take the word of God, or you can reject it...

Morowa
Why would you say that? How can I reject the word of God?

Pastor
Well, believe it or not, some people actually do... Because you
may doubt what I am about to say now, but I am going to go
straight to the point: your husband is a demon... recruited and
possessed by the devil... And because the devil is truly at play
here, I am sure that you have not suspected anything at all...

Morowa
Which husband?

Pastor
How many husbands do you have?

(SILENCE)

Pastor
I know you're in shock... I expect that...

Morowa

My own Sonny? A demon... Possessed by the devil? That's not possible...

Pastor

The message is clear... I have not added or subtracted from it... *Jeremiah 17 vs 7 says, 'Blessed is the man who trusts in the Lord, whose confidence is in Him...'* And that scripture is backed by I*saiah 41 vs 10 which says, 'Do not fear, for I am with you... I will strengthen and uphold you...'* It's not going to be easy... we're up against a real force... But the Lord says, the battle is His, not ours... As always, the Lord is in control... and it is in Him that we trust... Are you ready, Sister Morowa?

Morowa

Ready? For what? Sonny cannot be possessed...

Pastor

Believe me, when this was revealed to me, I was very upset as well... It's never easy telling anyone that their loved ones are the source of their problems... You won't believe how many people in church are in a similar situation... I won't mention names, but you are not alone, this is quite a common problem...

Morowa

This is all a bit too much for me...

Pastor

(Speaks in tongues)

I know you have given your life to Christ... and because you have done so, He will provide us with full instructions and directions on how to get out of this terrible situation... so that your husband can be unbound, cleansed and delivered... Even if you are not shedding tears outwardly now, I know you must be crying inwardly... But this is not the time for any tears, you have to be strong... tears just fuel the work of the devil, because he enjoys sadness... One important thing I have to stress is this: *you must not mention any of this our discussion to anybody...*

Morowa
Why not?

Pastor
These are not *my* instructions; they are from the Holy Spirit...

Morowa
OK...

Pastor
Don't get me wrong, your husband is not a bad man... at all... but he is possessed... that is the problem... When the appointed time comes, we will confront the demon in him... but now is not that time... You need to be spiritually strengthened for that confrontation... When I've given some people similar messages, they've treated their husbands or wives differently... Don't do that... carry on as normal with your husband... talk to him, cook for him, whatever... You sleep on the same bed?

Morowa
Yes... we've always shared the same bed...

Pastor
Don't leave your marital bed... at least not yet... At some point the Holy Spirit may instruct us otherwise... but as of now, stay put... You know everything that happens in the physical world, first happens in the spiritual? If you leave your bed now, without the proper divine prayers and processes, in no time female spirits may take your place... and make matters very worse...

Morowa
Female spirits?

Pastor
Oh yes... harlots of the underworld... *you* cannot see them, but *I*
can... If they get the chance, they will seduce and marry your
husband... and if that happens... believe me, what we are dealing
with now, will be child's play...

Morowa
So what am I supposed to do now?

Pastor
To start with, have you got any holy water and oil indoors? You
know I always advise that everybody should have these on hand
all the time...

Morowa
I have some Cherub Oil and holy water...

Pastor
That's not going to be enough... you definitely need the Rapture
and Wrath Oils as well... and the consecrated soaps... I've been
advising everyone to just get the holy hamper... everything you
need for payer for about six weeks is in there... Actually,
because you'll be needing intensive prayer now, it may not last
as long... but at £250, everybody's saying it's a bargain... The
thing is, we have a lot of work to do, and you can't afford to run
out of these things...

Morowa
OK...

Pastor
Don't delay... I'll send some passages to you now... read them as
often as you can... If you can kneel where you are, do so and let
us pray...

12 *Sunday 21 April*

Later in the day

DID HE MAKE YOU FEEL ANY BETTER?

Featuring Sizani, Morowa's friend.

Kira
Happy Easter... Where have you been?

Morowa
Happy Easter to you too... I told you Sizani invited me to her church... so I went down to her place... It was a different worship experience with South Africans... but really nice... I loved the songs and chants...

Kira
OK... How is she doing?

Morowa
She's fine... she asked after you too... Hmmm...

Kira
What was that heavy sigh for?

Morowa
I know you'll say I'm talking nonsense, but...

Kira
Let me be the judge of that...

Morowa
Joel just called me...

Kira
Aha... I might've known... if you're not quite right, he's likely to be involved somehow... What did he have to say?

Morowa
I told him I have a few things bothering me...

Kira
Don't we all?

Morowa
Well... I told him about the problems with the house back home... apart from someone else claiming the land is theirs, there's so much more going on now... Kira, if we're not careful, we might lose *everything*...

Kira
What are you saying? I thought Sonny sorted all that out the last time he went home...

Morowa
Well, to an extent... but new problems keep cropping up... and you know how it is back home... so difficult... almost impossible sometimes to get documents and paperwork... One of the twins... Yaa's son... he's been back and forward for the last six months or so, trying to get us just *one* land registry certificate... The whole thing is just getting messier... Our lawyer over there says we'll probably have to go to court...

Kira
Oh-oh... OK, so what did Joel have to say about all this now?

Morowa
Well in short, he says that Sonny is the cause of all my problems, and that I may never lay my head alive in the house in Ghana... He says because Sonny doesn't want me to...

Kira
What did you say? I don't think I quite understand...

Morowa
Well, he says Sonny is possessed... by the devil...

Kira
(Laughs dryly)
OK... So what did *you* say to *him*?

Morowa
Well... I know Sonny is not a demon or anything like that, but...

Kira
But what? You mean you didn't find a few choice words to tell him immediately, before slamming the phone down?

Morowa
Whatever the case, I think I need prayers...

Kira
Who doesn't? We all do... all the time...

Morowa
No seriously... I think this house thing is really getting to me now... And call him what you may, Joel does seem to have a special gift of prayer and anointing...

Kira
You know what the frightening thing is, Moro? That someone as sensible as *you*... can even be listening to someone like Joel... and actually tolerating him... Now look, you're nearly in tears...

Morowa
To be honest, I was feeling quite low even before he called...

Kira

But did he make you feel any better? Judging by the way you sound, I don't think so... Look, you need to come to your senses... right now... I'm warning you, I really am... Walk away from Joel, his stupid church and his nonsense...

Morowa

That's why I didn't want to tell you; I knew you'd go on like this... Look, Joel's come through for me a good few times... It was after his prayers that I was appointed head of department... then head of year...

Kira

Is that right? Because I don't remember it quite like that... What I know was that you were qualified and good enough... If you really and truly believe that you only got those appointments because of Joel's prayers, then I really don't know what to say to you any more... What power has he got? Look, the couple of times I've been to your church, I've not been impressed... at all... The last time I went, apart from the absolute nonsense they were preaching, they took collection four times... *four times*... and a fifth one cos one of them had a birthday... So *five collections* in total... I couldn't believe it... bare-faced, daylight robbery... carried out in the name of God...

Morowa

That's because it was a special service... Most of the time we have just two or three collections...

Kira

Just two or three? Is that all? Oh brilliant... And the money goes where, exactly?

Morowa

They do plenty charity... all over...

Kira

What 'charity'... 'all over' where? Please... you've got to be a bit more specific than that... But I bet no-one can really pinpoint where the bulk of the money goes... There'll be no proper accounts... nothing you can really put your finger on... When they do use some of the money, it's just for show... to try and convince people that they're doing *something*... The bulk of the offerings, donations and whatnot, go straight into the pastors' pockets... that's just a fact... and it's all so wrong... obscene...

Morowa

No... I know for a fact that they actually help people out... with all sorts of things... food, rent, scholarships, hardship funds... stuff like that...

Kira

I'm telling you, whatever money they supposedly help people out with, is just a fraction of what they've swindled out of the churchgoers in the first place... I couldn't believe the price of the anointing oils and soaps that they were practically forcing people to buy... then they had the so-called projects they wanted donations for... then they had the CDs, T-shirts, books, everything... I say it's daylight robbery... and it's going on in most of the black churches... It's just one big, blatant con...

Morowa

Oh, don't call it a con... it's not...

Kira

Oh yes it is... Look, I don't know who told some of our people that all they have to do to survive or get what they want, is to find the nearest greasy pastor, who probably needs more prayers than they do... and give them money for prayers or to buy any rubbish they may say you need... And as far as people are concerned, the more you give the pastor, the closer you come to getting what you want from God... whether it's a job, spouse, whatever you're after... Like magic... you don't even have to push yourself, you don't have to make any real effort... just give money to the pastor, sit back and wait for the miracle...

Morowa
It's not that simple...

Kira
That's the frightening thing, Moro... the ridiculously simple formula that these so-called men, *and women* of God, use to enrich themselves... preying on people... Show me where it says in the Bible that you have to go through people like them... through anybody for that matter... to get to God... As far as I know, the only person you need to go through, is Jesus Christ... and he didn't charge anything...

Morowa
You're confusing things a bit...

Kira
I'm not confused at all... *you're* the one who is... believe me... But I'm not surprised, because confusion is what some of these satanic pastors thrive on... And after they've caused the confusion in people's lives, they then carry on as if they have the solution to the problems they've deliberately caused in the first place... whilst taking your money for good measure as well...

Morowa
Look, essentially all we do is pay our tithes, sow holy seeds, buy holy oils and water that they've blessed, and stuff like that... that's about all really...

Kira
You say 'that's all'? Total things up... blessed oils... And

blessed by who anyway? The likes of Joel? Oh please... And what happens to your tithes? Which seeds? Wake up Moro...

Morowa
Look, Joel wouldn't deliberately just to try to upset me, my marriage, my home...

Kira
Oh yes he would... And you know why? Because people like him are anything but men of God... For some crazy reason you're refusing to see him for what he is and how much trouble people like him cause... And it's not just money some of them want... they want people's spouses... their property... some tamper with kids... just doing all sorts in the name of God... Weapons of mass destruction in their own right, if you ask me... just going around causing sadness for people... And someone like you... you're so good for business, because if others see somebody like *you* Moro, following someone like Joel, they want to follow him too... And I'm not trying to have a go at you, but if *you* can be taken in like this, then what hope is there for others?

Morowa
Now you're over-reacting... calm down...

Kira
I'm overreacting? The nerve of him to tell you that Sonny is a demon or whatever... Before you know it, next thing he'll be telling you that the Holy Spirit says you should tell Sonny to leave, so that *he* can move in... to your bedroom...

Morowa
Oh how? You're taking things too far now...

Kira
OK... But I'm warning you... don't say I didn't...

Morowa

So are you saying there's absolutely nothing good about our pastors and churches?

Kira

Look,we all know there are some really good, decent, God-fearing pastors out there... but they've been outnumbered... overshadowed by loud nuisances like Joel, who are just out to enjoy worldly things and acquire personal wealth... How can some of them, and not just the black pastors mind you... how can they justify owning private jets, mansions, fat bank accounts... living in luxury... all by taxing their church people the way they do?

Morowa

Look, they're human beings, so of course they don't get everything spot on... they make mistakes sometimes...

Kira

Oh, so that's your take on this? So Joel and the other ones with private jets and stuff... according to you, they're just a bit wrong sometimes? This is whilst some of the people they're preaching to and demanding money from are in rags... Well, I can't talk any more...

Morowa

I'm not defending these pastors blindly, but look... some people begrudge them having anything at all... expect them to live like paupers because they're doing God's work... I don't think that's fair... they have to survive...

Kira

Nobody's saying they shouldn't survive... But some of them are not just surviving... they're living in luxury... Jesus himself had nothing... absolutely nothing... he actually rode on a donkey...

Yes, I know the world has moved on a bit from then... But private jets and all those things? I know Joel is not quite there yet, but he's well on the way... after all, you have to start somewhere... Look at his car... look at the other pastors' cars... their wives' cars... their clothes, jewellery and all that... Come on now, Moro... when there's so much want and poverty in this world...

Morowa
Look, a lot of the pastors actually have other jobs...

Kira
That may well be the case... but I bet you, most of them get the bulk of their income from the church... Look, personally, I wouldn't begrudge any proper pastor being paid fairly, so he can live decently and be in a position to help others, because that's what all proper religions should be about... But that's not what a lot of these pastors are about, and you know it... And another very sad thing, is that there'll be young people aspiring to be like them, because they look prosperous and affluent and all that... But what are they in reality? Just monsters in fancy clothes... experts at swindling and cheating vulnerable people...

Morowa
No, no...

Kira
Oh yes... I wonder sometimes, is it hypnosis they use on the congregation? Or magic? Scare tactics? What is the technique? I can't believe the way you're actually sticking up for these evil, wretched, sick people masquerading as men of God...

Morowa
So, I shouldn't go to church, or what?

Kira

Did I say that? I didn't and wouldn't say that...

Morowa

You don't really believe in God, so...

Kira

I have never told you I don't believe in God... What I have told you over and over again is that I don't consider myself Muslim, Christian or anything else per se... I believe that I didn't make myself, there's a supreme being responsible for my existence, and I choose to believe that this being is a good one and a guide for me... And I'm convinced that if most people always try to treat others the way they would like to be treated, the world would be a much better place... that's it... Look, when it comes to pastors, you know I have my own story or two to tell...

Morowa

Hmmm....

Kira

I've told you what I went through with them when I couldn't fall pregnant... I don't like to think back to that time... What didn't they make me do? One time they made me walk barefooted... they made me drink some horrible stuff... one made me put some itchy leaves in my panties for weeks... One day when they started itching me at work, I nearly stripped myself naked in front of my colleagues...

Morowa

(Laughs)

Kira

It wasn't funny oh... These wretched pastors... made me do this and that... But did anything work? No... *nothing*... All they did was take advantage of my desperation... because that's what they do... I didn't dare let QC know what was happening at that time, because he would've said it was because of the pastors I wasn't getting pregnant... and he would've probably been right... And knowing him then... always looking for an excuse to misbehave... he would've given me hell accordingly if he'd found out was going on...

(They laugh)

Kira
QC has his faults, but he was actually very supportive at that time... One time I was actually quite shocked when I overheard him saying to someone: 'Do you marry just to have children? If you want them but can't have them naturally, what about adoption? After all, even some people who have kids naturally, adopt as well...' But to me he would just say: 'Stop stressing... one way or another, the children will come when they're ready'...

Morowa
QC is a good man...

Kira
Whatever... But he was right... when I'd almost given up all hope... boom, I was pregnant with Ralston... and just two months after Ralston was born, I was pregnant with Richie...

Morowa
Proper case of waiting for ever for a bus, then four come all at once...

(They laugh)

Kira
Seriously, Moro... as far as I'm concerned, some of these pastors are just plain dodgy... they're no good... they just make bad

matters worse... they should be avoided like the plague... Like now, Joel knows you've got issues with the house back home... obviously you're upset, and he's found an angle where he can milk you good and proper by offering spiritual help and advice... at a cost, of course... You think Joel cares if he causes problems for you and Sonny? He doesn't, because that's what he wants, I'm telling you... so it'll be like you've got never ending problems that only he can solve, and so you have to keep running back to him all the time for solutions... and as I said, we all know *his* solutions don't come cheap... Wake up Moro, because if you don't, by the time Joel's through with you, you won't recognise yourself, never mind anybody else...

Morowa
OK... I've heard you... I will pray about things... because I can't lie, I won't feel right if I don't go to church...

Kira
You think I don't know that? The church is meant to be a good place; it's bad, satanic people like Joel who are messing things up... Just do me a favour, OK? Find a proper church... with proper pastors ... they do exist... Joel and his setup... all wrong... and deep down, I think you know it... Look, if that fool can say that Sonny is a demon, or possessed, or whatever... then all I have to say is: it takes one to know one...

13 Sunday 5 May

I'M JUST TRYING TO HELP YOU

Pastor Joel calls Morowa... again.

Pastor

What's happening? I've been calling you... I didn't see you
again today in church... that's two, three weeks or so running...
You haven't bought your oils and stuff... I understand you're
even behind with your tithe... Do you know the implications of
not paying your tithe?

Morowa

I was up till late yesterday and overslept, that's all...

Pastor

You did not oversleep... That was no ordinary sleep, Sister
Morowa... Nothing is hidden from me... The devil bound you in
your bed...

Morowa

What?

Pastor

Oh yes... Be careful so you don't play into his hands... Not
attending service is the beginning of his power over you... doing
everything to make sure you don't hear the word of God... I
hope at the very worst you've been reading the Psalms and
passages I sent to you...

Morowa

I have...

Pastor
I know you know the importance and benefits of worship and fellowship... so I don't have to tell you that staying away from church is not a good thing... Anyway, as I warned you, I hope you have not discussed this your situation with anybody...

Morowa
Well... I can't lie... I was so upset... I just had to talk to someone... I only spoke to one person... my good friend...

Pastor
Let me guess... that your Sierra Leone sister... Kari... Karen?

Morowa
Kira...

Pastor
I felt it... It was revealed to me that you spoke to someone... But Sister Morowa, I categorically told you not to talk to anybody...

Morowa
She's the only person I spoke to...

Pastor
There's a reason why the Holy Spirit demands that you keep certain things to yourself... So what did you tell her?

Morowa
I didn't say much... basically, I just told her that I had problems with the house back home and that you'd prayed for me...

Pastor
Don't get me wrong, I am not specifically talking about that your friend... but take it from me... many so-called friends and well wishers make you believe that they have your best interest at heart, but in reality, that is not the case... at all... They will do everything they can to discourage you from listening to people

like me who speak the word of God... So you always need to be on your guard...
(Speaks in tongues)
Yes Lord... I hear you Lord... The Holy Spirit has just given me a very clear message about your building back home... Any funds you had allocated to put towards the house, you must channel those funds into sowing seeds for deliverance in church... immediately...

Morowa
I don't understand...

Pastor
You've suspended work on the building in Ghana, right?

Morowa
Yes... for the time being...

Pastor
We don't want that suspension to become permanent... So what you have to do, is put all the money you have saved by not building these past few months... be wise... spend it in church... These are not *my* instructions... they are from the Holy Spirit...

(SILENCE)

Pastor
Where are you?

Morowa
I'm at home...

Pastor
'Where are you?' That is the first question God asked in the Bible... *Genesis 3 vs 9...* Where are you with the Lord, Sister Morowa? Where do you stand with Him? What do you want to do: save money, or save and deliver the lives and souls of you

and your husband? Well, it's up to you... I was straightforward with you about the revelations... You yourself must know the urgency of arresting things before the devil gets his way; because if he does, things will surely spin out of control for you... Of course we don't want it to come to that... but I can't force you... our relationship with the Lord cannot be a forced one...

Morowa
I have to be honest with you... my husband won't agree to me making withdrawals... just like that...

Pastor
Ah... You mean you don't have your own account... your own money?

Morowa
Of course I do, but the bulk of our money goes into our joint account... so I just can't withdraw money from there anyhow...

Pastor
Look, I'm just trying to help you... But getting that money shouldn't be a *choice* for you; it should be a *must*... Look, I don't want to put you under any pressure... but if it comes to it, consider taking a loan, that's what some people in your situation do... You see the thing is: the sooner you sow the seeds, the sooner you will begin to tackle this spiritual attack you're facing... delay is dangerous... Noah only had seven days... *just seven days*... to gather all the animals on earth into the ark... Many people don't understand... as a pastor, I sometimes have to do things I don't really want to do... extraordinary things... even put myself at personal risk... just to help deliver others... so you should be prepared to do whatever it takes to follow the instructions of the Holy Spirit...

Morowa
Hmmm...

Pastor

You need to sow your seeds as instructed, and quickly... and in no time you will begin to reap the benefits... What I'm trying to say is, there's no point holding onto money or material things, if getting rid of those things will help to clear the obstacles that are clouding your destiny... They are just worldly things... you understand me? At the moment, your blessings are not flowing freely towards you at all... they're being held back... but you don't seem too concerned...

Morowa

Pastor... you sound a bit annoyed...

Pastor

I am a servant of the Lord... anger is not in my dictionary... But *Second Corinthians 9 vs 6-7* clearly states that God loves a cheerful giver... He does... It's like you're counting the cost... The thing is, we are divinely instructed to give without looking back... you've always done so in the past... What has changed? I am a bit frustrated, because it seems as if you're not fully understanding or accepting the urgency of things... And this is happening because you are not listening to the word of God as you should... as you used to... You never used to miss church... you're now listening to friends and suchlike... In fact, believe it or not, I actually have a spiritual message about that your Sierra Leone friend... but all I will say for now is, go and read *First Corinthians 15 vs 33*... and be very careful...

Morowa

Hmmm... OK...

Pastor

Anyway, as I say, at the end of the day, it's up to you... I have to go now, I have a meeting in half an hour... so if you can, where you are, kneel and let us pray quickly...

14 Wednesday 15 May

I'VE HEARD IT ALL NOW

Introducing Mama Razia who's visiting from Sierra Leone. She is staying with her son, Bolu and his wife, Nish, who is Kira's younger sister. Also introducing Faisal.

Morowa
Did you get my message to watch the cooking programme?

Kira
I did, but my neighbour came round with a box of chocolates... a little thank you for putting her bins in and out when she was away... So, of course, we chatted for a while, so I missed the start... but I caught the bit where they were using bamboo and banana leaves...

Morowa
Oh... that took me way back to days in the village when I was growing up... It's a very interesting series... it started a couple of weeks ago... they're featuring what they call 'tribal cuisine'... Did you hear the fancy names the oyibo cook was giving to the stuff we cook anyhow, all the time? *Flambéed* plantains with *pan seared* pig trotters...

(They laugh)

Morowa
But I actually tried one of the dishes they featured a couple of weeks ago, from Central Africa... it's called 'kanda ti nyama', or something like that... it's like spicy meatballs with pumpkin seeds... And my first attempt didn't turn out too bad, you

know... Sonny really enjoyed it... I'm going to try the East African dish they featured this week...

Kira

The one with the maize? That one looked a bit tricky to make... but we just have to try new things... from wherever... cos to be honest, one gets sick and tired of eating the same stuff over and over again... They put a leaflet through my door the other day for Sri Lankan cooking classes...

Morowa

I wouldn't mind doing something like that... but there's no time...

Kira

That's the problem... After work, if I manage to go to the gym a couple of times a week... after that I'm knackered... honestly... no time or space for anything else...

Morowa

When we retire we need to travel all over Africa... so we can sample and savour all the different foods and cultures...

Kira

Ah, it would be wonderful if we could do something like that...

Morowa

Just two grannies trekking across Africa...

Kira

That could be the name of our blog...

(They laugh)

Morowa

We could go and visit that your new found cousin, what's his name? The one in Botswana...

Kira
Oh, Faisal...

Morowa
Yes... we could start our trek and tour from there... They say
Botswana is nice oh...

Kira
So I hear...

Morowa
I really want go to those parts of Africa... Anyway... the chap
who presents the programme, the one who had the kente shirt
on... Did he remind you of anyone?

Kira
Remind me of someone? No... Who?

Morowa
Don't you think he looks like your brother-in-law... Bolu?

Kira
You think so? I'll look at him closely next time... Talking of
Bolu... Did I tell you the latest with him? Well, with his mother,
to be precise...

Morowa
Mama Razia? What is she up to now?

Kira
When is she never up to something? Just being her usual
nuisance self... Now she says Bolu needs more children... one
child is not enough...

Morowa
What? Where is she, anyway?

Kira
She came over about a month or so ago... She said she was
dying, so they brought her over for a quick check-up...

Morowa
Obviously she must be feeling much better now, that's why she's
piped up with this nonsense...

Kira
Of course...

Morowa
They should just fling her out... The last time she left, I thought
she said she would never come back...

Kira
Please... she says that every time she's leaving... always
threatening to *never, ever* come back, but...

Morowa
Why can't our people just come, sit down quietly and rest when
they come to visit?

Kira
No, not Mama Razia... She's allergic to peace and calm... All
she does when she's here is stress my sister out... Oh, by the
way, she's having a small lunch in a couple of months... and of,
course, we're invited...

Morowa
Who? Mama Razia?

Kira
Are you kidding? I hope she'll be long gone by then... Omar's
turning twenty-four, and Salma will be here for a few days

around that time... so double excuse for Nish to do something... although she was telling me Omar says he may not be there; he says it'll just be full of oldies...

(They laugh)

Morowa
Look, we don't want to see him either... We'll eat, drink and be merry in his absence... But come oh... *Twenty-four years...* So that's how long we've known each other?

Kira
Are you OK?

Morowa
What?

Kira
'Are you OK?' That's the very first question you asked me at the bus stop... I'll never forget...

Morowa
And the thing is, I'm still wondering... *'Are you OK?'*

(They laugh)

Morowa
I'll see if Kukua can do a small cake...

Kira
Oh, that'll be really nice... Of course Nish is going to stress me to do the bulk of the cooking... Actually, I'll probably just pay someone to do it... I can't be bothered these days... it takes too much out of you...

Morowa
Let Mama Razia make herself useful... Why can't she do some

of the cooking for the party? Keep her out of mischief...

Kira

I say I'm hoping she'll be gone by then... honestly... Talking of Mama Razia and food and cooking... I told you we nearly fought one time over a food issue...

Morowa

You and Mama Razia? I know you've had your problems, but you've never told me you nearly *fought*...

Kira

Oh yes... We nearly did oh... You know I've told you about Nish's miscarriages, the fertility treatment and all that... she really went through hell before she eventually managed to keep Omar's pregnancy... So anyway, one day she called me... Mama Razia had been abusing her for hours on end... non-stop...

Morowa

About her not being able to have a child?

Kira

What else? Of course, this was before she had Omar... This was happening virtually every day, apparently... as soon as Bolu left for work, the drama would start... One time Mama Razia slapped her... another time she tore her clothes... all sorts... Anyway, this particular day Nish called me... Mouthy as she can be, she was crying like a baby on the phone... things had just got too much for her... Luckily, I had the day off or something... so I made my way down to their flat in East London? You remember that place?

Morowa

Oh, yes... near that park... That was a lovely place they had...

Kira

They never gave it up oh... they bought it and rented it out...

Morowa

Oh, good...

Kira

Anyway, as soon as I walked in that day, Mama Razia turned on me... she was like a mad woman... She started shouting that I should just take Nish with me and get out... that she and her family had not bargained for this childlessness... at all... By then Nish had suffered about two or three miscarriages...she was desperate...

Morowa

Awww... I can imagine...

Kira

Anyway, I told Nish to get her things so we could go for a stroll or something... just to get out of the house and the situation for a little while... As soon as we said we were leaving, Mama Razia started again... Where did we think we were going... what was Bolu supposed to eat when he got back from work? She was shouting: other women were carrying babies... but look at Nish... all she could do was carry handbags, to go and roam around... aimlessly...

Morowa

Our people...

Kira

Anyway, we went into the kitchen, I think to get some water or something... Next thing Mama Razia sort of blocked us in, telling us nobody was going anywhere until after Nish had cooked *fresh* food for Bolu... She was saying after all Nish didn't have children to look after or anything much to do... so

why couldn't she cook for her husband every day? And it's not
as if there wasn't any food... there was plenty... but no... Mama
Razia said it had to be *freshly* cooked...

Morowa
Oh boy...

Kira
Anyway, she stood right in front of me, and of course I told her
to get out of my way... but she said she wouldn't... I couldn't
believe what was happening... Then she dared me to push her...
and God knows, I was going to... Next thing, I just felt Nish
pulling me back... I was so ready to push Mama Razia... right to
the ground, if I had to...

Morowa
Can you imagine if you'd actually pushed her? The drama...

Kira
Oh no... Every year she'd be taking people on a pilgrimage to
show them the exact spot where it all happened... and the
permanent scars she would be claiming I left on her that day...

(They laugh)

Kira
Anyway, she eventually moved out of the way, and we went out
for a while... But by the time we got back, Mama Razia had
recharged her batteries... now she was reciting poetry: that a
woman without a child was like a mirror without a reflection... a
spoon without a handle... a fart without a smell...

(They laugh)

Morowa
Oh, you remember all that?

Kira
I've even forgotten some.... there was plenty more... Initially we ignored her... but then she started on our family... how everybody knew that our mother and all the women in our family were just loose rubbish... she couldn't understand why her son had to get involved with such wretched people like us... she went on and on... Then at a point I'd just had enough and I just snapped... I don't know where the words were coming from... they were just tumbling out of my mouth... Nish was shaking in some corner, begging me to stop... but I didn't until I was satisfied... But do you know what, Nish said after that she had some peace for a while... Apparently Mama Razia would say: "Let me keep quiet... next thing you'll call your people to come and beat me"...

Morowa
She's just a bully, and when you gave her a dose of her own craziness, she realised that two can play that game... But what is it with our people anyway? It's like if you can't or don't have a child, you're somehow not quite whole...

Kira
Africans, we love kids, but sometimes we go a bit overboard... If you're struggling to conceive like Nish was... I think they expect you to die trying, if it comes to it...

Morowa
And God forbid a couple says, that for whatever reason, they may not want children...

Kira
What? You mean you can have children, but you don't want them? Or you're going to actively prevent yourself from having them... maybe with medication or whatever? No... our people can't compute that... they can't take or accept that... at all... that's beyond them...

Morowa
I actually heard of one mother who came over here and insisted that her son and his wife make love right in front of her...

Kira
Ehn?

Morowa
Apparently she was tired of waiting for grandchildren, and needed to see for herself that they were making every effort and doing things the right way...

Kira
I've heard it all now...

Morowa
If you can't have a child, that's an issue... have a daughter, they're still not quite happy, they want a son... have one child, that's not enough, they need more... Imagine Mama Razia now... Omar needs siblings... someone who's turning twenty-four in a few weeks time... You just couldn't make it up... Why is anybody listening to her anyway?

Kira
To be honest, I don't think anybody really is... I just feel sorry for my sister; Mama Razia's a serious nuisance...

Morowa
(Laughs)
You know why I'm laughing? You always complain about how cheeky Nish is, but you always have that your sister's back... always...

Kira
Look, if I pay attention to Nish's cheek, I won't let her anywhere

near me... honestly... In fact, sometimes when she starts her nonsense, I say to myself, 'No problem... Mama Razia... she'll chisel your rough edges for me'...

(They laugh)

Kira
But seriously, I wouldn't wish Mama Razia on my worst enemy... The thing is, my father made me promise to always take care of Nish, no matter what... so I always hear his voice when I've been on the brink of just slicing her off...

Morowa
You? Slice Nish, off? You couldn't... even if you tried...

(They laugh)

Morowa
Anyway, what do you think Omar would like for his birthday?

Kira
I usually just give him money... What can you even get these young people nowadays, anyway?

Morowa
Whatever the case, I'll get something for Nish... and Salma, of course...

Kira
Oh... So what about me?

Morowa
What do *you* want now?

Kira
You want to get something for my sisters and leave me out? It

doesn't work like that... Do you know how long ago you promised me shito?

Morowa
OK, I'll make some for the party, and set some aside specially for you... Happy now?

Kira
So, I have to wait till the party?

Morowa
It's not that far away... What is that expression your people have? They say 'sleep and wake'... the time will come soon enough...

Kira
OK... but *my* shito must come with kelewele oh... just like you did it the last time... remember? And you know there'd be no point... no balance to the whole thing, if you don't make some waakye, which of course comes with the stew... preferably that your fried giblet stew... And to round everything up nicely... peppered crab... that's all...

Morowa
OK... Are you sure 'that's all'? Nothing else?

(They laugh)

15 Monday 27 May

WE LIKE A BIT OF DRAMA

Morowa
Ah Kira... I don't think you should've called Joel, you know...

Kira
Ehn?

Morowa
He said you called him and told him all sorts... called him a criminal and all...

Kira
But isn't that what he is? And for the record, *he* called *me*...

Morowa
Well how did he get your number?

Kira
Have you been drinking, Moro? He's always had my number... Look, I've probably known Joel as long as you have... And you know what, he knew what he was doing, because he didn't call me from the number I have for him... he probably thought I wouldn't answer... and he's right; I probably wouldn't have... He called me from an 'unknown' number...

Morowa
So what was the problem?

Kira
I don't have a problem... I don't know what *you* told him, but he started off by asking me if I know why you haven't been to

church for a while... more or less insinuating that *I* was the one influencing you not to go... He was right, of course, but I don't owe *him* any explanation... I don't have any time or patience for him... none whatsoever... When he started, I was speechless for a few moments... I was a bit taken aback... But when I came to, I just stopped him in his tracks... I said to him: "Let me guess... You're phoning to tell me that I'm another possessed devil like Sonny, right?" I made him understand, in no uncertain terms, that I'm not one of the people he can manipulate...

Morowa
You shouldn't have spoken to him like that, Kira... I don't think he meant any harm...

Kira
First and foremost you weren't there... you didn't hear how everything went... And look, *you* may be under his spell, but he can't get *me*... I found the whole thing so irritating... Don't you see anything wrong with all this? What is he calling me for? And to talk such nonsense... That's harassment, you know?

Morowa
He said you said you hoped someone would give him a good thrashing and all... Was all that necessary?

Kira
Was it necessary for him to call me in the first place to talk such foolishness? How come you seem to be seeing things from *his* angle and not mine?

Morowa
Maybe if you'd just listened to him...

Kira
Listen to him for what? But didn't I tell you? He's going to

make you fight all the people who really care about you, so he can have you all to himself... so all you'll be doing is listening to him and his nonsense... He'll manipulate you, drain you and your bank account dry, without any interference... Just look at us now... arguing about this fool...

Morowa

You've never really given him a chance...

Kira

Do you know Joel is actually making you go a bit crazy? All you've been saying is 'give him a chance... listen to him'... I've said it: if he's got people like *you* on his side, fighting his battles for him, what more could he ask for? Look, I've got something on the fire... I've got to go...

Morowa

You haven't got anything on the fire... let's talk...

Kira

Look, I don't want to talk about Joel... But you know something, I don't think Joel should be taking all the blame here...

Morowa

So what are you saying? I'm to blame as well now, or what?

Kira

You want the truth, right? Yes... *you* have a few issues too...

Morowa

How?

Kira

Look, you have so much going for you and to be grateful for... nice family, good job, lovely home, etc... Then any time things aren't going quite your way, you think Joel can turn things round... it's as if you're not meant to have any problems in the first place... So you think everything should be smooth sailing for you all the time?

Morowa
No, I don't think that at all... the thing is...

Kira
Let me finish... please... Of course there's no harm in praying... prayer is important... but surely that's basically all you need... not predictions and all the extras that people like Joel come up with to create even more problems... They don't just pray... they must come up with a 'suspect', or two, responsible for whatever may be going wrong... You have a few hiccups with the house back home, and you run to him... a crook who needs a lot of help himself, if you ask me... Look at somebody like him... claiming he can see visions and the future... has two-way conversations with God, and this and that... You have to ask yourself: 'How desperate can God really be to have to talk to *him*?'

Morowa
(Laughs)

Kira
It's no joke... the amount of trouble people like Joel cause... Imagine him having the guts to tell you that Sonny is the cause of your problems... that he's going to make sure you don't lay your head in your house... so in short Sonny's going to kill you... What an insult... But for some strange reason, you don't seem to be seeing the seriousness of all this... I really can't understand why you're still tolerating him after all that rubbish... seriously...

Morowa
Look, I know how much to listen to, and how much to take with a pinch of salt...

Kira

Well not everybody does... and to be honest, I'm not too sure about *you* either...

Morowa

What do you mean by that?

Kira

You don't realise it, but you've been brainwashed, Moro... it's crazy... and scary... it really is...

Morowa

No... I know what I'm doing...

Kira

Oh you do most of the time... but not when it comes to this your church... Look, Joel's type... they've studied our people, and they've come up with a winning formula... They've mixed the two religions... black and white... elements of the Bible and elements of juju... Black people, we like a bit of drama and mystery... so that's where juju comes in... But let's face it, juju is a bit dark... and most people don't want others to know that they consult juju priests or people like that... And also, whether we accept it or not, we have a complex... everything else seems to be better than what *we* have... So that's where the Bible comes in, because essentially, it's foreign... Of course, it too has its mystery and all that... but it's more socially acceptable... it's more upmarket to go to church and talk about Jesus... So there you have it... People like Joel provide a perfect blend of the two religions... black and white... And they make people pay them for providing that blend... So clever...

Morowa

You're getting a bit ridiculous now...

Kira
Call me ridiculous or whatever you like... but when the scales
eventually fall from your eyes... which I pray they do, and soon...
you'll look back and realise that I'm telling you as it is... These
pastors... their tactics and manipulation are second to none...
What do they really give people in return for taking their money?
All they have to offer is fake hope, or fake visions of the future...
no concrete guarantees of anything whatsoever... And they
always have an answer or an explanation: so if by coincidence
things work out fine, of course they take the praise, as if it's all
down to them and their prayers... But if things don't work out,
then it's either they're still waiting on God's time, you can't rush
God... or the devil is responsible for the delay... They just make
me sick...

Morowa
I don't think you're looking at this whole thing the right way...

Kira
You keep saying I'm wrong... So are you really, seriously
saying that people like Joel and his cronies are right?

Morowa
Well, for starters, I know I don't mix the two religions...

Kira
I've just told you... you don't have to... people like Joel do all the
mixing for you... What people fail to realise is that some, if not
most of these pastors, are juju priests as well... so a lot of the
time they don't even need to consult anybody else as such... they
consult *themselves*... so they just come up with whatever they
like... unchallenged... To be honest, I don't have anything as
such against juju... it's the African way... My issue is the brazen
way these devils keep deceiving people... Look, I think one has
to choose... the Bible or juju... because I think it's the mixing of

the two that's causing most of the problems... particularly for black people... because we never seem to get the balance right... we never interpret things to our advantage... The message *we* seem to get from people like Joel, is that we should impoverish ourselves even further, by giving our last penny to them... for prayers and stuff that should be free in the first place...

Morowa
You haven't given me the chance to explain anything...

Kira
You don't want to explain... you just want to defend Joel... What were you telling me they called him one time? Joel the jewel... please... If you ask me, he's actually Joel the genius... because all he does is talk nonsense, deceive people... then these same people go and give him their everything in exchange for prayers and blessings and all that... If that's not genius, then I don't know what is... You know what, the more I think about it, the more I wouldn't mind talking to him again... In fact, tell him to call me... he took me unawares this time... next time I'll be well ready for him...

Morowa
Kira, this is not like you... at all...

Kira
This is not like you either... only Joel makes you this way... Look, I'm hungry... let me go eat something...

Morowa
OK... bon appétit...

16   *Monday 10 June*

WHAT KIND OF NAME IS THAT ANYWAY?

Featuring Pa Die-Go and Susannah.

Morowa
Eyd Mawlid Saeid!

Kira
Did you just wish me happy birthday... in Arabic?

Morowa
I did... I wanted to do it this morning when I spoke to you, but everything was muddled up in my mouth... I've been practising all day at work...

(They laugh)

Kira
Thank you... You're something else... And thanks for the card...

Morowa
Oh, I'm so happy you got it because I posted it quite late on Friday... I'll give you your present on Saturday at Mama Abena's... we'll celebrate your birthday there... I remember the first day I actually saw you write Arabic... I was just blown away... And you know and can sing hymns, probably better than me... You keep telling me that combining the two religions wasn't difficult when you were growing up, but...

Kira
It wasn't, I'm telling you... Actually, I think having a Muslim mother and Christian father was one of the best gifts in life my

sisters and I ever had... we knew nothing else, it was just normal
for us to worship both ways... And the thing is, the two religions
are similar in so many ways anyway...

Morowa
So I understand...

Kira
They are... You know my country has had its issues, big time...
but I'm sure we're probably amongst the top countries in the
world when it comes to religious tolerance... honestly...
Christians and Muslims have lived side by side for ever...
they've always intermingled and intermarried... no problem...
It's been a bit of a puzzle to me how much trouble religion seems
to cause around the world, when we've got it so right in that our
tiny, little country...

Morowa
Hmmm...

Kira
Let me tell you a story... something that shaped my stance on
religion... and sex... When I was twelve...

Morowa
You.... were you ever twelve? So when was that?

Kira
Do you want to hear my story or not?

Morowa
(Laughs)
Sorry, sorry...

Kira
I was getting ready for my Common Entrance, and my mum

decided that I needed extra help with English and Maths... She was desperate for me to make the grade so I could go to the same secondary school as Salma... TT... Taw Togsiwa... It was definitely the best school in my country at the time... and as far as I'm concerned, it was one of the best in the world...

Morowa
You're always bragging about that your school... What kind of name is that anyway? Taw Togsiwa... please...

Kira
You're just jealous... go and Google it... then you'll see what I'm talking about...

(They laugh)

Kira
Anyway... I just had to go to that school... So my mum was over the moon when Pa Die-Go put me on his lesson list...

Morowa
Die-Go? You Sierra Leoneans... Is that somebody's real name?

Kira
His name was actually Diego... I think they said his grandfather was from Spain or Italy... somewhere like that... He looked a bit foreign, you know what I mean? Anyway, apparently, as soon as he got to secondary school, Diego became Die-Go... for life... If you didn't call him Die-Go, no-one knew who you were talking about... I think he even called himself Die-Go...

(They laugh)

Kira
Apparently he was a lay preacher, ex-policeman, ex-teacher, ex-

everything... As far as people were concerned, he knew
everything about everything... he was consulted on every issue...
You know that type?

Morowa
Oh yes... every community has one or two like that...

Kira
Anyway, it's like everybody wanted Pa Die-Go to give their
children lessons; so I started attending his after-school classes,
probably a year or so before the exams... If I remember right, it
was twice a week, on Tuesdays and Thursdays... Most of us in
primary school lived within walking distance of school and of
Pa Die-Go's house... so on lesson days, a group of us would just
walk down to his place straight after school...

Let's take a quick trip down Memory Lane
with twelve-year-old Kira...

One day, Kira and her mates were walking to Pa Die-Go's house
after school, as they always did on lesson days, and as they
turned onto his street they saw a crowd. They pushed their way
through what was fast becoming a mob, to get closer to Pa Die-
Go's house; and to their dismay, they saw him being dragged out
of his yard by his trousers, blood all over his face and shirt.
Some people were pelting him and his house with whatever they
could lay their hands on, others were screaming, cursing,
threatening. A few jumped up and down on his car, an old VW
Beetle parked just in front of his house, clearly intent on
destroying it. It was just mayhem.

On the pavement outside his house, a few people were
aggressively interrogating and shouting at Susannah. She was

Pa Die-Go's teaching assistant, and she would come round to help him manage the lessons and the children. Some reckoned they were even having an affair. She had arrived at the house just a few minutes before Kira and her mates, and people wanted to know, what *she* knew about the goings-on in Pa Die-Go's house. She and a few others were appealing for calm and restraint, but they were woefully outnumbered and not making much headway at all.

What could Pa Die-Go have done to make so many people so very angry? It was clear that he was in real, big trouble.

And trouble it surely was: a little girl had run out of his compound, screaming and sobbing hysterically. She managed to explain to startled passers by, nearby traders, in fact anybody who would listen: she said Pa Die-Go had called her in to buy some of the mangoes that she was selling. She said as soon as she went into his compound, he had bundled her inside his house, up to his room, whipped off her little wrapper from round her little waist, pulled his baggy trousers down, laid his big bulk on her, and now there was blood trickling down her little legs.

What could've happened here?

Rightly or wrongly, when incidents like this happen in some parts of the world, such as where this was happening, people more or less answer questions like this themselves: they decide, there and then, what's what, and quickly form into groups; and most of these groups are usually united by the intention of ultimately taking the law into their own hands.

One group took physical charge of the little girl: at a point she appeared to be going limp, so they rushed her to a nearby clinic.

Another group went to find her family to inform them of events.

At the same time, another group decided to look into things a little further; forensically if you will. They rushed into Pa Die-Go's compound. A tray and some mangoes on the stairs which led up to his room, constituted the first, very telling clue, as far as they were concerned. The next clue was that Pa Die-Go had barricaded himself in one of his rooms. Why would he do that? Anyway, the door stood no chance, and was quickly kicked in; and Pa Die-Go's fate was more or less sealed, when some people noticed some marks on his floor and decided that they were blood stains, no doubt from the little girl; irrefutable evidence as far as they were concerned. Pa Die-Go was dragged out, quoting Bible passages and swearing by all he held sacred, that he hadn't done anything. Everything he attempted to utter was interrupted with swift slaps to his mouth and hefty blows and kicks to his body. In no time, he was bleeding from head to toe. His face was all swollen; he was almost unrecognisable.

Another group thought that stripping Pa Die-Go naked would be a good place to start with him, and in keeping with that theme, two young chaps announced that they would soon be back with a cutlass or two to cut off Pa Die-Go's 'you know what', after the intended stripping.

At this point, another group realised that things were escalating to a point where they would soon probably have a murder on their hands if they didn't move quickly, so somehow, they managed to wrestle Pa Die-Go into a car, and sped off with him to the general hospital.

At the time of the incident and in indeed in the following days, everyone seemed to have an opinion about what had happened.

Some people felt sorry for Pa Die-Go, and some were somewhat angry with the little girl for the embarrassment and humiliation she had supposedly caused him: a man of God, a trusted custodian of morals and propriety, a true pillar of the society. As far as they were concerned, if she wasn't mad (after all mental health problems can start at any age), then she must've been lying; children *do* lie, for whatever reason. Pa Die-Go simply wasn't capable of hurting or tampering with a young child, or anything like that. No way. Furthermore, there was no shortage of women that he could've befriended and who would've been happy to befriend him back: take Susannah for instance. What could he possibly want with a child? People like him just didn't do things like that. Did they?

Or could it be that the little girl had just seen her period for the first time, and the blood had frightened her, some wondered? Highly unlikely seeing as she was just a tiny little thing; she couldn't have been more than five or six years old.

A case of mistaken identity? Perhaps that was it: maybe someone in Pa Die-Go's compound was to blame. But the only other person in his compound at the time, was a young chap who had been home from work, apparently feeling a bit unwell. However, he had perked up really quickly, screaming his innocence when people had burst into the compound, and had questioningly and somewhat accusingly glanced and pointed towards him. In fact he wasted no time in frantically pointing out where Pa Die-Go was.

But there were some who were convinced that Pa Die-Go must have been playing these 'dirty games' for ages, and getting away with things; and now he'd been exposed at last. As far as they were concerned, this couldn't have been a 'first time' or 'one-off' incident; but even if it was, he deserved everything he got.

And indeed there were yet others, who claimed they actually knew of, and if challenged, could actually name, some of Pa Die-Go's 'victims'. They also thought that no punishment, no matter how harsh, would be enough for him.

Mobile phones simply didn't exist then, and even landline phones were few and far between. But news got round quickly, in fact very quickly in communities like the one Kira grew up in; so the police soon got to know that there was big trouble down Pa Die-Go's way. And events like this also evolve very quickly, so by the time the police arrived, Pa Die-Go was just being whisked away to hospital; and all they could really do, on the insistence of the crowd, was take Susannah and the young chap in Pa Die-Go's compound away to be questioned, for starters. The two of them knew they needed to clear their names, and quickly, because as far as people were concerned, things were very wrong in that compound, and the two of them were too close to Pa Die-Go not to be somehow in the know. And if they couldn't clear their names, well, everybody knew what could happen: groups would quickly form for them too.

It was a big mess; Kira and her mates had never really seen or experienced anything quite like this in their young lives.

The news quickly reached Kira's mother as well. She was a seamstress and her workshop was just at the front of the family home. It seemed like everyone passed by there every day, many stopping for a chat, even if they didn't have anything to have made or sewn up. On the day of the Pa Die-Go incident, before Kira got home, a few people were already in the workshop, feverishly explaining what they had seen and heard.

Kira's mother was just about to send someone to go look for Kira, when Kira ran into the workshop. Her mother more or less dragged her to one side, and her first words to her were:

"JhaKira, listen to me very carefully. Has Die-Go ever touched you?"

Whenever Kira's mother called her by her full name, it meant the matter at hand was at best extremely serious, and at worst life threatening; so Kira almost wet herself, went mute for a few seconds, but then heard herself asking her mother:

"Touch?"

"Look. answer me clearly before I slap you. I say, when you go for lessons, has Die-Go ever touched you?"

Kira's mother's words were stressed and clear.

"Yes... yes Ma."

"*What?*"

"He touches all of us Ma.'

"*You say what?*"

"Sometimes he holds us if he wants to cane us... when we get things wrong."

"Oh... Is that all?"

"Yes Ma."

"Are you sure?"

"Yes Ma."

That's what Kira's mother wanted, nay, needed to hear. She didn't probe any further. As she walked away, Kira heard her mother mutter, as if to convince herself: "Dic-Go is not a mad man; even if he touched everyone else's children, he wouldn't dare touch mine... he would not do it."

Largely due to his connections as a retired policeman, Pa Die-Go had been guarded round the clock in hospital; he had to be, as there was a very real and high risk of him being attacked right there on the ward. In fact at one point, news came that he had died. He hadn't, but his legs had been broken in several places, one of his arms had been yanked out of its socket, and needless to say, there was extensive bruising, internal and external. He also lost an eye, along with his longstanding respect and standing in the community.

Back to 2019...

Kira
Moro, the incident was the talk of the town for ages... everyone had an opinion... But what I knew was that the little mango seller hadn't been mistaken... she wasn't mad... and she hadn't lied... or anything like that...

Morowa
How did you know?

Kira
To use my mother's words, he had indeed 'touched' *me*...

Morowa
No... no...

Kira
Yes, yes, I'm afraid... a good few times as well... Of course I just acted stupid when my mother asked me... I knew there was definitely something not quite right with the way Pa Die-Go had 'touched' me... but honestly I didn't really know about sex as such, so I didn't know that he could've well gone even further... I just wanted the whole thing... in fact everything about Pa Die-Go... to just go away... but I instinctively knew that if I'd told my

mother the truth... things would not have just gone away... just like that... no way...

Morowa
Oh God...

Kira
And I guess you could say I was lucky, because he just didn't have enough time during lessons to go as far as he'd gone with the little girl... During lessons, he had to be real quick, there were too many eyes about... With this poor girl, who obviously didn't go to school, he had all the time in the world to go all the way... or so he thought...

Morowa
He miscalculated, the beast...

Kira
What would normally happen was this: we'd start lessons with lengthy prayers from him... then towards the end of lessons, he would ask who wanted to go upstairs with him to help prepare some refreshments: drinks and biscuits for all...

Morowa
Oh no...

Kira
I'd been there a few weeks when he picked me the first time... I was so excited... I dashed up the stairs... got into his room... and before I knew what was happening, he put his big, slimy tongue in my mouth... he put his big, sweaty hand in my knickers... and then he took my little hand and put it down his trousers...

Morowa
No...

Kira

I froze and went limp at the same time... It's been God knows how many years ago, but I can still smell him... horrible... The first time he took me upstairs, he explained to me that this 'hand to knickers and trousers' thing was a secret that had to be kept strictly between the two of us... He said everybody did it; it was normal, and it felt a bit strange just because it was the first time... and that after a few times, I would begin to enjoy it...

Morowa

Oh no...

Kira

He said to me that as long as I kept this secret between us, everything would go well for me... but if I didn't, the opposite would happen, everything would go really wrong.... He said if I ever explained any bit of this to my mates, I would fail the Common Entrance exam, but everybody else would pass... they would all go on to secondary school and leave me behind... And if I explained to any adult... the person I explained to would die... and even he might die as well... and I would still fail my exams...

Morowa

So as far as you were concerned, it was a lose lose situation, if you opened your mouth to anyone...

Kira

It sounds crazy now... but I believed him... totally... every word... Look, I was only twelve, and nothing like the grown up ones of nowadays... He even had a picture on his table of a boy and a girl... he said they were orphans... I remember I didn't even know what an orphan was before that day... Anyway, he said they were good children, but they hadn't kept 'the secret', so that's why their parents had died... and he had nearly died too...

Morowa
How calculated is that?

Kira
Of course I never put my hand up again to help with refreshments... but from time to time he would still pick me... I used to feel so sick... Then after a while, I started to think that maybe something must be wrong with *me,* that's why I wasn't enjoying it... And it wasn't just the *girls* he picked...

Morowa
Oh God...

Kira
As soon as I got home from Pa Die-Go, I'd run straight to our outside tap to rinse my mouth out... I think everyone thought I was just thirsty, but...

Morowa
So, you mean you didn't tell *anyone*?

Kira
How could I? As I say, I knew something wasn't quite right... But I also knew I had to keep 'the secret'... at all cost... how *I* felt about things didn't really matter...

Morowa
Oh Kira... Even after all these years, I can still hear *something* in your voice... As you say, nowadays the kids are so clued up about inappropriate touching and all that... Being a teacher, I know the influence we sometimes have over children... A lot of the time they listen to us more than their parents... Pa Die-Go was a teacher as well, an adult, an authority figure... So even though everything felt so wrong... you wouldn't have wanted to go against anything that miserable bastard told you...

Kira
Look, when they said he'd died in hospital, my little world
collapsed... completely... I couldn't eat, I couldn't sleep...
I thought somehow I must've caused his death... I remember
thinking maybe I'd mentioned this 'secret' in my sleep, and
maybe someone had overheard me, cos I knew I hadn't said
anything when I was awake... You can't imagine the relief
when they said he was in a bad way, but still alive...

Morowa
Look at that... so apart from the abuse, look at the mental burden
he put on you at that young age... making you think your actions
or whatever, could determine whether people lived or died...

Kira
That's paedophiles for you... they screw the children up all
round: mentally, physically, emotionally... making them feel
they're responsible for the whole nasty situation... Then they
even condition their victims to 'enjoy' the abuse... It's just
terrible... and it's something some victims just can't shake off...
some even end up killing themselves... And even those who
don't go that far... they usually end up with serious psychological
problems... lifelong... I see the nasty effects all the time at
work... Paedophilia has such a ripple effect...

Morowa
I know... we've always got kids at school who've suffered this
kind of thing... they need ongoing, long term counselling...

Kira
Well of course we didn't have school counselling or anything
like that in our time... People pounced on Pa Die-Go because
there was some awareness that what he was doing just wasn't
right... But even to this day in many parts of Africa, children are
being married off to big men... even elderly ones... sometimes as

third or fourth wives... So in a different setting, what he did wouldn't have been seen as such a big deal...

Morowa
It's mind boggling...

Kira
I only faced up to the whole issue as an adult... you know... when I started my social work course... It was then I was able to properly recognise and analyse what had happened to me as abuse... I sort of dealt with it then... But I don't think any amount of counselling can make stuff like that go completely away... it's always there... But as I say, I was lucky... he didn't go all the way... I've dealt with people who've been abused repeatedly... by teachers... sometimes even by their own dad... brothers... even by women in some cases... It's nasty business...

Morowa
Oh boy... And there's no way you and the little mango seller were Pa Die-Go's only victims...

Kira
Of course not... only God knows what the total tally must've been over the years... This was a man who was masquerading as some community VIP... Every other word out of his mouth was a Bible quotation... I think he's one of the main reasons why I have such contempt for people like Joel... using God's name and the Bible to destroy lives...

Morowa
So, I guess that was the end of the lessons?

Kira
Oh, of course... I don't think *he* even went back to his house again after that... You know our folks... very excitable at the best

of times... ever ready for action... It wouldn't have taken them two minutes to find an excuse to continue the assault on him...

Morowa
Assault? They could've *killed* him outright...

Kira
And then it would have been a case of 'Die-go' for real?

(They laugh)

Morowa
Over here, his type are on Easy Peasy Street... it's softly, softly, mwah, mwah, cuddle, cuddle... to more or less beg and bribe them not to offend again... If they manage to jail them... and that's usually a big 'if'... they're out in no time... fully refreshed and charged to go and molest and torment society again... with all the benefits you can imagine on release... from Killers Allowance to Rapists Support Credit... or what have you...
(Hisses)

Kira
(Laughs)
I don't think Pa Die-Go was in a position to do *anything* again... not with one eye, dislocated shoulder, damaged legs, etc, etc...

Morowa
Call it jungle justice or whatever you like, but back in our neck of the woods, we handle these issues a bit differently... Living here we've begun to see a lot of things through Western lens... when people are roughed up, we squirm... start calling it 'barbaric' and all that... God knows I don't advocate violence just for violence's sake... but I will advocate more than that if a man, or woman for that matter, is caught defiling a child...

Kira
Me too... But you know what, I've seen the other side of this

coin: people who've been wrongly accused of paedophilia... and it's not funny... In fact I honestly don't know which is worse... victim or being wrongly accused...

Morowa

To be accused of something like *that*... *knowing* that you're innocent... What could really be worse?

Kira

But it's like once you're in, you're in... If your name gets under the paedophile banner, rightly or wrongly... that's it... Even if you're declared innocent, you could take forever trying to get your name fully cleared...

Morowa

I know it's a bit different, but it's like hard drugs... whether you're using or selling... once you're in, you're in... you can't just walk away...

Kira

With drugs, you're at the mercy of the drugs people or the drugs themselves... one or the other is going to get you eventually...

Morowa

But before then, invariably you'll be in and out of prison, back and forth... And talking about in and out of prison, it was only when I came to this country, that I knew that prisoners would deliberately re-offend so that they could be sent back to prison...

Kira

Over and over again... because as you say, the set up behind bars is a little too cosy... I get to see behind the scenes sometimes, and I know that some criminals have really tragic stories to tell... really sad... But whatever the case, the penal system over here isn't much of a deterrent at all...

Morowa
Tragic stories or not, the criminals seem to get all the help, whilst most of the time the poor victims... they're left to sort themselves out... Look, the prison system back home ensures that after one stint inside... just one stint... if you survive that... the last thing on your mind will be to go re-offending... no matter what the challenges may be on the outside, or wherever...

Kira
That's a fact.... I went to the main prison back home one time... I wanted some information for a presentation I had to make over here... Look, I just couldn't take it... I couldn't have spent more than half an hour in there, but that was enough to traumatise me for a good while... The grime, the stench, the overcrowding... The prisoners were all in rags... most of the ones I saw seemed to have some skin condition... As for the food... Look, it was just bad all round... I can't imagine being locked up, for just *five minutes*, in those circumstances... I would die... How can you go through that and contemplate re-offending? No way...

Morowa
Flashbacks of your time inside are guaranteed to keep you on the straight and narrow when you're outside... forever and ever...

Kira
Amen...

(They laugh)

Morowa
Do you know something? In the last few months or so, it seems like I've learnt more about you than I have in all the years before that I've known you... really... strange but true... And I thought I knew more than enough about you...

Kira
Well... some things... you keep them buried... deep... It's like you don't need, or even want to visit them often... I'm sure there's a few things you probably keep right deep inside too... For instance, I've noticed you never really say much about your mum... Any time the topic comes up, you say very little, or you just change the topic completely...

Morowa
OK... So what did QC get you for your birthday?

Kira
See what I mean?

(They laugh)

Morowa
Look, Pa Die-Go's story has been more than enough for today... Thank God you got rid of him... like I've got rid of Joel...

Kira
You say what?

Morowa
You heard right... I've found a new church...

Kira
Are you serious?

Morowa
I am...

Kira
Look, I hope you haven't gone from frying pan to fire oh...

Morowa
Nah, nah... I've found this small church, not too far from us...

I've been a couple of times... and so far, so good... I think I like it.... it's just straightforward worshipping... hymns, address, readings... we pay collection... they've got a really good pastoral service and helpline... I just don't feel anything like the kind of pressure I was under with Joel to just spend, spend, spend all the time... I was in denial for a good while about what was *really* going on there... I didn't even have the courage to tell you some of the things Joel came up with... it was ridiculous...

Kira
There is a God... definitely... And as for Joel... there's nothing you can tell me about him, or any pastor for that matter, that'll surprise me...

Morowa
He was calling and texting me virtually every day... more or less suggesting different ways to manipulate... in fact lie to Sonny, so I could withdraw money from our account to give to him... Even his wife got involved at one point... she started calling and all...

Kira
Oh, as for her, you can see the greed in her own face... happily aiding and abetting Joel all along the way... I can't stand her...

Morowa
He went as far as to suggest that I should ask friends or relatives for money... or take out a bank loan... he just stopped short of telling me to go and steal... At a point, all I could hear was your voice telling me: 'I warned you, Moro'...

Kira
Well...

Morowa
At a point it was bordering on blackmail... he was telling me, if I didn't do this, or pay for that, by such and such a time, then I

shouldn't be surprised if this or that happens... It just got too much... I just had to accept, that whether I liked it or not, something was very, very wrong somewhere...

Kira
Well, as long as you've come to your senses at last, I will drink to that... after all Jesus turned water into wine when he was happy, and I am so happy to hear this... honestly... Although, let's not be too hasty... I think I'd better put you on probation for a while, because you've been under his spell for too long... I need to be fully convinced that you're completely Joel-free before I really start rejoicing...

(They laugh)

Kira
You know what, don't bother to give me a present on Saturday... Honestly... no present can top what you've just told me...

Morowa
As for Saturday... I can't wait... I've already ironed my ashoebi...

Kira
I needed to hem mine a little, but I'm good to go too... Talking of presents, I haven't got anything for Mama Abena... What do you think she would like?

Morowa
You never read the small print... the invitation says 'no presents'... She says just donate to one of her charities... She's chosen three charities, but you won't believe what one of them is... FFF [Fundraise For Fibroids]...

Kira
Really?

Morowa
And you won't believe what happened... I called her daughter-in-law to ask her to let Kukua do Mama Abena's cake... but she didn't seem too keen... she said they'll be using some fancy, upmarket bakers... So anyway we got talking, and she said that Mama Abena would like her guests to donate to charity, and I just casually mentioned FFF... I know for a fact that she hadn't even heard of them before then... Honestly, I couldn't believe my eyes when I saw it on the invitation...

Kira
So what are the other two?

Morowa
I'm not sure off head... check the invite... But of course, it's FFF for me... I'll definitely give them a few bucks...

Kira
You know what, let me go read my birthday cards... and listen to my messages, before the clock strikes twelve and the 10th of June is over again... till next year... So, I guess it's Tusbiheen ala khayr...

Morowa
You say what?

Kira
You were the one who started with Arabic... so I'm finishing... Tusbiheen ala khayr... that's 'goodnight' in Arabic...

(They laugh)

17 *Sunday 16 June*

GOOD MOVE... THINKING AHEAD

The day after Mama Abena's party.

Featuring Greg.

Morowa
What a night, eh? Mama Abena's people did it again...

Kira
But we knew they would not disappoint... My goodness... It was
just one wow after the other, from start to finish... It's been a
while since I enjoyed myself like that...

Morowa
Me too... even Sonny enjoyed himself... he was so impressed...
Yes, I know your people throw solid parties, but you have to
agree that yesterday's Ghanaian show was something else...

Kira
No argument there... superb... the food... music... ambience...
decor... everything was on point... nobody wanted it to end...

Morowa
I was actively looking around to find some fault... any fault...
but...

Kira
But you came away empty handed...

(They laugh)

Morowa
And I loved the speeches... they were just right...

Kira
Oh yes... very heartfelt... and not the usual lengthy, boring stuff...
well, apart from that her niece from Canada...

Morowa
Well there's always one...

Kira
Her accent and grammar... going on about 'this 'persi'... 'prespi'
princess'... whatever...

Morowa
'... this *perspicacious* princess of ours..."

Kira
Ah, see... you're an English teacher, you got what she was
saying...

Morowa
Don't even try that... your English is better than mine... The
thing is how would you get it when you were downing prosecco,
a glass in each hand... one after the other?

(They laugh)

Kira
It wasn't that bad... was it?

Morowa
It's a bit too late to be asking questions now... But you know
me, I don't judge people...

Kira
Yeah right...

Morowa

I'll leave all the judging to Facebook...

Kira

What? You mean they've posted them there already?

Morowa

So where do you think I got them from?

Kira

No...

Morowa

Calm down... calm down.... only kidding... The pictures I have
are the ones Sonny took... I've already sent them to you...
There's one where we're stuffing ourselves with those shrimp
canapés... I can't lie... we really look bad in that one... I hope
they haven't got that on video...

(They laugh)

Kira

But those shrimp things were nice oh... I must've had about
twenty... and it was out of shame that I didn't go for more...

Morowa

Me too... The finger buffet starters were just out of this world...

Kira

I have to admit, even the Jollof rice that most people just can't
get right, was on point...

Morowa

You Sierra Leoneans... I don't know what makes you think
you're the only people on the planet who can cook Jollof rice...
please...

Kira
Of course others, like your people, attempt it... and they usually come up with something similar to Jollof rice... but we're the only ones who can cook it *properly*... it's a proven scientific fact... proven and confirmed at the very highest levels...

(They laugh)

Kira
You know what... let's be honest... most things were really on point yesterday, but I wasn't too impressed with the cake... the taste wasn't that great...

Morowa
Even the design was a bit off... what kind of colour was that? It didn't match the theme at all... But I didn't want to say anything, because it would seem as if I was biased... Kukua would've done something spectacular, and for far less than what those 'fancy' bakers must've charged them... But you know with some people: more money equals better... But that's their business... I made sure I got the caterer's card though... they were spot on...

Kira
Ah... good move... thinking ahead, eh? For when our son-in-law in waiting.... what's his name again? Rotimi... for when he pops the question to our Debbie...

Morowa
Oh... look, I'm in such a good mood... don't upset me oh...

(They laugh)

Morowa
Moving swiftly on... Did you see the way they did Mama Abena's shawl and bag to match her slippers and her husband's hat and back of his shirt?

Kira

The organza and kente... masterpiece stuff... And that her husband... he looks damn good for his age oh...

Morowa

And do you know she's about three years older than him?

Kira

Older? Really?

Morowa

Didn't you hear her call him her toy boy in her speech?

Kira

I heard the *husband* say they'd known each other for nearly sixty-five years, or something like that...

Morowa

They've actually been *married* for that long... they were well ahead of their time... Can you imagine what they must have faced? For her, the woman, to be *three good years* older than the man... in Africa... at that time...

Kira

Just *three minutes* older would've been enough for our people to be telling him he's marrying his grandmother and stuff like that...

(They laugh)

Morowa

And you know, she just came out of hospital about a week ago?

Kira

Ah... what was wrong?

Morowa

I'm not too sure... you know our people don't want to tell you the full story when it comes to things like that: the daughter-in-law said it was acute arthritis, but somebody else said it was her blood pressure... maybe it was both, who knows? But apparently they nearly called the party off... but Mama Abena was having none of it...

Kira
You can tell she's quite tough... in spite of her age, you can see she has some sort of toned physique...

Morowa
She only stopped going to the gym a couple of years ago... They say she used to ride horses at one point...

Kira
No wonder... even the way she was boogying, particularly to the old highlife tunes...

Morowa
Talking of boogying... I see you had a very, very keen admirer yesterday... keen to keep you on the dance floor...

Kira
Oh, that one... he offered to take me home and all...

Morowa
Oh... but you should've agreed now...

Kira
What do you mean?

Morowa
Well, you say you don't want QC any more, so...

Kira
So because I don't want QC, I should settle for any LSC one that happens to come along?

lly glad you had a good time, cos we were
birthday too... Have you opened my present?

is it?

vhen you open it...

'm going to open it right now... Moro, my God...
ch... How did you know I wanted one of these?

ded?

an... the moment they know your issues, your
weaknesses... they find ways to keep reminding
'm never telling you *anything* again... nothing...

anks a million for this... I love it... I really do...

ld... enjoy...

Morowa
LSC? What's that?

Kira
Low sperm count... duh...

(They laugh)

Morowa
So how do you know he's got low sperm count, for God's sake?
But wait a minute... when did you start talking naughty like this
anyway?

Kira
Since *you* taught me, Moro... I've learnt from the very best...

Morowa
Well, you know they say a good master's apprentice often
overtakes the master... because that's definitely what's
happening here...

(They laugh)

Kira
He said he's Mama Abena's nephew...

Morowa
Oh I know him... Greg... his mother and Mama Abena are
sisters... Obviously you probably don't remember him, but he
was at her 80th...

Kira
OK... he said he came in just a few days ago from Ghana for the
party...

Morowa
I'm sure he's the one who brought those kente favours... Have

you seen anything like those before? Beautiful...

Kira

Oh, they're stunning... If they made them back home, they did well oh... they're top notch stuff...

Morowa

If you look inside the box it says 'Made in Ghana'... Africans can make and do some lovely things... Even look at our ashoebi... also 'made in Ghana'... yours really fit you so nicely... Who would believe the seamstress never set eyes on you...

Kira

But don't you think I've put on some weight, though?

Morowa

No... not really...

Kira

I think I have... My ashoebi felt a bit tight yesterday... compared to when I tried it on when I first got it...

Morowa

Well, it looked OK to me... You looked really nice and perky... and obviously Greg thought so as well...

Kira

Oh... here we go...

Morowa

Listen... he's a farmer... big time... he's into serious livestock and agriculture... and well in with the government back home... he's really loaded... well, maybe not down below according to you... but dosh-wise, I'm telling you, you could be onto something really sweet here...

Kira

With no wife or signifi

Morowa

Don't worry, I'll find o

Kira

No, Moro... I know yo
life... but don't go findi
looking for a man...

Morowa

OK, fair enough... but s

Kira

But of course...

Morowa

Well, that's all I'm tryir
here... say after me: 'Co

(They laugh)

Morowa

But seriously, we had a

Kira

Oh, we did...

Morowa

Look, we have all these
two... you mean not ever
engaged... give us an exc
party like yesterday's...

Kira

Who knows what they're

Morowa

Anyway, I'm re
celebrating *your*

Kira

Not yet... What

Morowa

You'll find out

Kira

OK, hang on...
thank you so m

Morowa

Wanted... or *ne*

Kira

You see black
problems, your
you of them...

(They laugh)

Kira

But seriously, t

Morowa

I knew you wo

Morowa
LSC? What's that?

Kira
Low sperm count... duh...

(They laugh)

Morowa
So how do you know he's got low sperm count, for God's sake?
But wait a minute... when did you start talking naughty like this
anyway?

Kira
Since *you* taught me, Moro... I've learnt from the very best...

Morowa
Well, you know they say a good master's apprentice often
overtakes the master... because that's definitely what's
happening here...

(They laugh)

Kira
He said he's Mama Abena's nephew...

Morowa
Oh I know him... Greg... his mother and Mama Abena are
sisters... Obviously you probably don't remember him, but he
was at her 80th...

Kira
OK... he said he came in just a few days ago from Ghana for the
party...

Morowa
I'm sure he's the one who brought those kente favours... Have

you seen anything like those before? Beautiful...

Kira
Oh, they're stunning... If they made them back home, they did well oh... they're top notch stuff...

Morowa
If you look inside the box it says 'Made in Ghana'... Africans can make and do some lovely things... Even look at our ashoebi... also 'made in Ghana'... yours really fit you so nicely... Who would believe the seamstress never set eyes on you...

Kira
But don't you think I've put on some weight, though?

Morowa
No... not really...

Kira
I think I have... My ashoebi felt a bit tight yesterday... compared to when I tried it on when I first got it...

Morowa
Well, it looked OK to me... You looked really nice and perky... and obviously Greg thought so as well...

Kira
Oh... here we go...

Morowa
Listen... he's a farmer... big time... he's into serious livestock and agriculture... and well in with the government back home... he's really loaded... well, maybe not down below according to you... but dosh-wise, I'm telling you, you could be onto something really sweet here...

Kira
With no wife or significant other?

Morowa
Don't worry, I'll find out what's happening with him...

Kira
No, Moro... I know you must've been a matchmaker in a past life... but don't go finding out anything... please... I'm not looking for a man...

Morowa
OK, fair enough... but surely you could do with some cash?

Kira
But of course...

Morowa
Well, that's all I'm trying to say... We can work something out here... say after me: 'Count cash, not sperm'...

(They laugh)

Morowa
But seriously, we had a good time last night...

Kira
Oh, we did...

Morowa
Look, we have all these young people around us... your two, my two... you mean not even *one* of them can get married, or at least engaged... give us an excuse to go crazy and throw a really good party like yesterday's...

Kira
Who knows what they're all waiting for?

Morowa
Anyway, I'm really glad you had a good time, cos we were celebrating *your* birthday too... Have you opened my present?

Kira
Not yet... What is it?

Morowa
You'll find out when you open it...

Kira
OK, hang on... I'm going to open it right now... Moro, my God... thank you so much... How did you know I wanted one of these?

Morowa
Wanted... or *needed*?

Kira
You see black man... the moment they know your issues, your problems, your weaknesses... they find ways to keep reminding you of them... I'm never telling you *anything* again... nothing...

(They laugh)

Kira
But seriously, thanks a million for this... I love it... I really do...

Morowa
I knew you would... enjoy...

18   Thursday 27 June

Earlier in the day

I NEED TO HEAR THIS

Introducing Elmy.

Kira
I got your message... What's up?

Morowa
You know, Elmy, my godson?

Kira
Of course... Milly's son...

Morowa
Attempted suicide oh...

Kira
No...

Morowa
He's in intensive care...

Kira
Intensive care? Ah-ah... What happened? Wasn't it just the other day we spoke about him?

Morowa
Yes... those earrings I wore to Mama Abena's party... I was telling you *he* gave them to me...

Kira
That's right... So what's going on?

Morowa
You know I switch my phone off at work... so when I turned it back on, I heard Milly's message... she was screaming... All I could make out was, 'Your godson... I'm finished...' Anyway, I managed to talk to her sister and she told me he was really sick... and she told me where they were... so I dashed down to the hospital...

Kira
What kind of trouble is this? So where are you now?

Morowa
I'm driving home... he seems to be stable anyway... I'll fill you in tomorrow, it's late now... I'm tired...

Kira
No, no... I need to hear this... tonight... I'm worried... What? Attempted suicide? Call me when you get in... Please...

19   Thursday 27 June

Later in the day

A BIT OVERWHELMING SOMETIMES

Featuring Morowa's friend, Milly, and her sons, Elmy and Rocco. Also featuring Gavin.

Morowa
It's me oh... excuse me for chewing in your ear... I'm starving...

Kira
Whatever... I'm used to you chewing in my ear... But seriously, what's going on? You say Milly's son *attempted suicide*?

Morowa
It's a long story... but he's stable... I think they got him to hospital in time...

Kira
Ah, thank God... that's the main thing...

Morowa
These our children... You know what, I think we have to accept that we, their parents... we are the... I don't want to say 'proper' Africans... but these our children are not like us... they're half and half... half African, half oyibo...

Kira
Hmmm... They just don't seem to have the backbone we've had to have...

Morowa

It's not the backbone... it's the *black*bone they don't have...

(They laugh)

Kira

True... the slightest thing, they say they're depressed... can't cope... telling you they're having mood swings, or they're feeling dangerously low... We didn't know all these things...

Morowa

Even if we did, what spare time did we have to have a mood swing? Our people kept us well busy... Did we have a hoover, washing machine, blender and all these things? Everything was done by hand... *our* hands... Then when you finished those chores, you had errands to run... you'd be sent to take or collect this or that... This was on top of schoolwork... church... So what time did you have to be depressed or anything like that?

Kira

Or even the privacy?

Morowa

Well exactly... when you're sharing a room and every waking moment with God knows how many others... *Suicide?* That was just completely out of our scope...

Kira

A lot of the things that these our children take to heart, we would just laugh at...

Morowa

And still do... The world isn't level at all... over here they have so much... they're pampered, comfortable... they have everything... excess in fact... but they're so fragile... Then you look at some of their counterparts in other parts of the world who have virtually nothing... every day and everything is a struggle...

Kira

On top of the excess over here, they want even more... in fact they want everything... and they want it *right now*... no delay... And a lot of us have come to these parts of the world and completely forgotten where we've come from... We've over-indulged our children to such an extent... pandered to them...

Morowa

Oh yes... and now it's all coming back to bite some of us ... in fact it's choking us... Because of course our children think like they do over here, that they must have everything, and they must win all the time... they don't make much allowance for failure or if things don't go their way... So the moment they can't afford something, or fail an exam, can't get a job, relationship not working out... anything that doesn't go according to plan... it's like the end of the world for them...

Kira

Just shouting at them... they get all upset... saying you shouldn't raise your voice...

Morowa

Look, shouting is part of our culture... When our people shouted at us, beat us, grounded us, whatever... we'd probably be sad for a matter of minutes... then someone would probably tease you about the shouting or the beating... before you knew it, you'd be laughing... playing... you'd completely forgotten about the punishment... you'd moved on...

Kira

Well this is it... After all, they didn't beat any of us to death... We just took those things in our stride... and I think that attitude, that approach, has helped us through life... and thank God for that... it has helped us deal with and overcome so much...

Morowa

We were raised to face problems and difficulties with optimism...
and hope... to be positive... One of our grannies would say to us:
'If things don't go your way... never give up... just keep praying
and pressing on... give it some time... be patient... the gods are
busy... you're not the only person whose prayers have to be
listened to and answered... but they'll get to you eventually'...

Kira

And we always had people around... and still do... to help you
see things differently, particularly if you're in some kind of
crisis... help you work things out somehow... Mind you, some of
the people who are supposed to help can be nuisances alright...
but their very presence if nothing else, will make it almost
impossible for you to do anything drastic... Can you imagine our
people's reaction, particularly our grannies, if they had heard us
say we wanted to kill ourselves when we were growing up?

Morowa

They'd trivialise the whole thing... They'd summon you and
then they'd say something like:

*'You... kneel down there... They say you want to kill yourself? OK...
fine... go on then... But there's just one problem: Who do you want
to do your chores when you're gone? Me? You must be joking...
Just look at your mouth... you've obviously had too much to scoff,
that's why you've got the energy to talk such nonsense... I dare
you... let me hear anything like this again... Before I open my eyes
again, if you haven't disappeared, see if I won't kill you myself...'*

(They laugh)

Morowa

Then as you'd scramble to your feet to run off, you'd hear them
hiss... the loudest, longest hiss you'd ever heard in your life...

(They laugh)

Kira

The thing is, as youngsters, our people knew we didn't know what to kill yourself *really* meant, even if we said it... If for one moment they thought you really did know or meant what you were saying, or that there was the slightest risk of you *actually* doing anything like that... they would've really panicked... because they would act all tough, but deep down, they couldn't bear the thought of us coming to any harm whatsoever...

Morowa

Just for a moment, imagine a situation where we could've imported those our grannies over here into this system... just the way they were... probably telling us to go and kill ourselves and stuff like that... Can you imagine what they'd make of them?

Kira

Oh no... over here they'd throw the book at them... They'd carry on as if no atrocity in mankind's history could even come close to what our poor grannies had said and done...

(They laugh)

Morowa

Oh yes... After circulating the worst mug shots they could take of them, they'd be diagnosed with psychopathic and sociopathic tendencies... and that's just for starters... Charges would range from child cruelty, to aiding and abetting suicide or murder... and everything else in between... By the time they would've finished with them, our grannies would be advising... in fact begging people not to have any children, never mind grandchildren...

(They laugh)

Kira

Oh, those our grannies... people of that generation... they were characters... the whole lot of them... a class act...

Morowa
Oh yes... Singularly and collectively... We owe them all so much... they were the making of many of us... God bless them all... Hmmm... Anyway, back to this Elmy one... apparently, he came out to his parents a year or so ago...

Kira
Came out... as in gay?

Morowa
Mm-hmmm...

Kira
Oh God have mercy...

Morowa
You know he works out of London, but we always keep in touch... He never misses my birthday or Christmas... and he always sends me something arty... unique... like the earrings... those kind of things... He gave me that vase by my entrance... and that ethnic looking scarf you nearly strangled me with, when you wanted to snatch it from round my neck...

(They laugh)

Morowa
He's given me some really beautiful stuff over the years... and I think he makes most of the stuff himself... he's very artistic... Oh God, please help him pull through... he's such a lovely person...

Kira
But did *you* know... that he was gay?

Morowa
No...

Kira

So you mean you never noticed *anything* about him?

Morowa

Like what? But you've seen him quite a few times yourself...
Did *you* notice anything?

Kira

No... nothing... But I guess it's not an illness where they
necessarily have to show signs and symptoms... So what did he
want to kill himself for now? What was the problem?

Morowa

Well, in the situation, I couldn't ask too many questions... but me
and Milly's sister went for a coffee... she filled me in on a few
things... She sort of just mentioned in passing that he was gay...
I can't lie, I was a bit taken aback...

Kira

They probably thought you knew...

Morowa

Maybe... but, I didn't... You know I would've told you...
Anyway, I think there's been a few issues since he came out...
For one Milly's husband and her other son, Rocco are not happy
at all... Apparently, I think things took a turn for the worse when
they found out that Elmy wants to marry the boyfriend now...

Kira

Oh-oh...

Morowa

Apparently Rocco went to Elmy's place a couple of days ago...
all hell broke completely loose... the police were called and all...
As for Milly's husband, he's siding fully with Rocco, and he's
blaming Milly for everything... According to him, she had been

too soft on Elmy when he was growing up, that's why he's gay...
I think the whole situation with his brother and family just got
too much for Elmy... The boyfriend came home from work
yesterday and found him unconscious... drug overdose...

Kira
Oh no...

Morowa
And I think he really meant business, because the boyfriend
wasn't supposed to be back until tomorrow or so... Luckily he
came back earlier and found him... Can you imagine? Look, I
know a lot of us don't quite understand this gay business, but I
think we have to try... really... I don't like what I saw and heard
today... Nothing can justify pushing someone to the point where
they want to end absolutely everything...

Kira
Well you've changed your tune now oh...

Morowa
How?

Kira
When I told you Richie doesn't seem to date black girls... and all
his girlfriends seem to be at least three or four years older than
him... you said an old oyibo granny would not be ideal, but better
than him coming to show me a man...

Morowa
Ah... but this is different now... we're talking life and death
here... And I'm saying it out loud for all to hear: nobody should
go kill themselves oh... Look, Millie's quite a tough cookie, but
I've never seen her in the state she was in this evening... She
was saying she just wanted her son to live... gay or straight...

Kira
Awww...

Morowa
You know I'm ready to see the fun in everything... but today in
the hospital wasn't funny *at all*... In fact I didn't even know
when I actually started crying myself... As for Elmy's partner...
he was a wreck... he couldn't even speak... you could see he was
just shell shocked... Look, when you have children, from when
they're quite young, you can't help thinking about their future...
that's what parents do... And one of the things you imagine is
the day they'll tell you they're getting married... stuff like that...
You imagine different scenarios... but I'm pretty sure most
parents don't really factor in your child coming with a gay
partner... you just don't... Look, let's be honest here: if any of
our kids tell us they're gay, we're not likely to jump for joy...

Kira
Look, we know we won't... I know some parents may readily
understand... in fact welcome it all... But we're all different... so
I know some other parents like myself... and I suspect you as
well... we may need some time... and maybe some space too... to
make some mental and emotional adjustments...

Morowa
Well exactly... And people should be allowed to do so without
running the risk of being called homophobic and stuff like that...
The thing is, whilst you'll be trying... probably even struggling to
an extent, to make those adjustments... because bottom line: you
love your child, and you desperately want to get to a comfortable
place of understanding and acceptance... for everybody... But
that's when you and your know-it-all colleagues are likely to
start: 'It's not about *you or your life*... it's about *your child and
their life*"... As if you didn't know...

Kira
(Laughs)
That is not how we handle such matters... at all...

Morowa
It is, I'm telling you... Some of your people are specialists in
making desperate matters even more desperate... Then apart
from the homosexuality, there's the other 'sexuals'... There's
pansexual... monosexual,... What's the one I heard the other day?
Paedosexual... What the hell is that now?

Kira
Actually, it does get a bit overwhelming sometimes...

Morowa
Very... I need to find out what some of these terms mean... just to
educate myself... Wait... I wrote some down... maybe
you can help me with the definitions... *binary... pangender...
demigender... androgynous... gender fluid... genderqueer...*
How are we meant to keep up with all this? Then you have the
ones who change from man to woman, or vice versa... then they
want to change back to their original sex... then they want to
have babies... For God's sake... someone can wake up in the
morning and say he's a man who identifies as a woman... by
afternoon he says he identifies as a man again... but by evening,
this same being can now say they feel like a cross between a cow
and a leaf, or whatever... and would like to be treated as such...
And through all these changing scenes of life... they'll say you
shouldn't call them 'he' or 'she'... you should refer to them as
'they' or something... I mean, come on now... Ah...

Kira
(Laughs)

Morowa
No Kira... I'm not mocking, or laughing at these people or these

situations at all... God knows I'm genuinely confused... So whatever time I may have left on earth now, I should use it trying to figure out *all* these things? I know as a teacher, I have to try and keep abreast of things... The thing is, a part of me really and truly does want to understand some of these things... at least a bit more or better than I do now... but another part of me seems to be saying: no matter how much I want to, and may even try to... I just won't get it... and maybe that's because I just can't...

Kira
Look, you have to be a bit more open minded... What you've just said sounds a bit discriminatory...

Morowa
Ehn? How? How am I discriminating because I say I don't think I may be able to understand? Just because this part of the world says all these things are OK, normal, whatever... doesn't mean I just have to understand and accept *everything*... just like that... Does everybody understand *me*? Ah-ah...

Kira
Look, we're not fighting...

Morowa
No... But is it a crime *not* to understand something? *Must* I understand everything? It's been hundreds of years of black people battling just to be tolerated, never mind understood... So excuse and forgive me if I don't understand one or two things in this my short lifetime... I'm sure my children and future grandchildren will get all this, but it's a bit difficult for me, I can't lie... The thing is, I've known Elmy all his life... I've watched him grow and he's my godson, and he's truly like a son to me... So I have a duty to him to at least *try* to understand *his* reality... his life... particularly the difficulties... As soon as he's better and up to things, I'll see him and we'll talk... Look, after

all, I just found all this out *today*... it's too much for me...

Kira
You know work has exposed and enlightened me to a lot of situations and scenarios... I've been forced to think way outside the regular, safe boxes that most people have to deal with...

Morowa
Me too... But as I say, it's just that it all gets too much sometimes... I'm getting too old for all this, honestly...

Kira
Nature itself comes up with things to add to the confusion... stop us in our tracks... You realise that not everything is black or white... there're plenty grey areas... A woman can have a baby with two heads or four legs... things like that...

Morowa
And a man can have two willies... we know all these things...

Kira
So which man is that now?

Morowa
Oh, we both saw the video now... the man had two solid willies... You were even saying, 'what a waste'... that if you could make contact with him, you would beg him to give your Gavin one...

Kira
Moro, when did I say that? And how is he now *my* Gavin?

Morowa
(Laughs)
I even felt so sorry for him... Remember? Ah... sad...

Kira
You... felt sorry for Gavin? I can actually tell by the way you're laughing even now, how very sorry you must've felt... Look,

I'm trying to make and come to a serious point here... about nature, and sexuality... how these and other factors may intertwine... and how people fall into certain categories... sometimes out of choice... sometimes not... It's complicated...

Morowa
That's what I've been trying to tell you... it's tricky... OK, so if I come home one day and Sonny's wearing my clothes, high heels and makeup and stuff, what should I do? Tell me... To start with, what category will that fall into? Cross-gender-dressing what or what? So I should just smile and give him a reassuring kiss... sit down and talk to him nicely... start exchanging clothes with him... in fact, go shopping together for a new female wardrobe and shoes for him... start going to social events as a couple?

Kira
The thing is you can't kill him... it's not the end of the world... With help, you'll work something out...

Morowa
He can go and get the help... he'll need it... Look, Sonny knows me... he won't be expecting an attack from me... If I find him like that, he'll actually be expecting a *frenzied* attack...

Kira
(Laughs)

Morowa
Don't laugh... I wouldn't be able to think straight... To be honest, for a while, I don't think I'd be able to think *at all* in a situation like that... Look, people are having dogs as their bridesmaids... in fact some are actually marrying the dogs... So what next? Look, let's just face it... the place, way and time we grew up, I think we're a bit too long in the tooth to process some of these things, just like that...

Kira
I think that's just it: we're from a different age, different era, different place... mentally, culturally... all round...

Morowa
But that doesn't mean we haven't been able to move with the times... we've tried.. The problem is, I think the so-called times are moving a little too fast for some of us to keep up... Oh wait... Milly's sister's just sent me a message...

Kira
Oh no... What now?

Morowa
No... it's OK... She's just thanking me for going to see them earlier... She says they left him stable...

Kira
Oh good... At least you'll be able to get a reasonable night's sleep... Don't worry too much; I'm sure he'll be OK... Maybe they'll let Elmy's partner stay overnight in the hospital... Where's he from anyway?

Morowa
Well... he looks white... but I think he has some black in him somewhere... his hair... you know...

Kira
And what is it with these our men, like Milly's husband... blaming everything they're not happy with or don't understand, on us, the women? So all this drama is down to Milly now?

Morowa
Oh yes... It's all *her* fault now... *nothing* to do with him...

Kira
It's like when Ralston didn't do well in exams... QC would say

he wasn't surprised... how *I* was the one encouraging him to mess around with bikes and other 'rubbish', as he called it... instead of making him concentrate on his schoolwork... God knows I tried... Richie, of course, was OK, no problem... but with Ralston... at a point, I just had to concede defeat... reading and things just made him so miserable... but give him any machine to fix or play with... and he would just come alive... By the time he was a teenager, I didn't need a handyman for anything...

Morowa
The time I knew we couldn't just dismiss Ralston's tampering, was when he repaired that my freezer... Remember? After a so-called professional had told me that I should just throw it away... I'd even started storing stuff in it... I couldn't believe it when Ralston actually got that thing going again...

Kira
And he was only about 13 or 14 at the time... I'm eternally grateful to you for pointing us in the NVQ, City & Guilds direction... He's just never looked back...

Morowa
A levels and university are all well and good... but not for *everybody*... Look at Ralston now, travelling all over the world... master of his trade... making a very good living and having a jolly good life... just by using his God-given talent...

Kira
Making at least three times what his brother makes... and Richie made a first class... so...

Morowa
I use Ralston as an example all the time... because his story played out right in front of my own eyes... I know at one time, most of us wanted *all* our children to go to university, whether

they liked it or could cope or not... but like everything else, we've all moved on a bit now... so people have come to realise, that even if a child has all the qualifications to pursue higher education, they don't necessarily have to...

Kira
Oh yes... there are so many other options available...

Morowa
And some are very lucrative and very fulfilling as well... Of course as a teacher, I've always sort of been aware of the other options... but I was keen on the girls getting a degree as a baseline, because for one, they were in a position to... and the idea, of course, was that they could build on that, or diversify, or whatever in the future... All the same, you won't believe... last Christmas, after Debbie and Kukua had had a bit to drink... well, drink is what I'm blaming it on... they confronted me... saying I had pushed both of them into careers of *my* choice, not *theirs*...

Kira
Oh... You can't win... So what was it they'd wanted to be... or not to be? That is the question...

Morowa
Well Kukua, she was a bit kind... she said, I shouldn't get her wrong, she loves her profession and all that... but she loved baking even more... and that if I'd maybe encouraged her in that, she could've probably had her own TV baking show by now...

Kira
Aha... trust Kukua...

Morowa
But she said she was sure I would've killed and buried her in an unmarked grave, if she'd had the courage... or nerve... to tell me

that she wanted to do *baking* instead of going to university... *at that time*... when, according to her, uni was more or less a life and death issue for us parents... particularly black ones...

(They laugh)

Kira
And our dear Debbie... how and where did you 'fail' her?

Morowa
As for her... Listen to this: she said I knew that she wanted to be a teacher like me, but I deliberately made myself look extra poor, haggard and confused all the time, and complained non-stop about work... just to put her off and steer her in the direction *I* wanted...

(They laugh)

Morowa
Now she says she doesn't feel fulfilled in the finance world... you know them... telling me it's not all about money and how much she's getting paid... Look, I found myself apologising to the two of them...

Kira
For what now?

Morowa
Well... by insisting that they become professional, independent women, and by encouraging and supporting them to do so... I guess that's where I obviously went wrong and ruined two, young promising lives...

(They laugh)

Kira
These our children, eh... I say you just can't win...

20 *Tuesday 2 July*

YOU CAN'T HAVE EVERYTHING

*Featuring Pa Magwa, Morowa's grand-uncle, her 'step-father',
Pa Aaron, and former neighbours, Carol, Trevor and 'Granny Five'.
Also featuring Kira's Grandmother Aisha and her Aunty Mahira.*

Kira
Hallo there...

Morowa
Hiya...

Kira
Hmmm... You don't sound yourself... Is everything OK?

Morowa
Yeah, I'm OK... It's my mother's fifteenth anniversary...

Kira
Fifteen years... already? My God... I really remember like it was
yesterday... Sorry eh...

Morowa
If I tell you I miss her, I'd be lying... She hated me... she really
did...

Kira
Hmmm... You want to talk about it?

Morowa
No... not really...

Kira
Look, no pressure... but sometimes it's good to talk... You've

told me bits and pieces about her, here and there, over the years, so of course, I know your relationship wasn't great... Most people from our background and culture would probably just want to sort of dismiss you... They'll tell you: 'That's not possible... mothers can never reject, hate or abuse their kids'... stuff like that... But I know that if you haven't been through certain thiings, you just don't know... you *can't* know...

Morowa
Exactly, so sometimes people should just shut up... honestly...

Kira
I didn't experience anything like that first hand, thank God... but through life and work I've come across some pretty rough situations involving some mothers... in fact some parents... because of course, many *fathers* are very wrong too...

Morowa
But we mothers always seem to be held to a higher standard...

Kira
And I suspect that's how nature planned it... cos somehow your father letting you down just isn't quite the same as when a mother does... But then again, can you tell someone who was sexually molested by their father all through childhood, or something like that... and I've dealt with a few cases... are you going to say, well because it was their *father* and not their mother, the abuse couldn't have been *that* bad?

Morowa
Well no, of course you can't say that...

Kira
You know Richie and his animals... when he was younger, I watched loads of nature programmes with him... and I learnt so much... The fact is, even in the animal kingdom, not all mothers are the nurturing, protecting, ready to give their lives for their

kids creatures that we're made to believe they all are... For whatever reason, some just aren't... Some animals reject their kids outright... really maltreat them... some actively drive their kids away... some shred them to pieces... literally... they kill them outright... then some even go as far as to eat them... And this is sometimes after carefully selecting the kids they prefer and want to look after... Just like some human mothers have their favourites among their children...

Morowa
Well, we are animals after all...

Kira
We are... and mothers having serious issues with their children... particularly their daughters... it's not that uncommon, you... it's just that it's a taboo subject that people just don't want to deal with, because it goes against everything we've been conditioned to believe, or even want to believe... And it's not just women... you'll be surprised to know how many *men* also have a story or two to tell about their mothers... there're some horror stories out there... So if it's any consolation, you're not alone... at all...

Morowa
Look, they say you never forget how someone makes you feel... and my mother's left me with a feeling that I wouldn't want to leave my enemies with, never mind my children... So I'm so happy... in fact grateful, that she never really knew my kids, and they never really knew her as such... She would've used the girls... manipulated them to get at me...

Kira
You think she would've gone that far?

Morowa
I really do... Look, she went out of her way... actually put things in place to make us, *her own children,* knock our heads

together... So tell me, why would she have spared *my* kids, or anyone else's for that matter, if she'd got the chance?

Kira

Hmmm... But you and your siblings are very close... I know that much...

Morowa

We always have been, thank God... but that wasn't down to our mother... I'm pretty sure, left to her, we'd probably be at each other's throats for the rest of our lives... just like she was with her own siblings...

Kira

Oh... so she had problems with *her* siblings as well?

Morowa

She had ten siblings... four full and six half ones... she fought the whole lot... And as for my grandmother... her own mother... she just gave her hell... all the time... If there were any family problems, you could bet your last dollar, either my mum started it, or she was in the middle of it.... it was just so unpleasant all the time... At a point, most of her siblings just sort of cut her off... ostracized her... I think for their own sanity... She wore them all down...

Kira

But she must've got on with *some* people...

Morowa

Oh yeah... But when I look back, she surrounded herself with lapdog kind of people... you know the kind who would never argue with or challenge her, even when it was crystal clear sometimes that that's what she needed... a bloody good challenge... But as far as she was concerned, she was *always* right, she always had to have *her* way, and most definitely had to have the very last word...

Kira
Look, some people are just like that... but it's one thing to fight with friends and colleagues and even some family members... but to take *your own children* on... So how was she with your dad?

Morowa
Well you know he died when I was just six, so I was too young to be able to assess their relationship... But I know this much... my dad's people didn't have a good word to say about her either, because... surprise, surprise... she took them all on as well...

Kira
Really?

Morowa
Oh yes... Then a few years after my dad died, she got involved with Pa Aaron...

Kira
Wusi's dad?

Morowa
Yeah... he was a really nice man... at least to us children he was... But he and my mum... not good... at all... The thing is, for starters, he was a married man... we were young, but we'd often hear them quarrel about his wife... But look... that's another story altogether... a story for another day... Anyway, Wusi came along... but after a while we began to see less and less of Pa Aaron... until he more or less disappeared off the scene...

Kira
Hmmm... Who knows? Maybe something went wrong in *her* childhood... somewhere, somehow along the line... She probably had some psychological issues or whatever, that needed sorting out... But our people weren't equipped to diagnose or look into those kind of things back then...

Morowa
And besides, this was in the village...

Kira
Look, whether she was in the village, town, city, wherever... there's definitely something wrong somewhere, if you're sort of fighting everybody... all the time...

Morowa
Hmmm... I've often thought to myself: maybe *I* did something to her... because she was quite hard on my siblings as well... but she was just awful with me...

Kira
Did something? Like what? So what could *you*, Moro... what could you possibly have done to her, that no-one has ever done or heard of before? Look, your mother was your mother... and you were her child... you weren't mates... you weren't rivals... And in my book, no mother has the right to make her child feel the way you obviously do, even after all these years, without having an almighty showstopper of a reason... and it would have to be *really* good, because there can't be much some of us haven't heard... Look, even mothers of mass murderers, love and stand by their children... so please... One granny who lived near us back home would say: 'A child is like an axe; even if it hurts you, you still have to carry it on your shoulder... you don't have a choice'... Bottom line, I actually feel sorry for your mother... I think she missed out on not having you in her life... She could've done far, far worse than have you as a daughter...

Morowa
Hmmm... Wait a minute... Is that meant to be a compliment?

Kira
I'm not too sure myself now... but you know what I mean...

(They laugh)

Kira

But seriously... the thing is, you obviously didn't follow in her footsteps... rather you've followed your own instincts and made your own way in life... cos I've known you a long, long time, and crazy as you can be, I haven't seen you waging non-stop war on all the people around you...

Morowa

Just remembering and thinking about it all is exhausting...

Kira

I bet it is... You know what I'm going to recommend? Some counselling...

Morowa

No, I don't need that... I'm OK...

Kira

No you're not you know... you don't really outgrow some of these things... stuff like this never completely goes away... but you'll be amazed at what some good counselling can do... You know I was reluctant to go for counselling over QC... but you made me go... To be honest, I didn't think it would help, but it really did...

Morowa

OK, I'll think about it...

Kira

Look Moro, you've ticked a good few boxes, girl: good marriage, good children, good career... and I think the list goes on... The thing is, you could've had a *wonderful* mother and all that comes with that... but a *horrible* husband which of course equals a horrible marriage... maybe awful kids and all... The thing is, you can't have everything...

Morowa

I know... but I must confess, I think I've always sort of envied people like you, who had a straightforward, normal upbringing... two normal parents... the impression I've always got from you was that they were close and loving and all that... fairytale stuff...

Kira

True, my parents were the best... they really were... But a lot of things...if not *most* things... are never quite as they seem...

Morowa

So what does that mean now?

Kira

Therapy session over... I'll send you my bill... Look, I'll tell you everything some other time... I promise...

Morowa

Oh... so there's something to tell? No, you must talk... and as they say... no time like the present...

Kira

Hmmm... OK then... brace yourself... Remember when I sent you that picture of my cousin Faisal... the one in Botswana? You remarked on how he looks more like me than my own siblings...

Morowa

But you know that's how it is... some cousins look more alike than siblings... It's like people always say Kukua looks more like me than Debbie... So what's up in Botswana?

Kira

Well... Faisal's my cousin alright... and he's my brother too...

Morowa

Hmmm? Well, we're Africans... all our men folk... cousins... close, distant, whatever... even people from the same village... we call them our brothers... But there's more to this, right?

Kira
Uh-mmm... You know my mum was from the Gambia... that's
where she and all her siblings were born, grew up, went to school
and all that...

Morowa
Yes... I think I know that much...

Kira
Anyway, when my mum's big sister, Aunty Mahira got married,
she moved to Sierra Leone to be with her husband... When she
fell pregnant, she sent for her sister... that's my mum... to join
her... to come help her out, as they do, or at least used to do in
those days... So that's how my mum actually came to be in Sierra
Leone...

Morowa
Oh, OK...

Kira
So my mum's now in Sierra Leone, and next thing, even before
my aunty had her baby, my mother was pregnant too... and
initially she wouldn't name the baby's father... she couldn't...

Morowa
Couldn't?

Kira
So my aunty threatened to send my mum back to Gambia, and I
think things got quite messy... Cut a pretty long story short...
eventually... my aunty's husband had to own up...

Morowa
I don't understand... Own up? To what?

Kira
Do you really want me to spell everything out? What do you
think, Moro... what do you think?

Morowa
Wait a minute... Forgive me if I'm wrong... but are you saying
your aunty's husband... he got your mother pregnant? No... that
can't be it... or?

Kira
Yes... that is indeed it...

Morowa
Ah... As you would say, 'Am I hearing this?'

Kira
You are I'm afraid... You can imagine the scandal... it was
bad... My mum nearly lost the pregnancy, because my aunty
apparently beat her to within an inch of her life when the whole
story came out...... It tore my mum's family apart... completely...
And then the bombshell... my dad chose my mum over his wife,
my aunty... So in a nutshell, that's how my parents met and
eventually got married... My mother had fallen pregnant with
Salma... then of course after Salma, me and Nish came along...
You know what, I can just imagine your face now...

Morowa
My dear... I don't think I can even find my face at the moment...

(They laugh)

Kira
Anyway, so, my aunty had to go back to Gambia... she went and
had the baby there... So that baby, of course, was Faisal...

Morowa
So Faisal's mum and *your* mum are actually sisters?

Kira
They are... same mother, same father... And me and my sisters
and Faisal have the same father...

Morowa

This is movie stuff... You've had some drama in your life, you know... Pa Die-Go... now *this*... So, did you know about him... Faisal... or any of this when you were growing up?

Kira

Well, sort of... but it was all sketchy... Me and my sisters picked up bits and pieces from gossip and chit-chat here and there, you know... but nothing definite... nothing 'official'... But one time I'll never forget, I was quite young, and my mother had a problem with a couple of her customers over some dresses... Between these two women, there's nothing under the sun they didn't call my mum... a witch... a shameless dog... I didn't even understand a lot of what they said that day, but I knew it was really horrible... But what really hit me was when they called her a thief who'd stolen her sister's husband...

Morowa

Oh no...

Kira

I just couldn't get that out of my head... And of course as we got older, me and my sisters... we were able to piece more and more of the story together...

Morowa

You know what, I don't even know what questions to ask...

Kira

(Laughs)

You're too nosy... there's nothing to see here...

Morowa

Oh yes there is... Family gatherings and stuff like that... how did those go?

Kira

Well, as always in such cases, my mum and dad had a few close relatives and friends who sort of supported them... my mum's mother, Grandma Ashia... she used to come from Gambia to see us... quite frequently actually... There were always people around... but there was something a bit off that me and my sisters just couldn't put our finger on... but as kids, growing up at that time... we couldn't ask too many questions...

Morowa

I know... in those days... kids... ask questions... with that kind of issue in the background? But tell me, your mother and her sister... what the hell was their relationship like?

Kira

Well, they didn't talk until my mother died... My aunty's still alive... she's lived in the US for years...

Morowa

OK... Do you think you'd like to meet her?

Kira

Please Moro... one thing... one person at a time... I'm just getting used to Faisal... I've only spoken to him a couple of times... Of course, he's the one who filled me in on the details about his mum... Actually, thinking about it, I probably *would* like to meet her... But the question is: would she want to meet *me?*

Morowa

Oh I'm sure she would... She must be quite old now, and she knows whatever happened had nothing whatsoever to do with you or your sisters... you weren't even born when all the drama started... So Faisal and your dad... did they have a relationship?

Kira

I don't think so... Apparently my dad tried to make contact with him over the years... but my aunty... she wouldn't hear of it... I think initially, she actually went mental... At one time they say she even had a dog named after my mum...

Morowa
Oh my God...

Kira
We social workers are all about parents having access to their children... usually no matter what... But as a woman, I can see where my aunty was coming from... I probably wouldn't have wanted to see my dad or want him anywhere near my child either... honestly...

Morowa
So you mean you've never actually met Faisal in the flesh?

Kira
Never... It was his daughter who found Omar on social media...

Morowa
Imagine that... He must've wanted to find you guys, cos he obviously gave his daughter the relevant information... Awww... So as far as you know, Faisal was your dad's only son, right?

Kira
As you say... as far as we know... but who knows who else is out there waiting to be found?

(They laugh)

Kira
And you know what, the first time I spoke to him... his voice... he sounds identical to my dad on the phone... it was actually quite spooky...

Morowa
Genes... you can't argue with them... But come oh... so when you sent me his picture, you knew he was actually your brother?

But you told me he was your cousin... Why did you lie to me, Kira; why were you so untruthful... to me of all people?

(They laugh)

Kira

Don't be so melodramatic... Look, I didn't lie... after all, technically he's my cousin as well... The thing is I couldn't explain things to *myself* properly, never mind anyone else... I was in shock... I think I still am... I always wanted a brother... When I think about all those wasted years... Crazy, eh?

Morowa

Well, they say 'better late than never'... you guys can take off from here and now... and try to make the best of things moving forward... make up for some lost time...

Kira

Oh yes... Salma's invited him to her party next year... and he says he won't miss it...

Morowa

Oh, that'll be nice... we'll all get to meet him then... But look, I'm still curious... and intrigued... So you mean your parents never explained *anything* to you and your sisters about *all* this?

Kira

Not really... The thing is, where would they have started... or ended, for that matter? Actually, my mother did tell me a few things... just once... but she didn't say too much...

Morowa

Let me guess... on her deathbed...

Kira

Funny you should say that: she wasn't on her deathbed... actually she was fine... but it was the last time I saw her and spoke to her face to face... Somehow, something must've told her that she'd never get the chance again... She told me she somewhat regretted the upset she'd caused in her family...

Morowa
Awww... It must've been difficult for her... because whatever upset she may have caused, or thought she caused, she couldn't have regretted having you and your sisters...

Kira
Well this is it... and I know she didn't regret meeting my dad either, because they were good together... a really good match...

Morowa
Life is just never straight, is it? You could say if only your dad had met your mum first... that is, before your aunty... then everything may have been fine... But that wouldn't have been so fine for Faisal, because then he may not have been born...

Kira
The thing is, my parents may not have even met at all, but for my aunty... then me and my sisters wouldn't have been born... so...

Morowa
What did I say? Life just isn't straight...

Kira
I think another thing that bothered my mum, was that she and *her* mum had a few unresolved issues...

Morowa
Oh here we go again... more mother-daughter issues...

Kira
Well indeed... Actually, it was one major issue, to be honest... my granny wanted us to be initiated...

Morowa
Are you saying what I think you're saying?

Kira
I think so... FGM [Female Genital Mutilation], I guess that's the modern term for it... Actually, my mum wanted us to have it done as well... initially...

Morowa
Your mum? No...

Kira
Well, I can't really knock her for it... it was their custom... still is... and has been for centuries.. All the women in her family were initiated, so of course she was as well...

Morowa
Hmmm...

Kira
Anyway, my mum said the only time she and my dad ever had a really serious issue... in their whole relationship... was over this FGM thing... Apparently he made it very clear to her that he didn't approve of it at all... I think it would've been a game changer for them if my mother had insisted... The thing is, I know it's a big deal for those who practise it, so I think my granny just couldn't understand why we weren't having it done... I've often thought to myself, that maybe my granny was thinking that if we'd had it done, it would've been such a significant step to take... that it might've helped to heal things in her family... help get her family back together somehow... I dunno...

Morowa
Awww... Maybe that was what she was thinking, you know...

Kira
Bottom line, I think me and my sisters are just happy it didn't happen...

Morowa
The thing is every culture moves on... evolves... customs and

traditions need to be looked into... they need to be modernised, adapted, whatever...

Kira
Or even done away with, if need be... but change isn't something our people embrace with open arms...

Morowa
Embrace? We actively resist it... and sometimes for no good reason... Sometimes you can readily see the clear benefits of some change... but no... our people just won't have it... And that mentality holds us back a lot of times... Look, we don't need to change just for the sake of change... there're many things that don't necessarily need changing... but there's a whole lot that needs looking into... and FGM has to be on that list...

Kira
Oh yes... But I have to say though... in spite of the FGM thing, and the family scandal between my mum and her sister and my dad, and God knows what else they probably hid from us as kids... my grandmother never rejected my mother... or us... Looking at things with adult eyes now: I realise it must've been quite difficult for her, on so many levels... For starters, I'm sure just having her daughters in that situation with my dad, would've been more than enough for any mother... But I guess, it was what it was... and it is what it is... And there you have it, my dear Moro... the origins of Kira...

Morowa
Wow... As you say, it's good to talk sometimes... everything makes a bit more sense now... Now I understand why you're so good at finding package holidays... and there's always good deals to Gambia... but even when I point them out to you... you always come up with a reason or something for us not to go... Well all that's going to change... I'm going to hold your hand, and we're going to go to the land of your forefathers...

Kira
Foremothers more like...

(They laugh)

Morowa
Look, that's your parents' and grandparents' story, not yours...

Kira
So, do you still envy me?
(Sobs)

Morowa
Are you crying? What's going on here? Look, if anybody should be crying today, it should be me... it's *my* mum's anniversary, not yours... So what are you crying for now?

Kira
Moro, many people have things on their minds... things that have been bothering them, in some cases, for years... but they think... or even *fear* sometimes... that there's no point saying anything, because they might not be taken seriously... I'm not saying *you* wouldn't have taken me seriously, but... I don't know... Sometimes, I think I'm cursed... some kind of generational, family thing...

Morowa
What? Why would you think that?

Kira
I've just told you where it all began for me and my sisters... my family... it's like we're probably not entitled to happiness because of the situation with our parents, my Aunty Mahira, Faisal and all that... No wonder QC left me... Why should I or my sisters be happy? Because of us, my aunty's marriage broke up... Faisal didn't have a dad... I know this all sounds a bit crazy... and I'm the one who deals with people's social issues

and problems like this all the time... but that's how I feel... and I can't help how I feel...

Morowa

You're right... it *does* sound crazy... particularly coming from *you*... You need to stop right there, Kira... First of all, *you* left QC, not the other way round... And were you or your sisters there when your parents met? Did you have any say in things? I don't think so.... So how can you be responsible, or suffer for what they did or didn't do at that time? Listen, no-one on earth had a say in how they were born... you just find yourself where you find yourself...

Kira

You're right, but...

Morowa

But what? There's no 'but' here... Look, there's no such thing as an ideal way to be born... or an ideal family... or anything like that... they just don't exist... Trust me... every single family... rich, poor, black, white, whatever... has a story they'd prefer to keep quiet... sweep well under the carpet... make disappear if they could... And the more squeaky clean some families try to come across, the more scandal they're sometimes trying to hide...

Kira

But some stories are worse than others, Moro...

Morowa

So what are you trying to say now? This your family story is the worst of the worst? Please... Look, you always say there's very little you haven't heard... And you know full well that there are worse stories... far, far worse...

Kira

But it's a bit different when it's *your own* family...

Morowa

Because when it's *your* family, you know all the gritty details, and those details sort of get amplified in your head, so you *think* it's the worst... that's just human nature... But I'm telling you again: *nobody's* from a pure family or background... from royalty down, the world over... so no-one has the right to turn their nose up at others, or make anybody feel not quite right about themselves... And you're not cursed... don't say that again...

Kira

I think too deeply sometimes...

Morowa

You tend to do that... and I've warned you about that before... So are you saying you and your sisters should be conscious of yourselves, sort of looking over your shoulders for the rest of your lives, whilst murderers, rapists, paedophiles, those sorts... they can relax, whilst campaigners fight for their rights round the clock? And mark my words, the crazy way things are going... it's just a matter of time before we wake up to breaking news: that rape and paedophilia aren't crimes any more... and that in fact everybody who was ever convicted of those 'former crimes' should come forward for compensation...

(They laugh)

Morowa

Look, we're talking about all this stuff now... my mother and your parents... because in spite of the pain or whatever, we actually *can*... Do you know there are some stories you cannot really discuss as such... they're that bad... there's just no words... That your poshy poshy friend in Wales... what's her name again? So is this *your* story worse than *hers*? Come on...

Kira

Oh my God... that's on a different level altogether... just wrong...

all round... whichever way you look at it...

Morowa

Oh-oh... so you see... Look at a situation like that... but she's getting on with her life... somehow... What can she do? They say: when life gives you hot pepper, make hot pepper soup...

(They laugh)

Kira

Well, actually, when I stop and think about *her* story, I guess my parents were just a bit naughty...

Morowa

I would call them 'unconventional'... but I guess 'naughty' will do just fine... Look, trust me... if you have an election between 'Naughty' and 'Nice'... 'Nice' will win... and you know why? Because people have to keep up appearances for the audience... they have to be seen to be doing the 'right' thing... But do a *secret* ballot, and see if 'Naughty' doesn't win... hands down...

Kira

(Laughs)

Morowa

Trust me on this: most people want a bit of naughtiness... we all do... In fact we *need* it, because that's what makes the world go round... makes life interesting... and enjoyable for that matter... Life would be so damn boring... just unbearable, if everybody followed all the rules all the time...

Kira

That's not up the PC alley... but I guess you're right...

Morowa

It's just a fact of life... And as for your parents; they were human beings, that's all... OK, maybe they broke some rules, but what's new? Who hasn't? People always do and always will... no matter what... Some of our grandparents... even *great-grandparents* wouldn't have been born, never mind some of us or our parents, if people hadn't broken some of the so-called rules along the way... In fact when you stop and think, who makes some of these rules anyway? Look, to the rule breakers who made it possible for some, if not *most* of us, to be here in the first place... and who make life juicy and interesting, I raise my glass and say: 'Keep up the good work... and don't ever stop'...

(They laugh)

Morowa
Look, my granny's brother, Pa Magwa... he would always tell us that in life, the beginning of many things may not be so good... in fact it could be quite bad even... But then, out of that bad... some real good could come... He would tell us this story time after time, because it was really *his* own story: apparently, a nun... a missionary... found his mother collapsed on some bush road... with him, tied to her back... he was aged 2 or 3 or so at the time...

Kira
Really?

Morowa
Yes... The nun revived his mother, but I think she must've suffered a stroke, because from what we could understand, she was never quite right after that... I think she had problems with her speech and movement... Mind you this was all probably well over a hundred years ago now...

Kira
Wow...

Morowa
Anyway, after that, his mother started going to church with her children, of course including Pa Magwa... and the nuns now took the family... particularly him... under their wing... He and his

siblings, including my granny, went on to attend the missionary school... Apparently the nuns were so fond of *him* in particular... at one time they even wanted to send him to Ireland to finish school... but his mother and grandmother refused point blank to let him go...

Kira

They probably thought: 'If these people take or send this our son away... that's it... we'll never see him again'...

Morowa

And they would've probably been right... I don't think he ever really got over not going to Ireland... he always talked about it... But all the same, he did well in life... he became a big man in customs... very well known and highly respected... And looking back, a lot of what he got from those nuns was more or less private tuition... he said he had special access to their library and all sorts... So from being quite young, he got to read and know about so many things... that's why he seemed to know at least something about everything... every subject... And you could never get tired of listening to him... whether he was explaining something, or telling a story... And no-one could tell a story like he did... whether it be an African or oyibo story... he'd patiently explain the meanings of names, proverbs and sayings... those kind of things... very witty... and very kind...

Kira

You probably inherited your way with words from him...

Morowa

Probably... But what about his wit and kindness? Are you trying to say I didn't inherit those?

(They laugh)

Morowa

And talking about words: before I came to England for the very first time, I went to see Pa Magwa to say goodbye... as it turned out, that was to be the last time I would see him... he died a couple of years after I came here...

Kira
Awww...

Morowa
I miss him till today... But anyway, he gave me a prayer book, which I still have and treasure... He signed it: 'From Your Grandpa Maguire, in brackets 'Magwa'... That's when he explained to me that the nuns had actually given him the name 'Maguire'... but our people... they Africanised it to 'Magwa'...

(They laugh)

Kira
Trust them... Oh to be a child again... none of this adult stuff... worrying and analysing all these things we've been talking about today... no worrying about children, paying bills, workplace issues and this and that... I'd give anything now, to just sit for hours and listen to someone like your Pa Magwa, telling stories about why leopards have spots and stuff like that...

Morowa
Me too... But seriously... the point of all this explanation is that, as Pa Magwa said: good came out of a not so good situation... He would always say, but for that fateful encounter with the nun that day, the chances of him ever going to school, would've been very slim... The fact is, the course of his life changed for the better... but all because of a sad event... his mother's collapse with a stroke... And for someone like *him* not to have gone to school... that would've been a crime... illiteracy wouldn't have suited him *at all*... So my dear, look... your parents may not have had an ideal start... but at the end of the day, I think things turned

out pretty good... for *all* of you... end of story...

Kira

I guess you're right...

Morowa

There've been so many instances in my life where the beginning of the story was not straightforward... or a bit of a nightmare in fact... but by the end, things turned out OK... somehow... When things are rough, it's like I hear Pa Magwa saying: 'It looks bad now... but just find a way... any way... to keep moving forward... and you'll see... everything will be fine'... The thing is, no matter how rough things get or actually become, you just have to believe that things will eventually work themselves out... How do you face the never-ending challenges of life if you don't sort of think that way? In fact why bother to face them at all? You might as well just give up... throw in the towel...

Kira

You know what... every time I hear that expression: 'throw in the towel', I think of that your neighbour... Carol...

Morowa

As for that one...

Kira

I blacklisted her completely after that pad thing... I think it's the words 'throw' and 'towel'... It's funny, but it must be... I think the fact that she *threw* a sanitary *towel*... a used one for that matter... over your fence into your backyard... as soon as I hear 'throw in the towel'... somehow it just brings it all back... urgh...

Morowa

Well, *you* probably need some more counselling to help you erase that tragic memory...

(They laugh)

Kira

But seriously, *that* definitely took some beating... How does someone even *think* of that, never mind actually do it?

Morowa

Carol... she was just wrong... on so many levels... This is someone married to a Caribbean man, with three mixed race kids... but she'd keep telling me to take my kids back to Africa... You just couldn't make it up...

Kira

And as for the husband... What was his name again?

Morowa

Trevor... one time he was standing right there when she was telling me to 'fuck off back to the jungle'... but he just sort of smiled sheepishly... Actually he was quite a nice chap, but...

Kira

Imagine what she would be saying to him behind closed doors...

Morowa

Well according to the girls, they heard them quarrelling one time, and she was calling him a 'bloody black beast'...

Kira

Oh the 'threebies'... Is that all? Oh that's not too bad, bless her...

(They laugh)

Morowa

It was like every other day she'd call the police on me... until that time when she was right up in my face, and I told her to stop pointing and spitting... and she says to me: 'I'm not spitting in your face, but I will if you're not careful"... So of course I told her if she tried it, one of us would end up *dead*... Next thing she calls the police... as usual... that I was threatening to kill her... But that was the very last time she called the police on me...

Things didn't go quite the way she'd hoped for at all... Because that my elderly neighbour... Granny Five...

Kira

Oh Granny Five... I wonder if she's still there...

Morowa

Where will she go? Anyway, she told the police that Carol had started all the trouble... Carol just couldn't believe it, because they were good friends... or at least supposed to be... But you know these old oyibo people... they know everything and everybody's business on the street... who's coming and going... what they're coming and going for... very nosy... But by and large, they speak the truth...

Kira

And nothing but the truth... even to their detriment sometimes... Most of that generation... they just don't know how to lie...

(They laugh)

Morowa

So anyway, to my delight, Granny Five explained things to the police even better than I did... So as you know, Carol ended up with a caution...

Kira

Oh yes... no-one was more deserving...

Morowa

She brought out a side of me that *I* don't even like about myself... But after that night Trevor collapsed, she came to her senses... because if Kukua and Debbie hadn't given him CPR, that would have been it for him... no two ways... even the ambulance staff said it... they were so impressed with them... Look, I was taken aback as well... *I* didn't even know Kukua and Debbie knew all that CPR stuff... I just stood there looking in amazement... So, anyway, after that near death experience, Carol now became *Saint* Carol... over-the-top nice, so grateful, apologetic... offering to do this and that for me... baking cakes and all that...

Kira

So was she really expecting you to eat her food?

Morowa

Can you just imagine? God forbid... may I never be that hungry... or desperate... As soon as she turned her back, everything would just go straight in the bin... But the bottom line is: things didn't start out good for me and her... at all... in fact things were pretty rough for a good while... And I can't say we became the best of friends, but at least we didn't part as enemies...

Kira

Well, as your Pa Magwa would say: 'Some good came out of some wrong'...

Morowa

I guess... And can you believe we moved away from Carol and her wahala nearly six years ago?

Kira

You mean you've already done *six years* in your place? And I still call it your 'new' place... Time flies oh... You know what, I'm actually thinking of moving as well... downsizing... But my fear is: I've been so relaxed here... I don't want to move and probably end up with a new neighbour like Carol... I just won't have the energy to deal with somebody like her now...

Morowa

But if you look at things like that, you won't do anything... Your next door neighbour could wake up tomorrow and decide to sell, or move on, or whatever... Next thing, who do you see packing in next door to you? Jack the Ripper and his extended family... struggling to introduce themselves to you...

(They laugh)

Morowa

What do you do then? I don't think you'd be looking for advice at that point... You'll be snatching the first offer you get, so you can scramble as far away as possible...

Kira

True... You know what just crossed my mind? I've just remembered how *we* met...

Morowa

What? So what made you think of *that*? Just out of the blue...

Kira

I really don't know where that came from... I guess the mind just wanders sometimes... it does some sort of scan and then just randomly lands on something... But anyway, I've often thought to myself, but for that wretched so-and-so who nicked my pouch at the Elephant & Castle, we may never have met... we'd have probably just walked past each other... You were my own personal Good Samaritan that day... you didn't just walk on by like everybody else... You didn't know me from Adam, but you gave me your very last penny...

Morowa

So who told you I gave you my very last penny? Did I look crazy to you... to give you my *very last penny*?

(They laugh)

Morowa

Anyway, what's all this granny, sentimental reminiscing for now? Look, the question you should really be asking yourself is this: "How the hell would I have coped... survived even... if I'd never met Moro?"

(They laugh)

Kira
But look oh... funnily... again, good came out of wrong... I think your Grandpa Magwa is somehow trying to reach out to you today... trying to tell you one or or two things... maybe he wants to tell you a story... like he used to...

Morowa
No... let him just stay quietly wherever he is... please... I'm fine, thank you...

(They laugh)

Kira
Just say a prayer for him... In fact you know what... say a prayer for your mother too... it's her anniversary after all...

Morowa
Actually, I pray for them... all the time... I hope they're both at rest... But today I'm going to be a bit selfish... I'm going to pray for *myself* for a change... Look, only God knows what *my* children will have to say about me if and when the time comes for them to say something... but I guess that's their prerogative... The thing is, no parent gets it right all the time... it's impossible... But *my* prayer is this: I hope I have played my cards with them in such a way, that when's it all over for me... when it's all done and dusted, I hope Debbie and Kukua remember me with genuine fondness... When I think about it, that's all I really want from them... nothing else... nothing more... If I achieve that, wherever I may be, I know I'll be at peace...

21 Saturday 6 July

Earlier in the day

TALKING ABOUT TREATS

Featuring Racquel, Kira's friend.

Morowa
You're still at home? What are you doing at home at this time?

Kira
Should I be somewhere? We don't have anything on today, do we?

Morowa
The christening... don't tell me they didn't invite you... They were practically begging me to attend... but I told them I won't be able to make it, but I'll send a present for the Little One...

Kira
Christening?

Morowa
The Royal Christening now... what else?

(They laugh)

Morowa
Actually, today's that FFF... fibroid fundraising thing...

Kira
Oh... but you didn't say... we'd said we would go...

Morowa

I only found out *this morning* that it was today... they'll be almost finished by now... I don't think they advertised it properly this year... last year information and flyers were all over the place...

Kira

Oh, that's such a shame... we would've been there...

Morowa

Definitely... Anyway, I've just seen your message... theatre tickets and a meal afterwards...

Kira

So are you game?

Morowa

Why won't I be game? I'll be at a teachers' conference that afternoon, so it'll be so nice to unwind in the evening... So how much will I be owing you for that?

Kira

No, no... it's on me... I'm actually treating you and Racquel...

Morowa

Ooh nice, thank you... I haven't seen her for ages... your oyibo sister from another mother...

(They laugh)

Morowa

I just love her company... she's so funny...

Kira

Racquel... she's special... She'll be in London for a couple of days, so I thought we could all meet up... I just needed to make sure *you* could make it... so I'm going to go ahead now and book a table at this new African fusion place... someone at my gym told me about it... they say it's really good...

Morowa
Oh yeah? Which one's that?

Kira
It's called Dine With Dzifa...

Morowa
Spell that...

Kira
Well, it's Dine with D-Z-I-F-A...

Morowa
(Laughs)
I thought so... that's a Ghanaian name... you didn't pronounce it right... DZ is pronounced as 'J'... Dzifa... I'm pretty sure she's the one I heard on the radio... and I'm sure she was talking about this restaurant... If I'm not mistaken, it's in Covent Garden...

Kira
It is... it must be the one... I've checked the reviews... apparently some celebrities and stars go there regularly... so I thought we could go and rub our poor shoulders with them... we'll go and act all fake there, as if we're used to the high life...

(They laugh)

Morowa
I'm sure Racquel will like it too...

Kira
Oh definitely... you know she's up and ready for anything African...

Morowa
I was so impressed with her the last time she came and she wore that ankara top and skirt to your barbecue...

Kira
With head-tie and all... She said she couldn't understand all the attention... She said to me: 'Africans wear European clothes all the time... nobody gives a damn... So what's the big deal?'

Morowa
Well exactly... Anyway, that's an evening to look forward to... Then the following week we're at Nish's... for Omar's birthday... and after that I'm off to the Lake District...

Kira
So you're actually going? I thought you were joking when you said you'd be holidaying in the UK this year...

Morowa
Sonny decided we should do that for a change... he says there's so much to see right here in the UK...

Kira
He's right you know... Do you know I've never been on the London Eye? Never been to the London Dungeon...

Morowa
Me neither... and it's been ages since I went to Madame Tussaud's... The Aquarium... places like that... There's quite a few places... landmarks... even outside of London... we really need to make time to go see some of them... have a few fun days out... just treat ourselves...

Kira
You're right... But hey, you know what... talking about treats... I've actually got one for you right now...

Morowa
Really? What is it?

Kira
Courtesy of no other than... Her Royal Highness... or Lowness rather... Mama Razia...

Morowa
(Laughs)
Haven't they bundled her back home yet?

Kira
After what's happened now, I'm hoping she'll be off sooner rather than later... she just couldn't keep her miserable mouth shut...

Morowa
What did she say now?

Kira
She recorded herself...

Morowa
Doing what?

Kira
She recorded herself on the phone, by accident... bitching about my sister...

Morowa
No...

Kira
Oh yes... Let me not spoil it for you... check your phone in a couple of minutes... I'll send the recording to you... That's the my weekend treat for you... enjoy...

22   MAMA RAZIA'S MESSAGE WAS RECORDED ON...

Wednesday 3 July

Mama Razia is visiting the UK from Sierra Leone. She's staying with her son, Bolu and his wife, Nish (Nausha), who is Kira's sister. Bored at home one morning, Mama Razia calls her niece, Hauwa, for a chat. She uses the landline phone, and presses the record button by mistake. They speak in the lingua franca of Sierra Leone.

Also featuring Mama Razia's grandson, Omar, and nephew Deji.

Mama Razia
Hauwa, my daughter... is that you? So you don't care about your Aunty any more? You haven't even come to collect the stuff I brought for you...

Hauwa
It's not like that, Aunty... work, work, work... they're killing us in this country... The only reason you caught me now is because I've taken the morning off today... I'm waiting for a delivery...

Mama Razia
Oh, this white man's land... no-one to help you... you have to do everything yourself...

Hauwa
We're used to it now, Aunty... But wait a minute... How come you're using the house phone? So you know my number off head?

Mama Razia
My own phone is charging... Bolu showed me how to call you by just pressing 8 on the house phone... he is no 2, and that

witch, Nausha, is no 1... as if I would ever call her... For what?
God forbid...

Hauwa
Oh, I see... I'm on speed dial... Aunty Razi, Razi...you're sharp
with this technology thing oh...

Mama Razia
We have to keep and measure up now...

(They laugh)

Hauwa
How are things?

Mama Razia
Come and see me, my dear... I'm just here on my own like a
scarecrow... no company... nothing...

Hauwa
Aunty, this is our life over here oh... Why don't you watch TV?
Eat... drink... relax...

Mama Razia
I can't just be eating anyhow... Me too, I'm watching my
figure...

(They laugh)

Mama Razia
As for TV... most of the time, when the white man is talking,
I don't understand what they're saying... and my eyes begin to
ache if I watch for too long anyway...

Hauwa
Well, you can go stretch your legs, go for a walk...

Mama Razia
Me? Walk? No-oh... The last time I was here I fell down... in

the street... strangers had to pick me up... you know me and my
knees... And it's not easy to find your way around anyway...
Sometimes when I ask for help or directions, people don't
understand me... And look, it's very cold... let me be indoors...

Hauwa
Cold? This is the warmest time of the year... It doesn't really
get much warmer than this oh...

Mama Razia
Look, me, I'm an old African... this your country is never warm
enough for me... Any time I have to go out, I have to dress up
with layers and layers... But you know what, my daughter? I
can't hide anything from you... I don't feel like doing anything...
I don't want to eat, or drink, or go out, or anything...
(Sobs)

Hauwa
Ah-ah... Aunty, what is it?

Mama Razia
My heart is full... it's heavy, Hauwa... Since I came to this
country, I've been crying almost non-stop... It's your brother
Bolu oh... it's Bolu... When last did you set eyes on him? Bolu
is finished... completely finished...

Hauwa
Ah... What's wrong with him?

Mama Razia
I'm sure you haven't seen him for a long time, because if you
had, I know you would have alerted me... I've told you people to
keep an eye on each other... If you see him, you will cry too...
he's just like the leather the shoemakers use to make slippers...
dry, no oil, no flesh... he looks so haggard... my fresh, handsome
son... Oh... what has befallen me at this latter stage in my life?

Hauwa

Aunty, calm down... stop crying... But I saw him and Nish just a couple of months ago actually... Bolu looked fine... he was OK...

Mama Razia

He's not OK... at all... Since I came I've been cooking for him... trying to build him up a bit... But do you know, Nausha won't let him eat my food?

Hauwa

What? Why not?

Mama Razia

How would I know? Ay Bolu! Nausha has finally got my son where she wants him... She won't cook properly for him; she never has... When I cook for him... things I know he likes... he'll just manage a couple of spoons... next thing she's forcing him to eat her rubbish 'passa' or pasta or whatever she calls it... She makes him eat salad and all these dry, tasteless oyibo foods all the time... she says it's healthy... Bolu never liked salad... I'm so surprised to see him eating it the way he does now...

Hauwa

Aunty, sometimes over here, after work, we get home so tired... you just feel like eating some light food... nothing too heavy... or just something different...

Mama Razia

Why won't *she* eat light food then... and let Bolu eat some meat for a change? You need to see the amount of beef and fish *she* eats at one sitting... Oh Bolu... this is what happens when you don't listen to your parents' advice... From the very first day I set eyes on this Nausha, I knew she was bad news... I just knew it... and I did not keep quiet... I said it... loud and clear, but...

Hauwa

Hmmm...

Mama Razia
Then when I did my homework and dug into her background...
mother, father, uncles, aunties, grandparents... the whole lot of
them, all sleeping with each other anyhow... I knew this is where
we would end with a girl from such a family... wretched people...
Of all the girls Bolu could've married, he settled for this one...
Now look... Even her name... 'Nausha'... What is that? And as
for that her un-brought up, rude sister who wanted to fight me...
that oblong-shaped Kira... Well, my own husband stayed with
me till the very end... Where is hers? Tell me... Where is QC?
Of course he's not stupid like Bolu... he ran for his dear life... he
couldn't cope with her rudeness and nonsense... Poor boy... he
even left his children behind... I'm sure he went looking for a
woman with some hips, to start with... So tell me... what is Bolu
waiting for? What is he benefitting from being with Nausha? In
fact, what has he *ever* benefitted?

Hauwa
Aunty, calm down...

Mama Razia
When you see him, you see someone whose life is in reverse... If
this is not witchcraft, then what is it? So Nausha and her people
want to finish my son the juju way? I see... You know me very
well, I don't like trouble... And don't get me wrong, it's not that
I don't like her... I do... Nausha knows very well that in spite of
her behaviour, I've always been very kind to her... I've supported
her... But if it's the juju way she and her people want to take
things, then so be it... I will also make them understand that not
everyone who says 'goodnight' goes to sleep... Simple...

Hauwa
Aunty, listen to me...

Mama Razia
One thing for sure is this: Nausha is going to pay dearly for these

tears I'm shedding now... No mother will see what I'm seeing now and keep quiet... Bolu is dying right in front of my eyes... My grandmother was a born and bred Yoruba woman; she named Bolu after my brother, your father... Boluwatife... meaning 'as God wishes'... so it can't be as *Nausha* wishes... She will not be able to kill him, because that is what she wants, I'm telling you... So she can reap where she did not sow... take all Bolu has worked and struggled for, to go and enjoy with another man... that's how all the people in that her family are... everybody knows them...

Hauwa

Nish is not my favourite person either... Even me... I told Bolu ages ago, to get rid of her... not once, not twice... Some years ago I even tried to pair him up with one or two of my friends who would've been really good for him, but... Anyway, they seem to be managing somehow... I guess they're happy enough...

Mama Razia

Happy? What kind of happiness is this? You can't imagine the amount of nonsense going on right in front of me in this house... *She* drives the car to work, whilst *he* takes the bus and train, and walks... for miles... The other day he came back from work, I almost didn't recognise my own son... looking like a madman, with beef, yams, onions, plantains, and other foodstuffs... almost tied to his back like a baby... Bolu... forced to go to market... like a houseboy... and you're here telling me he's happy...

Hauwa

(Laughs)

Aunty, we don't have house help over here like back home, so it's nothing unusual or strange for our men to help with the shopping and housework... they just have to help out...

Mama Razia

Don't tell me that nonsense, Hauwa... I wasn't born yesterday...

Imagine this... Nausha will be watching television whilst Bolu's in the kitchen... battling with the cooker and pots and pans... Then worst of all, she sticks her fat self down to actually scoff the food he has cooked... So tell me, is that right? The other day I wept like a baby when I heard him telling someone on the phone that he *enjoys* cooking... So it has come to this? Bolu has a wife... supposedly... but he has been reduced to the point where he actually *enjoys* cooking... To the extent, he even ties the wrapper around himself... you know the one the oyibo people use when they want to make food...

Hauwa
(Laughs)
Oh... the apron... Actually, no-one can blame him for cooking for himself though, because Nish can't cook properly... at all...

Mama Razia
But how can she when she wasn't properly home trained? The other day she was acting all busy and important... she didn't know I was spying her from my bedroom... she wasn't doing *anything*... whilst poor Bolu was changing bed sheets... next thing I saw him using that electric broom thing... hoover... Oh, my eyes have seen too much... Luckily his father is not alive to see and hear all this... But come oh... I hear that over here in the white man's land you can go for an operation, and they can actually change you from a man to a woman... Is that true?

Hauwa
Well, it is...

Mama Razia
Ehn? Wahala oh... Look, if I don't arrest things *right now*, mark my words... that's the next thing she'll make Bolu go for...

Hauwa
(Laughs)

Mama Razia
No wonder I keep dreaming all the time that Bolu's being chased
by chameleons... Chameleons change, so Nausha wants my son
to change... to a woman... Lord God... it's all crystal clear to me
now... Hmmm... I have to move very quickly before Nausha gets
the upper hand here... I don't even know what you're laughing
at... honestly... Actually, you seem to be taking her side...

Hauwa
No Aunty... how can I take Nish's side?

Mama Razia
You don't know anything... she's probably sorted you out with
juju too... So there goes my whole family... you included... And
I should just fold my arms? No way... She's taken advantage of
Bolu because I don't live here in this country... She should ask
Deji's wife... You know my sister is quiet, so she couldn't deal
with that her daughter-in-law... But me... Just before I came this
time, I washed, dried and pressed that one into shape back home,
when she started trying to display her cockroach tactics to us...
Imagine that one too... another nuisance like Nausha... thinking
she could tell us what to do in our family... By the time I was
done with her, she was thanking me for the couple of slaps I was
forced to give her, and for the opportunity to kneel down and
apologise to me and my sister... her mother-in-law... because at
the end of the day, she realised I did it out of nothing but love for
her and for her own good...

(SILENCE)

Mama Razia
You're not saying anything?

Hauwa
Aunty, what do you want me to say now? I've told you to calm
down, but you won't...

Mama Razia

How can I calm down? Even Omar, my own grandchild, Nausha has turned him against me... Do you know he's only been here to see me twice since I came... just twice... Is that right?

Hauwa

Aunty these our children over here don't have time for all these family politics and things... Omar is a busy man...

Mama Razia

What do you mean? And do you know he lives with a Chinese girl now? The last time I was here it was a white girl he came with... now Chinese... This is all down to Nausha... she did not train him properly at all... in fact she spoilt him... I kept saying it from when he was small... but nobody was listening... now look at the outcome... Bolu tried... everybody knows he tried... But Omar is not like us at all... he's ended up like Nausha's people...

Hauwa

Aunty, these children nowadays... they're different... they mix and mingle with everybody...

Mama Razia

So tell me, is that good? Mixing with everybody anyhow? Isn't that how the trouble comes into families and doesn't go? The other thing that's really bothering me, is the fact that Bolu doesn't even have any other children...

Hauwa

Ah... Aunty... Where's all this coming from now?

Mama Razia

So you mean you don't understand what I'm saying, or what? Bolu should have gotten another woman ages ago to have more children... there's nothing wrong with *him* oh; *he* can definitely have more children... It's not as if I haven't been telling him over the years... There are so many nice girls from solid families who could've delivered the goods for us by now... But of course, as I say, you seem to be supporting this Nausha... Anyway, what do you even know about life? You're just a child...

Hauwa

Aunty, I'll be forty-nine next month...

Mama Razia

Oh... so you think you're a big woman now? I was the second person to hold you in this world when you were born in your granny's house, because your mother couldn't make it to hospital in time... so you can never be a big woman for *me*... never... Look, my son needs more children... his father had eleven...

Hauwa

That was a different time, Aunty... our fathers had several wives then... I have my two boys and that's fine for me...

Mama Razia

I've noticed that when you people stay abroad for long, you start to lose your senses... Don't you know there's a big difference between two and one? Your children have each other to grow with... Who does Omar have? Look, if I have my way, Bolu must kick Nausha out... not tomorrow... left to me, she will leave *today*... Look, by the time I come back to this country again, my name is not Raziana-Iman, if I don't see to it that he gets a nice, young, juicy girl who will look after him properly for me... take the cooking pots out of my son's hands for a start... give him some young, fresh blood, instead of the stale, sickly blood that he's been getting all these years...

Hauwa

(*Laughs*)

Mama Razia

By the grace of the Almighty, I will soon have more grand-children from Bolu to enjoy before I die... Poor Omar, because

he was all alone when he was growing up... no wonder he's
looking for Chinese people and all now... So are you telling me
he doesn't see black people... black girls... or what? Suppose he
says he wants to marry this one now... Can you imagine that
kind of trouble? Where would we start with those people?

Hauwa
(Laughs)
She's a very nice girl, Aunty... really... And she's *not* Chinese,
you know... she's from a place called Laos...

Mama Razia
From where?

Hauwa
Aunty don't worry...

Mama Razia
No, teach me... I'm old, but I can still learn... spell it for me...

Hauwa
L-A-O-S...

Mama Razia
Which Lagos? She's not a black girl oh... he brought her right
here, I saw her... Once in a while my ears play up, but my eyes
are not that bad... She's definitely Chinese... Or has he got a
black girl somewhere that you know about? Aha... that's it...
maybe you think that's the one he came with... Look, if he has a
black girl... please... he shouldn't waste my time... he should
come and show her to me instead... quickly...

Hauwa
Aunty, you need to calm down about everything... seriously...

Mama Razia
Look, I can't keep everything bottled up... I will talk...

Hauwa

So, you think you can tell Bolu to drive Nish away, and she will go, just like that? We all know he could've done so much better than her... but forget it... he's not going to drive her away...

Mama Razia

Do you want to bet me? She will go...

Hauwa

They've been together a long time...

Mama Razia

And so? Better late than never... You know that my neighbour back home, the one who lives almost opposite us... the policeman... the one with no neck and big, bulging eyes...

Hauwa

PC Cole... How can I forget him?

Mama Razia

Well, just imagine him in that condition...

Hauwa

(Laughs)

Mama Razia

Ah... he looks much better now... I knew him when he was going to school... my God... if you saw him then... He was chasing after me in those days... and I thought: 'you and who'? Anyway, last year he left his wife... after over *forty years* of marriage...

Hauwa

Oh... very pretty woman...

Mama Razia

Oh yes... it was a beauty and the beast situation... only God knows how and where they met... Anyway, so many people begged PC Cole on his wife's behalf... we all did... but he said 'no'... enough is enough... So if an apology like him can take such a stand, what is wrong with Bolu? Tell me... Look, when I'm done with Nausha, she will pack her things and run for her life... In fact, what is she even packing? What did she bring to my son's house in the first place, apart from bad luck and juju? After I make her confess to witchcraft, she can just clear off for good... to make way for better people and better things...

Hauwa
Aunty, if Bolu hears all this, it won't be good... at all...

Mama Razia
Oh, leave me alone... I've kept quiet for too long... I want him to hear me and come to his senses... My son is no fool, but somehow Nausha has managed to turn him inside out... The way he looks now, is that how he looked when she met him? If I don't take action now, by the time I come next time, I'll probably meet him walking around the streets of London, carrying things on his head to sell... maybe groundnuts or onions... or whatever Nausha may decide... after she would've probably forced him to change to a woman... That's if he even survives in the first place... Oh...

Hauwa
(Laughs)
Nobody's changing to anything, and nobody's dying, Aunty...

Mama Razia
You don't seem to understand what I've been trying to tell you all this time... at all... Anyway, whether you understand or not, I've made up my mind... I know what I have to do to save my son, and so help me God, I'm going to do it... just wait and see... Anyway, how are my grandchildren? I'm sure they must be big men now...

Hauwa

They're fine... they're both taller than their father now...

Mama Razia

What? Wonderful... Make sure I see them before I go back oh... My daughter, what soup will you bring for me when you're coming?

Hauwa

What would you like?

Mama Razia

But you know what I like now... maybe dried cockle stew...

Hauwa

Aunty, where do you want me to get dried cockles from?

Mama Razia

Oh, you've run out? I brought plenty for you... you will collect them when you come... OK, prepare anything with fish for me... but the only thing: don't bring it when Nausha is home...

Hauwa

Aunty, I can only come at the weekend when she's likely to be home... And it's her house anyway... Will you keep the food in your room? You can't... at some point you'll have to put it in the fridge for all to see... and even eat if they want to...

Mama Razia

Listen to me good, Hauwa... and learn... When you're dealing with people like her, you have to be ahead of them all the time... I say don't bring anything for me when she's here... I know what I'm saying...

Hauwa

Hmmm... OK Aunty... Oh, I think the delivery people have arrived... I'll call you back later, OK?

23 Saturday 6 July

Later in the day

IT'S LIVE... REAL LIFE

Morowa
Wow oh wow... So people like Mama Razia actually still exist?

Kira
They do... very much so...

Morowa
Oh my God... Talk about shooting yourself in the foot...

Kira
I know Nish can be troublesome and all that, but just to keep the peace, I know she's put up with a lot from that her mother-in-law... always gives her the benefit of the doubt... Even Bolu has told me he admires the way Nish puts up with his mother...

Morowa
So did they make her know about the recording?

Kira
Oh yes, of course... they played it for her... But was she sorry? Hell no... Apparently her initial reaction was: can't she talk freely in her son's house? How can they have something that can record people just like that?

Morowa
So no remorse?

Kira
None... But then they told her that it would probably be better if she just went back to Freetown, more or less immediately... Of

course she wasn't prepared for that at all... to go back, just like that... So then apparently the crocodile tears began to flow... how she didn't really mean any harm... Nish is like a daughter to her... after all she has other grandchildren, so why would she be insisting on more... you know the usual nonsense... Imagine her going on as if Bolu is some starving orphan who has to fend for himself... You saw how big he got one time... The doctors warned him to pull down... or else...

Morowa
And he has oh... Remember, I couldn't recognise him in that picture you sent me some time ago... he looks really good...

Kira
All thanks to Nish insisting on a proper diet and exercise and all that ... I feel sorry for Nish, honestly... but I guess she's used to Mama Razia now...

Morowa
Is it possible to ever get used to someone like her? She's never going to change...

Kira
She can't... Did you hear the bit where she said how QC ran away for his life from me? Imagine her actually having the nerve to say she's always liked and supported Nish... And as for that Hauwa one... how she'd told Bolu to get rid of Nish several times... how he could've done better... She's even looked for other women for him... Hey...

Morowa
I had to rewind a few times, because even though I understood most of it, when they spoke fast, I couldn't get some bits... But Hauwa... she's Bolu's cousin... the tall one, right?

Kira
That's her...

Morowa
You can tell she thinks she's something special...

Kira
Oh, she does... she was telling us one time that anywhere she goes, she can feel the eyes on her... people are always looking...

Morowa
Of course they're looking... in absolute horror...

(They laugh)

Kira
Nish said she just couldn't believe her ears when she heard Hauwa on the recording, because she always goes on as if Nish is one of her favourite in-laws... She will definitely be at Nish's lunch... I must tell her one or two things then... It's people like her who've undermined my sister from the very beginning...

Morowa
If she has any shame, she won't go to that lunch... but if she does, just ignore her... don't say anything to her... For God's sake, just look at her from head to toe... *you* don't have to say anything to her... you can tell that life itself has already had a word or two with Hauwa; it's just that she's not listening...

(They laugh)

Morowa
Look, we've got much better things to do with our time than waste it on life shorteners like her and Mama Razia... Hang on a minute...

(Morowa talks to her husband, Sonny:
Sonny, I'm on the phone... Are they finished? You want me to check them? OK, I'll be down in a minute...)

Morowa

Sorry... it's Sonny... he's baking sausage rolls... peace offering for wrecking my laptop... I wanted to take it to a professional to sort out... he said it wasn't a big problem, he could fix it... Now the laptop isn't even in two halves... it's in three or four halves...

(They laugh)

Morowa

Thank God I back everything up, otherwise that could've been another crisis altogether for me... Anyway, let me send you a picture of the sausage rolls before they went in the oven... I can't keep this to myself... I must share...

Kira

No! Wait a minute... What's actually going on here? Which part is the sausage and which part is the roll? I don't think I've seen anything quite like this before oh...

Morowa

I don't think anybody has... Look, you're just dealing with a picture... for me it's live... real life...

(They laugh)

Kira

But you're quite bad you know... you should've taken charge before things got to this stage...

Morowa

Look, I was in the shower, so I told him to wait for me... but he didn't... So by the time I got to the kitchen, this is what I was confronted with... There was absolutely nothing I could do to save the situation... we just had to put them in the oven like that... No, tell me, what could I have done?

Kira

Do you know there're some websites where you can send

pictures of stuff like this? I think they're called 'cooking fails', or something like that... They'll pay for this particular picture, I'm telling you... This is nothing short of a crime scene...

(They laugh)

Morowa
The story doesn't end there oh... he says wants to try his hand at palm oil soup next...

Kira
Oh no...

Morowa
If I'm lucky, I'll just go into a coma after eating the sausage rolls today... but after the palm oil soup... my chances of survival will be very slim... it'll really be touch and go at that point...

(They laugh)

Morowa
As things stand now, my life is at risk... Look, I'm relying on you to make sure Sonny doesn't get away with things... please help the police all you can with their enquiries... Don't let them reduce the charge to manslaughter... it should be first degree murder...

(They laugh)

Kira
Ah, don't worry about that... I've got the evidence right here on my phone... no judge or jury will free him after seeing this...

Morowa
Look, I'd better go and assess the final damage now... I'll keep you posted... that is if I pull through, of course...

(They laugh)

24 *Tuesday 13 August*

EVERYBODY AND EVERYTHING IS USEFUL

Morowa is back from holidaying in the Lake District.

Featuring Aunty Lois and her grandson.

Kira
I saw your missed call... Is everything OK?

Morowa
You know there's never a dull moment... After eating all that oyibo food in the Lake District, I felt like some good soul food... So yesterday I called Aunty Lois to see if she had some kenkey... She always calls back, so when I didn't hear from her I got a bit worried, cos she lives on her own... or so I thought... Cut a long story short she couldn't answer because these phone scam people called her pretending to be her bank...

Kira
Oh no...

Morowa
So she was busy sorting that out with the police and all that... so that's why I couldn't get her...

Kira
They keep warning people, particularly the elderly ones... but they just won't listen... *Do not engage in any conversation on the phone unless you know exactly who you're dealing with...*

Morowa
I don't know what more they can do or say to warn them of the

dangers... I don't know if they're looking for conversation or what... Depending on the mood I'm in when these stupid scammers call: sometimes I just put the phone down... other times, I take them on and abuse them good and proper...

Kira
So how much did they take from this poor woman now?

Morowa
Look, she made a very narrow escape... and you won't believe who saved her? That her grandson...

Kira
Which one?

Morowa
The one who went to prison... he's living with her now...

Kira
Since when?

Morowa
Since they released him a few weeks ago...

Kira
Ah... Are you sure he's not involved in this scam?

Morowa
I really hope not... honestly... As I understand the story, after the scammers called and said they would come to collect the bank cards...

Kira
You mean they went to her house?

Morowa
Oh yes... apparently her grandson told her not to open the door when they came... he told her just to confirm that they had come

for the cards... So when they came and knocked, she answered them from inside... but to the shock of the scammer, it was the grandson... freshly out of prison... who actually opened the door... So apparently he just lifted the scammer up... I don't think his feet touched the ground until the police arrived...

(They laugh)

Kira
I can imagine the scammer's shock...

Morowa
Oh yes... he knocked on the wrong door this time... Apparently he had an accomplice on motorcycle... I think that one just sped off when he saw his mate suspended in the air...

(They laugh)

Morowa
Anyway, Aunty Lois is singing her grandson's praises... listen to her now: how everybody and everything is useful in their own way, because if not for this her grandson, troublesome as he is, God knows what would've happened to her...

Kira
Aha... So she'll be in no hurry to ask him to leave now...

Morowa
Oh, he's safe and sound and cosy now... Apparently, when they released him, he told his granny he had nowhere to go...

Kira
Lie... Why didn't he go to where he was before he went to jail? Or to his parents?

Morowa
His parents? What? He dare not... apparently his father has

disowned him... completely... But I was wondering... don't they give them accommodation when they're released?   I thought they say they give them all these perks...

Kira
Well... I think a lot of the stories about perks and all that, are a bit exaggerated... and when it comes to accommodation... I'm not too sure what they get... But whatever they may have offered him on release, couldn't have come with an in-house granny cooking and fussing over him round the clock... so whatever the case, I'm sure this arrangement suits him just fine...

(They laugh)

Morowa
How did you know? Aunty Lois more or less cut our conversation short yesterday, so she could go and make food for him...

Kira
Well, there you go... This boy... his siblings... they're medical people, right?

Morowa
The brother's a dentist and the sister's a pilot... Remember they featured her on TV one time... she was encouraging young girls to take up so-called male professions...

Kira
Oh yes...

Morowa
Apparently this chap... he's the youngest and he had the best of *everything*... private school, this and that... And they say he did so well in school... according to his granny, he's actually brighter than those his two siblings...

Kira
Well, let's hope being in prison has sobered him up a bit...

Morowa
My worry is: I hope it doesn't become a pattern... you know this isn't his first time inside...

Kira
Hmmm.... You said it was drugs, right?

Morowa
And a few other things... Bottom line, just bad company... My grandmother would say: the cloth maker does everything to make sure his cloths are nice and attractive, but after he's sold them, he has no say over what they will eventually be used for: a wedding dress or a shroud...

Kira
Here we go with the parables and proverbs... What does that mean?

Morowa
Come on now, it's self explanatory: you try to treat your kids the same, do your best for them... but you can't tell how they'll eventually turn out... There but for the grace of God go all parents and carers...

Kira
Oh, as for that... you can say that again... Even identical twins, with identical DNA, identical upbringing, identical everything you can think of... as time goes by, one can turn out a saint, whilst the other one could end up being the total opposite... apprentice to the devil himself...

25 *Thursday 15 August*

TWO CRAZY OLD BIRDS

Morowa
So what's with the profile picture on your phone? You want to create a very false impression that you understand and appreciate wildlife, nature and stuff like that...

(They laugh)

Kira
The parrots... they're really beautiful, aren't they? They're my virtual grandchildren for now, courtesy of Richie... He's helping a friend look after them for a couple of weeks... As soon as he sent me the picture, I thought wow... profile pic for a while...

Morowa
They look really nice...

Kira
Dia and Spora...

Morowa
You say?

Kira
That's the parrots' names: Dia and Spora... The owner is one of these arty types... really eccentric... a theatre or art designer... something like that... Apparently she's got a cat and a dog as well... one's called Trial and the other's called Error...

(They laugh)

Morowa
You know what? It reminds me of when we were growing up...
some troublesome ones... they'd go and get a dog or a cat... and
then give them a name that was like a message... to torment or
threaten a neighbour they had a problem with... So the poor
animals would end up with names like, 'Wahala-Suits-You'...
or 'Poverty-is-Your-Portion'... and stuff like that...

(They laugh)

Kira
Africans... we're characters... it was exactly the same when I was
growing up as well... And then of course, to retaliate, the
neighbours would go and get their own animals... sometimes
even goats or chickens would do... and they'd give them names
like 'Time-Will-Tell'... or 'We-Shall-See'...

Morowa
And just to cause maximum irritation, they'd be calling the poor
creatures at the top of their voices, all day long... most of the
time they'd call them for absolutely no reason whatsoever...

Kira
Maybe that's why there are so many stray animals back home...
poor things... I'm sure most of them are runaways with mental
health issues... brought on by the stress of the constant name
calling...

(They laugh)

Morowa
Anyway, those two... they must be husband and wife...

Kira
Hmmm? Who?

Morowa
The parrots...

Kira
You won't believe this: apparently they were sharing a cage for a while and the owner was expecting them to mate, but they just fought all the time... It was only when they took them to the vet for their jabs or something, that they found out that they were both actually female...

Morowa
No wonder they were fighting... they were hormonal... they needed their space... And they're probably just as crazy as their owner as well...

(They laugh)

Kira
Exactly... Anyway, now they're in separate cages, their relationship is much better, and apparently they talk to each other all day long...

Morowa
Two crazy old birds...

Kira
And apparently they know each other's names... so they say sometimes they just start calling each other back and forth: 'Dia... Spora... Dia... Spora'...

(They laugh)

Morowa
You know what they probably need to round things up nicely? A husband...

Kira

You want to sort the parrots' love life out as well? This is insane...

Morowa

Look, the thing is, they don't even need a husband each.... they can share... one can be the wife, the other can be the mistress... it's a win win situation...

Kira

Only you could come up with something like this... only you...

(They laugh)

Kira

But come oh, Moro... on a serious note... if those parrots are putting words and sentences together... why can't you do the same and finish that play off for the competition?

Morowa

So as far as you're concerned, it's just a question of putting sentences together? You're stressing me... If you know how many books and papers I have to mark... please...

Kira

You've done most of it anyway... you just need to finish it off... If I could write like you, I would've entered the competition myself... honestly... The thing is, the deadline is the end of this month... Please now... do it as a personal favour to me...

Morowa

Look, I'm not going to win, so what's the point?

Kira

But what's the harm in entering? You don't lose anything as

such... well apart from a bit of your time and energy, of course...
But just think about it for a minute... if you *do* actually win... it's
a safari trip... But another thing that really attracted me to the
competition, was that you could possibly get a publishing deal...
Who knows where that could all lead to?

Morowa
Look, stop... I'm not that good...

Kira
Says who? But look... even the runner-up prizes are not bad...
Be and think positive... you just never know...

Morowa
You seem to have it all sorted...

Kira
I do... You just do the writing... I'll do absolutely everything
else... the hoping... the worrying... the accompanying on the
trip... Just leave everything else to me... I'm your self-appointed,
unpaid agent...

(They laugh)

Kira
OK, seriously now... it has come to this... Is there any way I can
bribe you? What do you want from me to finish this play?

Morowa
Actually, there *is* something you could do for me...

Kira
I say name it... anything... your wish is my command...

Morowa
I'll finish the play off... on one condition: if you go for a meal

with QC... Do that and the play is as good as written...

Kira
You can't be serious...

Morowa
Look, just a meal... nothing else...

Kira
What kind of deal is that?

Morowa
Look Kira, life's too damn short... Face it: you've never stopped loving QC...

Kira
Maybe not... but we all know, sometimes love is not enough...

Morowa
So what's enough, then? Look, he made a few mistakes... OK, maybe many... but surely we're not counting any more now... What I know is that you're the love of his life, and he's the love of yours... Both of you have had enough time and space apart to calm down and sort yourselves out... It's time to stop all this foolishness and delaying tactics, and just get back together...

Kira
Thank you very much Oprah...

Morowa
You know what he keeps saying to me?

Kira
Honestly, I don't care...

Morowa
When he starts, I almost feel like crying...

Kira

Oh here we go... this has got to be a joke...

Morowa

I'm not joking... and *he's* not joking either... You know he's one of the company's directors now... a serious shareholder and all that... he's done really, really well...

Kira

Of course... after nearly impoverishing me...

Morowa

How? Look, a whole professional company executive... he's reduced to like a teenaged boy when he's talking about you... He says you're what's missing in his life... he doesn't want anybody else... He's *always* said you've been the only genuine woman to him...

Kira

Whatever...

Morowa

Whatever indeed... *whatever's* happened, *whatever* he's been up to, he's tired now and just wants to settle down... quietly... don't you?

Kira

Maybe... but not with *him*...

Morowa

Look, I'm not the only one who's tried to match you up with a few other people... some really nice people... But it never works... and it never will, because let's face it, deep down *you* don't want anybody else either... you just want your QC... nobody else will *ever* do... So what is it anyway? Do you want to be a... what's the name for a female eunuch? You want to be a female eunuch for the rest of your earthly days, or what?

Kira

So what's your problem if I'm a 'eunuchess', or whatever the name is...

(They laugh)

Morowa

Your wellbeing, which of course includes your love life, is of paramount concern to me, Madam... Look... just a meal for old time's sake... that's all... absolutely nothing else... If you go for that meal and you're not happy, we'll take things from there...

Kira

What do you mean: 'we'll take things from there'...

Morowa

(Laughs)

Because we will... Look you go for a meal, I finish the play... simple... Deal or no deal?

Kira

No deal... I'm not interested, Moro...

Morowa

You're just being awkward for the mere and sheer hell of it all... Look... just go for the meal and talk to him...

Kira

About what?

Morowa

He says he'll take you anywhere in the world... just for a meal... and I know he means it... Tell him you want supper in Dubai, or somewhere like that... or wherever... He's always travelling all over the place... he'll take you along... you just have to say... Some women would give a whole lot to be in your position now... and you know it...

Kira
I'm not hungry and I don't want to go anywhere...

Morowa
You're difficult oh... you really are...

Kira
Look, if I end up going for a meal, or meeting up with QC in any way, and get I get really worked up, which I honestly suspect might happen... I may just kill him, there and then...

Morowa
OK, you know what... fine... kill him... You know I'll never abandon you... never... I've always had your back... I'll never miss a court hearing, or prison visit before they finally give you the lethal injection, or hang you for his murder... I promise, I'll be there all the way... till the bitter end...

(They laugh)

Morowa
In fact, you never know... you may be lucky... they might see it as a crime of passion and just jail you for life... obviously without parole... We'll take that... with open arms... no quibble...

(They laugh)

Morowa
But seriously now... I'm sure QC will give up all his wealth and trappings... everything he has now... in exchange for you... I'm not kidding...

Kira
Now you're getting well and truly carried away... Give everything up for me? This is a black man we're dealing with here...

(They laugh)

26 *Tuesday 27 August*

IT'S GOOD FOR THE SOUL

Morowa
Check your phone... I've just forwarded something to you...

Kira
You've finished the play at last?

Morowa
Hmmm... I say check your phone...

Kira
Mama Abena! Oh my God! What happened?

Morowa
I don't know oh... I don't know... her daughter in-law just sent it to me... I've been trying to reach her, but of course all their lines are busy...

Kira
Can you imagine? This life eh?

Morowa
Tell me about it... you never know what's just round the corner... Fair enough, she was 90, but it's still a big loss... Look at how full of life she was at her party...

Kira
Oh my God... She was saying goodbye to us all at her birthday... in grand style too... Her husband will be devastated...

Morowa
To be honest, I can't see him lasting too long after this...

Kira

And here was I thinking my day just couldn't get any worse...

Morowa

What else now?

Kira

No, no... nothing anywhere near as serious as Mama Abena at all, but... But can believe, my hairdresser chopped half of my hair off?

Morowa

No!

Kira

She said that's what I told her to do...

Morowa

Well, this is what I can't stand... instead of just putting her hands up and apologising, she's talking nonsense... How could you've told her to do that, for God's sake?

Kira

I told her to trim the back and shape the sides... like I *always* do... I don't know what the hell she's done... Let me send you a picture...

Morowa

Why couldn't God give us the kind of hair that you can just shampoo, rinse and go?

Kira

Ralston says black hair is like black people: curls, bends and twists... but beautiful when properly cared for...

Morowa

Let him be talking his poetry there... It's OK for the men, but we black women... our hair is a big, big issue...

Kira

Massive issue... Look at me now... sitting here, confused, stressed... sleepless nights are sure to follow... all because of my hair... Now my only saving grace will be head wraps... for God knows how long... I don't like covering my head, particularly at work, but that's what I'm going to have to resort to until the hair grows out...

Morowa

I'm looking at it now... it doesn't look too bad...

Kira

Ah... look properly... Can't you see part of my scalp is showing? Suppose it doesn't grow out?

Morowa

Why wouldn't it grow out? But then again, I know someone that happened to, you know...

Kira

Trust *you* to know someone like that...

Morowa

Well... it wasn't their *head* hair...

Kira

What do you mean?

Morowa

Remember the lady who did my curtains? She went for a Brazilian wax... about three years ago... since then... nothing... desert...

Kira

You mean there's nothing down there?

Morowa

Completely bald apparently... Short of applying acid and poison, she said there's nothing she hasn't tried to get it to grow again...

(They laugh)

Kira

How did we get from Mama Abena's passing to hair below?

Morowa

I know not... The thing is I was just getting ready to send you a cheeky message, to say you'll be pleased to know that I've finished the play... at last... next thing I see this message about Mama Abena...

Kira

Awww... Do you know when I went to wish her happy birthday, she remembered my name, and that *my* birthday was the same week as hers...

Morowa

Oh, she's very sharp... well... *was* very sharp... This is unreal...

Kira

It is... Anyway, you say you've finished the play?

Morowa

I'll send the final draft over to you... I want to send it off latest tomorrow... so please read through and give me your final feedback... ASAP...

Kira

I will... well, some good news on a pretty rough day... but you're cutting it fine oh, Moro... if I'm not mistaken, the deadline for submission is this Friday...

Morowa
What more do you want from me? I've finished it... Look, the next time you try to get me entangled in any competition, or anything like this again, I'll stop you before you finish the sentence...

Kira
I'll remind you of all this when you win and we're on safari, riding camels whilst sipping champagne...

(They laugh)

Morowa
I wish I had the confidence in myself that you seem to have in me... It's like the competition judges have already told you: 'And the winner is... Moro...'

Kira
Look, I only back winners...

Morowa
Well how come you're not backing QC?

Kira
Oh, leave me alone... please... In fact you know what my problem is now? I have to brace myself for a meal with him... all because of this play... This is so childish...

Morowa
Look, when Kukua and Debbie were younger, they used to say adults are boring, and they were right... a bit of childishness now and again never hurt anybody... it's good for the soul... What's so childish about two adults going for a meal, anyway? And

actually, if I check the small print of our deal... you should've gone for the meal *before* I finished the play, not after... so don't force me to get technical and enforce the rules here...

Kira
Give me a chance... Is it even up two weeks ago that we 'signed' this miserable meal deal?

Morowa
Whatever... But let me warn you right now... if you try to be smart... i.e. make me submit this play and then you don't go for the meal... then you'll see my true colours...

Kira
I don't take well to threats...

Morowa
You call this a threat? Don't go for the meal, then you'll see...

(They laugh)

27 Wednesday 4 September

THAT 'SOFTLY, SOFTLY' APPROACH

Featuring Bev, who attends Morowa's church.

Kira
Holiday over... back to school... What's it like being back at work after weeks of idleness and unemployment?

(They laugh)

Morowa
To be honest, I was getting a bit bored, so it was good to be back... but I know the good feeling won't last... it never does... How can it? For one, the stabbings and things have already started again... And this is just week one...

Kira
I've just seen it on the news...

Morowa
Apparently the boy was running away... but a rival school gang or something caught up with him... he's fighting for his life now... So these ones who do all these stabbings and things... were they just waiting for school to re-open so they could resume, or what?

Kira
I don't think they really stopped during the holidays... I think it's just that there's too many incidents to report, so they just focus mainly on the extreme or special cases now... Maybe this one's made the news because it's the first stabbing of the

academic year... I dunno...

Morowa
You think so? Well, if it's the first, I hope to God it's the last...
honestly... we can't go on like this... So are you telling me this is
just normal... business as usual now? How did our children get
to this point, for God's sake? So a good fight is just not enough
any more... Blood must be spilt... someone must die?

Kira
So it seems... One know-it-all at work was saying it's the West
Indians versus the Africans... I asked her whether she could tell
the difference... because I don't think I can...

Morowa
(Hisses)
Well exactly...

Kira
Look, I know we're being a bit defensive, but we have to face it:
some of our children are a big problem... This gang business...
it's mainly black children who are in gangs... or am I wrong?

Morowa
No, that's a fact... And whether we like it or not, something
needs to be done... and fast... But the majority of our kids are *not*
in gangs... which seems to be the general impression...

Kira
Thanks to the press... The fact is: there's a hard core out there...
out of control... no doubt about that .. but they are in the
minority...

Morowa
But they're the ones we hear about all the time...they're the ones

who give the many, many law abiding, peaceful children and black people in general out there, a bad name...

Kira

If you go by the media: it's as if *all* black kids are roaming around with weapons of mass destruction from the moment they can walk and talk... Our children are always made out to look like the worst of the worst... it's not fair...

Morowa

Look, every society has its rules and regulations when it comes to raising children... official and unofficial... But if some of us had blindly followed the rules and stuff laid down over here when it came to our children, there'd probably be much more trouble going on in black communities than there is now... You see this system isn't set up for us or our children... and of course, we don't expect it to be... But many times, to avoid trouble... we've instinctively had to tweak, adapt, revise... in fact, sometimes totally deviate from the so-called guidelines and handle our kids *our way...*

Kira

And that doesn't mean we were just beating our children all day every day... or anything like that...

Morowa

Who had or has the energy to be doing that? Half of our time was spent on pushing our kids to do as well as they could at school, because not much was expected of them there... the other half was spent putting a good dose of the fear of God in them, so that they'd stay well clear of trouble...

Kira

Exactly... we didn't want any unnecessary contact or dealings with the police or authorities, or anything like that... And most of us didn't have that 'it takes a village to raise a child' back-up over here that we sort of grew up with... so essentially we were on our own as parents... working really hard to just break even whilst raising them... If I think back to those times when the kids were really young... only God knows how some of us made it... It wasn't easy... at all... And you know what... big kudos to those parents who took one look at things over here and decided to send their kids back home to school... even if just for a while...

Morowa
Oh yes... The education system back home isn't perfect... at all... but there are some aspects of it that seem to work for our children... somehow... For one, there's a discipline element if nothing else... and not just in school... In some cases you could clearly see that nothing short of disaster lay ahead for some children if they hadn't been taken out of this system... I *personally* advised a few parents to send their kids back if they could... and I'm actually yet to meet anyone who's regretted it...

Kira
Regret? As you say, if some hadn't been taken away, it wouldn't have been good for them or their families... for anybody... And you know what really annoys me? The so-called experts... the ones who confidently... in fact arrogantly, try to explain to us what the black issues are and how to deal with them... particularly when it come to our children... They won't listen to you as a black person, when you try to tell them what you actually *know* as opposed to what they *think* they know...

Morowa
Instead of *listening,* they'll be showing you some statistics and research and reports... theories and stuff that only make sense to *them*...

Kira

Sometimes you just want to tell them to clear off with their reports... they just don't get it...

Morowa

They can't... When I want to make the point to some people, I tell them about your Richie when he landed back home for the first time... He was just five, right? Imagine him, asking you, on African soil: 'Who brought all these black people here, Mum?'

(They laugh)

Kira

I'm laughing now, but at the time it hit me that he'd *never* seen so many black people together, in one place... He was looking round the airport... totally baffled... I'll never forget the look on his face...

Morowa

It was probably quite frightening for him actually... It was an innocent question from an innocent child... but a deep one... He'd always been part of a minority, bless him... so in his young head, he just couldn't process being part of a majority...

Kira

And I think we underestimate what constantly being part of a minority can actually mean for our children...

Morowa

Even for us as adults ... I think we develop a minority complex... and I don't think that can be avoided... it sort of comes with the territory... Of course we can't send *all* our kids back home to school... but what I say is, where possible... funds allowing and all that... take the kids home on holiday as often as you can... make it a priority... it gives them that sense of belonging and identity... You may see the effects as just temporary, but each time you take them home, it builds up a bit more... and a bit more... and it's an investment that money just cannot buy... no-one can ever take that away from them... If they decide to come back... a good many of them don't, they stay home... but if they do, it helps them to face and handle things better over here... the racism and all the challenges which they just can't avoid at virtually every level... school, work, relationships, media...

Kira
As for the media... it's like we're some kind of sport for them: they downplay anything positive and amplify the negatives about us... all the time... Why?

Morowa
Why not? It's not down to *them* to change the narrative, as they call it... The media actually benefit from our problems... it's like we're a never-ending source of juicy headlines for them... and juicy headlines and unsavoury stories equal big bucks for them... So why would *they* want to change things? *We're* the ones losing out in all this... so it's down to *us* to change whatever needs changing... make people see the positives about us... nobody else is going to do it for us... But black people, we don't seem to understand that you know... It's like we're waiting for others to come and help us out and promote us, and all that...

Kira
True... Every other group of people... when they're unhappy with things, persecuted or whatever... they come together and they form pressure groups that just won't stop until people take notice and something's done... they make sure change happens... But not us...

Morowa
If we do manage to make some noise on an issue, invariably it's

not as a solid, united front, because we're usually fragmented... disjointed... and of course that works against us all the time... So whatever noise we manage to make, dies down... quickly... and that's usually the end of the matter... We've got no stickability...

Kira

Then of course there's the money issue: because let's face it, our communities and groups never usually have any or enough... and what can you really do without money? But if and when we do manage to raise some funds, what happens? One or two people usually decide they're going to take it all for themselves... So naturally a quarrel breaks out... then of course the main focus is lost, because the argument now shifts to accountability... so nothing's achieved... And then we're back to square one... Ah...

Morowa

The thing is, unless and until we come together to *seriously* address *all* these things that are holding us back... and find strategies to tackle them... we're just wasting our time... We're not going to be taken seriously or respected by the media or anybody else for that matter... because it's like we're not taking *ourselves* seriously, so why should anybody else? We can cry and whinge and complain all we like, about all the nonsense we have to put up with, day in day out... racism, poor jobs, bad press and this and that... but things are just going to ride on and continue as they always have... The media is not our friend, so it's not going to help our cause or help us out in any way... *we have to help ourselves*... simple as that...

Kira

And if you think about it, even among ourselves as black people, do we spread good news about each other? Do we really celebrate each other the way we should? So why should the press, media or anyone else? It's like good news about each other seems to more or less upset us...

Morowa
Strange but true... Say for instance a child does very well... let's say gets a double first class in quantum molecular physics or some serious stuff like that... Will our people spread that news around? No way... If they do, ten chances to one, it'll be accompanied by something to take the shine off the whole thing... Before you know it, they'll say the child probably spied in the exam... or the mother slept with the lecturer... they must say something to make you stop clapping for that child...

Kira
'The mother slept with the lecturer', you know...

(They laugh)

Morowa
Oh yes... If there's something not quite right... something bad or sad about you... no wildfire can match the speed with which our people will spread it... I'm sure it's the same with your people... I often wonder at how quickly the news of someone's passing flashes round in my community... Virtually within minutes of the person's passing, you start getting messages from all over the world alerting you... I really wonder how they do it... But good news doesn't move that fast.... if it in fact moves at all...

Kira
True...

Morowa
Look, some time ago I was somewhere in South London, minding my own business, next thing I see one of my church people... She goes: 'Sister Morrow'... you know these West Indians, that's how they call me... 'Sister Morrow, do you

know Bev's daughter?' She described her and all... I know Bev, of course... very nice Jamaican lady... but I didn't know her daughter, and I said so... But that wasn't going to be a barrier... whether I liked it or not, I was going to hear the story...

(They laugh)

Morowa
In a nutshell, she said this Bev's daughter was heavily pregnant for a married man... this was her third baby father... but she was still living with the second baby father, or some story like that... So, tell me honestly... what kind of image do you immediately get about the girl in question?

Kira
Well... not a very bright one, that's for sure...

Morowa
Look, when I eventually got to see this daughter... I thought this *cannot* be the girl they were telling me about... no way... Sister Bev must have another daughter... somewhere... Cut a long story short... this *was* the daughter in question... in fact she doesn't have another daughter... This girl... or woman should I say... is a consultant software analyst or something like that... she's got her own business, employing how many people... highly sought after... internationally...

Kira
The one with the three baby fathers?

Morowa
Yes... She looked so good, so well groomed... she spoke so well... oozing class and confidence... I mean the whole package...

Kira
Really?

Morowa
Fair enough, I think she's had her issues with a few men... things
happen... they just do... and to the best of us... But whatever may
or may not have happened to this girl, she's a success story... no
two ways about that...

Kira
Oh, our people... they usually get just half of the story... and
most of the time, even that half isn't quite right...

Morowa
Look, accuracy isn't what our people are after, because usually
the accurate story isn't juicy enough to spread and cause some
mischief with... As long as there's potential for some scandal...
the incorrect half will do just fine for spreading purposes...

(They laugh)

Morowa
Quickly... turn to Channel 7... they're showing the mother of the
boy they stabbed... Look at her... This is so sad... I think the
general attitude seems to be: it's black on black... just leave them
to kill each other... good riddance...

Kira
Talking about the media: look at the reporter's smug face...
they're always happy to cover anything that goes wrong for us...

Morowa
The reporters are a bit better... after all, they're just reporting...
What I can't stand are the ones they ask to comment on issues...
be it politics, health or whatever... the so-called experts... the
way they talk and analyse things... I ask myself, 'Come oh... am
I just thick? Is it just *me* who doesn't get what they're saying?
They'll say something like: *'Exponentially, there's a polarised*

pseudo quasi effect, that's homogenous to a parochial genre'...
For God's sake...

(They laugh)

Kira
I thought it was just me... When they start, I think to myself:
What are they actually saying? You see everybody nodding and
clapping... so I think to myself, 'So you mean everybody gets
this... they actually understand what they just said? Everybody
gets it... apart from *me*?

Morowa
Look, I teach English, but hey... they lose me all the time...
Anyway, I console myself... after all English isn't my first
language... I may be able to handle the language to a certain
extent, but I don't think in English... in fact I can't...

(They laugh)

Kira
Some of these media people really make me sick...

Morowa
But some of these our black kids make me even sicker... If you
ask me, some of them just need a couple of solid slaps to steady
them up sometimes...

Kira
But you know where 'just a slap' has landed some parents,
particularly some dads in this country... The whole system has
come crashing right down on them... People have even found
themselves behind bars for trying to discipline their kids...

Morowa
I know... And, as we say, it's not about just wanting to slap or

beat children up anyhow...that's not it at all... We all know there are some very creative punishments that can sting much worse than a beating... but it's like the parents' hands are completely tied because of these plenty children's rights that have just got more and more ridiculous over the years...

Kira
Oh yes... So now we've ended up with more and more parents... even some grown men, in tears, because their children are out of control and it's like there's not much they can do about things... And it's not just the oyibo men... you know they cry anyhow anyway... but now our own brothers have joined in as well...

Morowa
No surprises there... you know *we* must find a way to follow and copy everything everybody else does... and the more ridiculous the better...
(Hisses)

Kira
Of course... One of my colleagues... tough looking guy... lifts weights... that type... came into work some time ago... All of a sudden, he breaks down crying... sobbing seriously... Next thing he's explaining to us that his children were ganging up on him, and his wife was supporting them... Ask me how old these kids are...

Morowa
How old?

Kira
Six and eight...

Morowa
Not even teenagers? No... he probably has some mental issues...

Kira

He just looked so pathetic... Well, they say the men should get in touch with their feminine side, and this and that... so this is where we've ended up... the men are crying all over the place... Even the children don't cry any more...

Morowa

Why should they bother, when their dads are crying on their behalf instead?

(They laugh)

Morowa

But you actually feel sorry for some parents... some of them really try their best... If you know the amount of them who come to school... some even go directly to the police to report that their kids have weapons, drugs or whatever... begging for some kind of help... But what tends to happen after that? Nothing much... if anything...

Kira

Look, *I* feel like crying myself when sometimes it boils down to: not much can be done as such, often because the child is supposedly under age... they start pussyfooting around them... They make it sound as if that's the civilised, cultured way to deal with children... but it's not, it's just stupid... How can it make any sense whatsoever, to wait for a 10 or 12-year-old with a knife, to turn 16 or 18 before anything can seriously be done to tackle that child? All they do is give them a good few more years to become more hardened and seasoned... or better still, until they actually kill someone...

Morowa

Then of course, when they do something as drastic as that, they start with their miserable enquiries, supposedly to find out what went wrong... At that point you just want to scream: 'What are you really looking for now, when the questions and answers have been staring at *everybody* in the face, *for years*... way before the crime was even committed?'

Kira

The fact that more and more of them keep getting weapons shows that as far as they're concerned, there's nothing to fear... I'm just fed up...

Morowa

In days gone by, if I saw young black boys in groups, I had no fear of them whatsoever... Fair enough, some of them looked a bit rough, but they were quite harmless... They would greet you, carry your shopping, crack a cheeky joke... real characters, some of them...

Kira

But as you say, that was then...

Morowa

Now, thanks to way the system has evolved... *deteriorated* if you ask me... when I see some of them, I panic a bit, because some of them have no boundaries... they have no fear of authority, or anything, or anybody for that matter... They can take anybody on anywhere... fight the police bone to bone, if it comes to it...

Kira

What are you talking about? Some of them even fight their *parents* bone to bone, never mind the police... the police are small fry for them... And as for some of the girls... they are even rougher than some of the boys...

Morowa

Are you telling me?

Kira

As we say, not all of our kids are out of control criminals... most of them aren't, thank God... But some of these kids seem to be so bitter and angry... and they don't know how to control or manage the anger, or whatever it is they have... too young to understand or analyse things... the serious consequences of some of their actions and behaviour...

Morowa

I think some of them understand, at least a bit... but some of them are from such deprived, dysfunctional homes... poverty, poor parenting and all sorts... Poor things... some of them, when they're from those kind of backgrounds, it's very hard to get through to them... they've already been so let down by everybody and everything... you're just another adult nuisance to them... and they really don't care what you have to say...

Kira

But then again, some of these kids are just bad... no excuse...

Morowa

Oh, that's a fact... But anyway, I try to talk to and guide *all* children... good, bad, black, white, whatever... But I do impress on the black ones that they have to be *extra* careful... they have to stop and think properly... probably a little bit more than others, before they do anything... because things are seldom weighted in their favour...

Kira

Oh yes... if they slip up, they don't usually get the benefit of the doubt, or the sympathy vote... When you try to explain to some of them that some consequences and punishments are long term... even permanent... a lot of the time, all you get from them is indifference and defiance... Their attitude is: if they end up in prison, or even dead, so be it... What's the big deal?

Morowa
Look, like charity, raising and disciplining children should begin
at home... but I see first-hand how difficult it can be sometimes
for some parents in this system...

Kira
I always tell people, *I* wasn't going to leave raising and
disciplining my children just down to school or this society...
No way... I had my own in-house rules which, by and large, had
to be obeyed... *You* know very well that I more or less fought
Ralston and Richie... physically, when I had to... and I have no
regrets whatsoever... And I don't care what the law says... if a
few skirmishes and a few torn shirts and stuff behind closed
doors helped to keep my sons out of prison... or the cemetery for
that matter... I'd do it again... and without hesitation...

Morowa
But you know what I went through with the girls as well... We
all descended into hell a good few times... before we all re-
surfaced again... At the time they didn't find it funny... neither
did I... As for Sonny... you could see he just wanted to run away
and leave us when some of the arguments and things took off...

Kira
Poor man... must've been the stuff of nightmares... stuck in the
middle of three arguing women...

(They laugh)

Morowa
But looking back, we all have a good laugh at some of those
crazy moments now, because they can actually see and
appreciate what we were trying to do then... In this society,
being black is a minus to start with... the last thing you need to
add to that, is a criminal record... or anything like that...

Kira
Something that could handicap and dog you for ever... To be honest, I didn't have too many issues with Richie really... but that Ralston... he was something else... Remember that time you had to stop me from calling the police... when he didn't come home until about 4 o'clock in the morning?

Morowa
How can I forget?

Kira
That day they'd rumoured that there was going to be some demonstration, or riot or something... so I told him categorically not to go out... But of course, as usual, he defied me... By the time I got back from work, he was gone... Then I couldn't get him on his mobile... There's no scenario that didn't come to mind... I thought maybe he was in police clutches...

Morowa
Hmmm... horror of horrors, because we know absolutely *anything* can happen to our children if the police lay their hands on them... *anything*... Just the mere thought is giving me goosebumps... honestly...

Kira
Then I thought maybe he was lying somewhere... stabbed or even killed... I was in bits... Look, when he eventually decided to turn up...

Morowa
I was actually on the phone with you when you screamed: 'Moro, he's back!" And I know the rest was history...

(They laugh)

Kira
I was so mad, I couldn't control myself... I just jumped on him...

rugby tackle style... Richie was trying to pull me off... Anyway,
next thing Ralston starts shouting: 'You're gonna kill me...
Richie call the police... you'll go to prison for this, Mum... I'm
not worth it'... When he said that, I just burst out laughing...

(They laugh)

Morowa
Look, our children are lovely... whether they're born at home or
abroad or wherever... but I don't know whether it's the melanin
or what... but a lot of them have got some kind of energy... some
kind of fire that sometimes needs to be sort of harnessed... So if
you're dealing with a bit of fire, sometimes that 'softly, softly'
approach doesn't work too well with a lot of them...

Kira
That's just a fact of life... But let's face it... even in the real
world, how far does 'softly, softly' get you? For minor things,
probably yes; but not when serious things are at stake... Just
'talking' doesn't really work sometimes... When it comes to
some issues and you *talk*... then you're seen as just that... a
talker... You're seen as someone who doesn't actually *do*
anything... you're no threat, so you don't necessarily have to be
listened to or taken seriously... The Western world.... did they
acquire their power, prestige and wealth from their slaves and
colonies by being all 'softly, softly'? I don't think so...

Morowa
Don't mind them... Forget those far off days... even right now,
in modern times... they may start off with 'dialogue' and
'negotiation'... and all the high grammar they can come up
with... but the moment they realise that that's not really working
for them... they're not really getting their way, or they meet
serious resistance... the gloves come off, and they're ready to
fight and kill to get what they want... no ifs, no buts... If they

decide that a good fight or some blood spilling will probably get
them what they want, then so be it... That's how they are... that's
how they've always been... and that's how they'll always be...

Kira
And after they've started the trouble as usual, and people want to
follow their example and fight them back, then they have the
cheek to start preaching 'non-violence': *'You don't achieve
anything or get anywhere with violence; it's never the answer'*...

Morowa
Yeah right... And of course they have fancy words for when *they*
attack or fight people... it's just a 'bit of a clash' or 'dispute'...
but when *we* fight, then it's a 'brutal massacre', a 'slaughter'...
When they're caught out, they're just 'misguided' or they
'misjudged' the situation... but with us, it's we're 'criminal' and
'corrupt'... God punish them all... honestly...
(Hisses)

Kira
Well... there's no point getting upset... But the fact is this: until
we wake up and wise up as black people, we will continue to
have no say... others will continue to dictate the pace... set the
rules and standards for us and for everything... they'll decide
what's what... what's a conflict and what's a massacre... and so
on and so forth... It's as simple as that...

28 Monday 16 September

THEY HAVE PLENTY TO ANSWER FOR

Featuring Kira's teacher, Mr Yeboah, and Dorle Cia, a talk show personality.

Kira

That video you sent to me... those poor children eating from the rubbish heaps... oh... What is all that?

Morowa

Oh Africa... When I saw it, I couldn't eat... my appetite vanished completely... Even Sonny was taken aback... he usually says I get worked up easily about nothing, but this really shook him...

Kira

So who's to blame now? The white man as usual, I guess... *(Sighs)*

Morowa

Oh, of course... blame the white man, whilst some of our own leaders are consulting each other... exchanging notes on different strategies and ways to wreck Africa...

Kira

You're right you know... most of them must be consulting each other, because their methods are just too similar for it to be just coincidence... As if they graduated from the same colleges of corruption and confusion...

Morowa

As long as they can line their pockets, they just don't care who

suffers... Kids eating from rubbish dumps... water off a duck's
back to them... doesn't bother them one little bit...

Kira
How can they claim to be in charge... governing... and allow
some of our children to live like those ones in that video? Some
animals are better off... How do they sleep at night?

Morowa
I can assure you, they sleep better than you and I ever could...
And why do even we insist on calling them 'leaders'? Very few
really qualify for that title in Africa... Where are most of them
leading us to? If those kids were actually eating each other in
desperation, I don't think it would shake most of them...

Kira
And in Africa we claim to have some of the brightest minds...

Morowa
Oh yes... you know our people go out of their way to make
everybody know they've had this 'superior' education, with
PhDs and XYZs, from some of the best institutions in the
world... how they've mixed and mingled with all the people who
matter, and this and that...

Kira
But how has all that benefitted us?

Morowa
Only God knows... we've got plenty, plenty graduates and
learned people from everywhere, in every area and discipline you
can think of... But it's like you put them in charge and sooner or
later there's bound to be a story... from accountability issues... to
substandard work... everything that can possibly go wrong,
seems to on our watch... So eventually, to salvage the project,

repair the damage or whatever... the foreigner... invariably the oyibo, has to come to our rescue and take charge of things... That's just how it is...

Kira

It's like we just can't cope... we seem to let ourselves down all the time... Then we start complaining all over the place that's it's the white man's fault... they did this and that to us... Fair enough, we know they're not blameless... even they themselves know they're not... they know they have plenty to answer for... But what have they done to us that *we* haven't done a thousand times more to *ourselves*? As someone was saying the other day... to start with, no other race sold their people out to slavery like Africans... so we have to face up to some of these things...

Morowa

Oh come on now, Kira... we were simple folk... naïve... ignorant even... For God's sake, the majority of our people are still that way today, not to talk of hundreds of years ago... The fact is, we were going about our own business in Africa... whether we were dancing with giraffes in huts or trees, or whatever... that was our way and our business... we weren't bothering anybody... we were in our own world, doing our own thing... *They* went and met us out there...

Kira

That is not in dispute...

Morowa

They called it the 'Dark Continent'... but they didn't stop there... they decided that we were primitive... by their own standards, mind you... next thing we're in chains and on boats... Then they colonised us so that they could continue to control us and our resources, more or less for ever, if possible... It's been an ongoing story of abuse... they've never really left us alone...

Kira

And they're not going to... Why would they, when we've got so much that they need?

Morowa

And the thing is, they're actually more corrupt than we are...

Kira

But they taught us... And we've taken things to another level... But ours is not a case of the apprentice overtaking the master... Oh no... with us, it's like we didn't learn properly... didn't get the formula quite right... as usual... You see the oyibo people, *they* massage things... they do their own corruption with finesse and style... and they're clever enough to make sure most of their people have a reasonable standard of living, so no-one really focuses too much on the dodgy things their leaders get up to all the time... But with *our* own leaders... they just go completely berserk... just grab, grab, grab, to excess... and for their own *personal* benefit... So you just can't help but focus on their own corruption, because it's so damn glaring when you look at their lifestyles compared to the pitiful condition of their people...

Kira

When some of our people go to these high powered meetings, usually with *so* much at stake, I don't think they pay any attention to the small print...

Morowa

They don't pay any attention to *anything* as such, apart from how much they're going to get in kickbacks... Instead of taking qualified people along who can look properly at the paperwork and the finer details of the negotiations and stuff, they go with clueless party supporters... Everybody else goes to those meetings armed with the right people, desperate to get the best deals for their countries... they're focused on what they're there for... they have their aims and their goals and they ruthlessly try to achieve them for their countries... but not us...

Kira
Those meetings and things bore our people... they just can't wait to get out of them... As soon as they get what they're *really* there for... i.e. as soon as they settle on an amount to credit their private bank accounts with... in the hurry to leave, they end up signing away all our resources and heritage for peanuts...

Morowa
The things is, we have a few African leaders who are really trying hard for their countries... everybody can see that... But what I can't understand is: Why does it seem as if most of the other leaders don't seem too keen on following those good examples?

Kira
We just don't know how to play the game... we just don't get it...

Morowa
But you know something, I know we all complain about Africa, and everything's that's wrong, and how things should be better and all that... but I don't care what anybody says: a lot of things are just not our fault... And I get well irritated with some people, who just don't seem to understand that a lot of the issues we're facing today... if not most of them... are largely down to what's happened to us in the past... And leading on from that, you have the ones who say that slavery and all that happened a *long, long* time ago, so we should be well over things by now... It doesn't work like that... They didn't just take us away; they maltreated us... good and proper... they dented our spirit... Who's to say how long it should take to recover from such trauma that went on... not just for a couple of years or so, but for hundreds and hundreds of years... from one generation to the next... and to the

next`? They shook and tore up the whole continent... forced
alien systems and stuff down our throats... they completely
confused and destabilised us... we've never really recovered...
to this day we just haven't been able to pull ourselves together...
Even some of us who think that in spite of everything that's
happened we're okay and we've arrived... we're just fooling
ourselves somewhat... We're *all* scarred in one way or the
other... They should've just left us where God put us... we
would've evolved and developed in our own unique way... Now
it's like we can't find our way... we're just lost and on so many
levels...

Kira
But the sad fact is, they did what they did, and it is what it is...
And no matter how upset we get, we can't change that... We're
never going to be able to go back to what we were, with the
opportunity to just be and evolve as you say, in our own way...
And whether we like it or not, oyibos are still in charge and still
running the show... The question is: going forward, are we black
people prepared to stay like this: at the bottom of every pile,
disrespected, abused, taken advantage of and all that... *for ever?*
And if not, what are we going to do to change things?

Morowa
Hmmm... Those are indeed the questions...

Kira
The thing is, no matter how bad a situation is, if you look hard
enough, you'll see something in it that you can use to your
benefit or advantage... they say stars shine brightest in the dark...
We should be drawing sense, savvy and energy from our past
experiences and history... and using that to demand and force
things to work in our favour... or at least work a little better for
us than they do now... Look, only a handful of oyibo explorers
went around and conquered the world to benefit their people...

they weren't that many at all... Surely by now, we should also have more than enough educated, enlightened and determined Africans to take charge of Africa's destiny like those explorers... After all Africa is not the only place they colonised; but everyone else seems to have wriggled free... at least to a degree...

Morowa
How can we wriggle free when it's our own leaders, who are supposed to look out for us, who are keeping us tied up in knots... more or less in bondage... they've made poverty, illiteracy, misery, hardship... in fact our leaders have made everything wrong, the norm for our people...

Kira
The problem is, most of our leaders don't see themselves as *servants*... they see themselves as *masters*... overlords in every sense of the word... who have a right to keep their people down whilst they live large and enrich themselves...

Morowa
The thing is, our people are confused... dangerously so... and our leaders are the products of that confusion... Because if our people weren't confused, would they be dancing and cheering for these leaders... all over Africa... time after time... leaders who, when they or their family members, or girlfriends, or whatever, have just a toothache, they're on the first flight out to get state of the art treatment abroad... but these same leaders can't ensure that ordinary people have at least just painkillers when they fall ill...

Kira
Apart from being confused, they're ignorant as well...

Morowa
Well there you have it: confusion and ignorance... How far can you go with that combination? Tell me...

Kira

And even when you try to make some of our suffering people see some sense, they can easily turn on you... They'll tell you to leave the politicians and 'big men' alone... that you're just jealous of them and their money and lifestyle...

Morowa

All just because, at election time these politicians probably give these poor people a bag of rice or some cheap fabric... alongside the empty promises, of course... Then after they've got the votes, they're off... they abandon them... leave them to languish... for years... Sometimes they don't see these politicians... *at all*... until the next election... Then the cycle starts all over again... some rice... cheap fabric... empty promises... abandonment...

Kira

And it's not as if we're a weak race... we have so much to be able to fight and claw back with, and take some control of things... but instead of coming together and clawing at our enemies, we claw at each other... fight each other to a standstill... Just pure self-destruction...

Morowa

It's not just 'self'... we're just destructive all round... when it comes to ruining and wrecking things, you can't beat us... Look at your education system in Sierra Leone... you were telling me that it hasn't recovered since that horrible war you people had...

Kira

No... it hasn't... it's a shambles...

Morowa

As a teacher, I think that's such a big shame... It's like your people were the frontrunners in education in West Africa at one time... Pa Magwa, my granny's brother, used to talk about your country all the time... he was such a big fan... He made Sierra Leone sound like it was abroad... oyibo-land... even the way he pronounced it, made it sound like some exotic island... He said that anybody who was anybody in West Africa in those days, had some Sierra Leone connection... either they went to school or university there, or got married to your people... According to him, your place was 'the Athens of West Africa'...

Kira
What do you mean, 'according to him'? It's according to the well documented, historical facts...

(They laugh)

Kira
He was absolutely right though... We had some of the oldest and best of everything... the best institutions... schools, colleges, hospitals and stuff... and some even claim not just in West Africa, but in the whole continent of Africa...

Morowa
He told us you even had the oldest prisons and all...

Kira
You see black man... you must drag me and my glorious history down... Which prisons? I don't know about any oldest prisons...

(They laugh)

Morowa
Seriously, he would've just loved to meet you, honestly...

Kira
I keep telling you all the time, when you're with me, you're in the presence of greatness, but you don't seem to get it... at all...

Morowa

I do Your Majesty... I do...

(They laugh)

Morowa

You guys were a real force to reckon with at one time... It must've been a case of big things coming in small packages... because you're just a tiny little place, but you seemed to be in charge... right at the forefront of everything in those days...

Kira

Oh we were... but things fell apart... big time... When I think of my country sometimes, I feel really sick... the height we've dropped from... Anyway, you Ghanaians, we saw you guys as quite special too, you know... very calm and cultured... Our chemistry teacher, Mr Yeboah... he said he was from Cape Coast... You know kids... we used to laugh at the way he pronounced some words... When he wanted us to do our work he would say: 'Ladies, you must do your *wek* now'...

(They laugh)

Kira

He was nice... very easy on the eye, as they say... all the women teachers and girls were falling for him...

Morowa

You know, the education and social setups we enjoyed back in Africa in those days... we just took them all for granted...

Kira

As youngsters do... Our education was first class... could've rivalled the best in the world...

Morowa

Easily... But we had no idea how well seasoned and grounded

we were... until we came abroad and were put to the test... big time... Without realising it, we'd been equipped to face and overcome some very serious odds and challenges in these foreign lands... and we didn't just face them, we survived them...

Kira
I think we've done a bit more than just survive...

Morowa
You're right... And you know what? I'm going to drink to that...

Kira
Any excuse for a quick swig...

(They laugh)

Kira
Oh no... You'll never guess what they're showing on the telly now... Those begging adverts... you know the ones with the little children in Africa, drinking water that even a dog would say 'no thank you very much' to... Look, after that video with the children eating rubbish, now this... Look, I've had enough for one day of black kids and their poverty... we get the message...

Morowa
As for those miserable adverts... they've been showing those since we came to this country... almost unchanged... same format, same everything...

Kira
True... Surely they could find some creative people to come up with nicer images to put their points across... What real purpose do those adverts serve anyway? Apart from making everybody... particularly kids... see Africa as this most hopeless place...

Morowa
Well, the fact is... if and when we actually *do* stop begging all

over the place and get our act together in Africa, there'll be no place... in fact, no need for these humiliating adverts and things... Let's face it: who really likes beggars? When you see them, you give them what you can spare... but you don't really *like* them... And if you think about it, Africans being seen as wretched beggars on the world stage, just helps to fuel racism and resentment towards us... it really does... And I do worry about the effect that some of these images must have on young minds... In fact they're not good for *anybody*... old or young...

Kira
Look at the time I took the boys home for the first time... imagine the two of them telling me they didn't want to go to Africa... telling me to leave them with their Aunty Nish and to go on my own, because they didn't want to see all the children over there in rags, with flies in their eyes and noses, and all that... obviously based on what they'd seen on telly...

Morowa
But at least you were able to take them home and show them that things may not be perfect over there... in fact far from it... And even though they were quite young, at least they could see for themselves that people don't live in caves, drinking black water, roaming around in rags all day long...

Kira
But I told you the time we went on my friend's building site... you know the raggedy clothes the men carrying the cement and stuff usually wear back home... looking really rough and threadbare... The boys saw some of them... next thing they're shouting out: 'Mum look, The Flintstones..."

(They laugh)

Morowa
Look, beggars, poverty, all these things... if you didn't know

better, you'd think it's a strictly third world, African thing...

Kira
Of course we know that's not the case... but let's face it, Moro...
Africa's situation is a bit unique...

Morowa
I know, I know... it just doesn't add up... at all... One of our
friends says: 'Two and two makes four everywhere else in the
world... apart from in Africa... There, two and two decides for
itself what it wants to make...

(They laugh)

Kira
We've been blessed with absolutely *everything* on that
continent... from resources, to manpower, to weather... we
couldn't really ask for more... But nothing seems quite right...
Why? Sometimes, I just don't like talking about Africa, racism
and all these things... I get so upset...

Morowa
As for racism: I can honestly say, I only really became aware of
it when I came to this country...

Kira
It was an experience for a lot of us from back home... and a
pretty bad one to be honest... to come over here and be called
nasty names and funny stuff like that... To actually be treated
differently... in fact treated *badly... cruelly...* just because of our
colour... I don't think some of us have ever quite gotten over
the shock...

Morowa
We never will... we've just learnt how to live with it all... The
thing is, we grew up and went to school with people from all

sorts of backgrounds... rich, poor... and all sorts of races... white, Lebanese, Germans, Indians... but race was *never* an issue...

Kira
The thing is, Africans like strangers... we respect them... obviously a bit too much for our own good a lot of the time...

Morowa
But how do you think slavery didn't just happen, but flourished as well? All down to our almost childlike admiration and trust of strangers... and us not putting much premium on ourselves and on our own ways and things...

Kira
We never took advantage just because we were in the majority...

Morowa
We never do... black people... we're not really wired that way... When we're in the majority, we never seem to appreciate or see the advantage of that... If we did, a whole lot of things would just never have happened to us as a race... We idolize, almost to the point of worshipping, almost any and everything foreign... That's why in the past, just one or two tumbled down oyibos... dropouts... ex-convicts... they would send them to go and control *millions* of Africans... and they did... with ease...

Kira
Of course it was easy, because for one, they could rely on the unflinching loyalty and help of our own black people when it came to keeping their fellow blacks under control...

Morowa
Instead of ganging up on the slave and colonial masters, it's like we began to actually *enjoy* being kept down... It's mind boggling... We tend to treat everybody with such deference; we are the most hospitable of people... but just not to each other a lot

of the time... And it's strange, because it's like we somehow disconnect from each other... and particularly when it really matters... when we need each other the most...

Kira

Exactly... Yes, the white man tricked us into slavery... they took advantage of us... they did us a lot of wrong... we know all this... But it's like being in an abusive marriage or relationship... at some point you just *have* to stand up and say 'enough is enough'... and find the strength... from somewhere... wherever... to fight back and get out of that situation... if not for yourself, then for your children... and you have to fight in such a way that you can't be ignored... Because otherwise, is Africa never, ever going to get out of this crazy situation we seem to be in? Or are we always going to end up the victims... the losers in *every* equation? Or how long is it going to take for things to change for us? How long?

Morowa

How long is a piece of string?

Kira

OK... they say Africa has the largest youth population, right? If that's true, then surely that should count for something... The youth... I think they probably hold the answers for Africa...

Morowa

Past generations have tried... but the results aren't too good... at all... If I think about it all, I just feel like crying...

Kira

If you start crying for Africa, you won't stop oh... But honestly, I think if the youth of Africa can use that strength that our forefathers took for granted... that strength that everybody else, apart from us, seems to have recognised and exploited... If they could take it and have the courage to stand up and say to the rest of the world, particularly to our exploiters: *'As for our fathers, grandfathers, forefathers... all combined... we really don't care what they signed or said in the past... We, the youth, who represent the present and future of Africa... we're not accepting the terms and conditions that they agreed to any more...'*

Morowa

In theory, what could be more brilliant than that? But it's one thing to insist on being in charge of our destiny and all that... but what'll be the point if we can't run things properly by ourselves, standing on our own two feet... unaided? We have to step up our game as Africans... big time... There's a whole lot of things we need to look into... so many things need addressing... For starters, we need to educate our people so they can understand the electoral process a bit better than they do now... the importance and benefits of electing the right leaders... And maybe that'll help us to stop settling for mediocrity all the time... because all we seem to do is 'manage this' and 'make do with that'... All the wrong people are hailed and respected in our communities... from these small village and church associations right up to government... It's like we just haven't got standards... *anything* and *anybody* will do...

Kira

As you say: confusion and ignorance... What else could it be? We need a complete and total overhaul of things... The authentic African is tough, hardworking, resourceful, resilient... but increasingly it's like they've grown so lazy and helpless, and just want to rely on handouts... from God, pastors, family, government... from everybody... anybody... depending on others has become a way of life for a lot of our people now... Even the money you send for them to manage, sometimes they forget that it's a gift... they begin to feel entitled, as if you owe them... As you say, we have to develop systems and a culture of helping,

managing and depending on *ourselves*... and on every level for
that matter...

Morowa
But that's not going to be an easy task... at all... And let's be
honest: it's not just the people back home that need to change...
even those of us abroad who've been exposed to a few things,
and who ought to know a bit better when it comes to certain
things... we contribute to the problems going on... When we go
home, flashing money... doing all sorts of things we know we
won't get away with over here... jump queues, don't want to pay
the going rate for things... give bribes... all that kind of stuff...

Kira
The oyibo people do all those things too oh...

Morowa
Are you serious? So you want to actually compare them and us?

Kira
No... not really...

(They laugh)

Kira
But look, I'm not trying to make excuses... but back home they
can make some things that should be simple and straightforward,
so awkward and difficult... almost impossible sometimes... They
deliberately frustrate you, almost to the point of madness...
particularly when they know you're from abroad ... and then it all
finally boils down to: the choice is yours... it's either you bribe
or you suffer... take your pick... they more or less back you into a
corner... I can't lie to you... I've succumbed a few times...

Morowa
Look, we all have at one time, or in one way or the other... but,
as you say, it's no excuse... But the thing is, if we're really

serious about wanting to change things for the better, we have to be honest and humble enough to see whether we can adopt and adapt some... not all... but some of the things and ways that other societies benefit from... give them an African flavour and twist, if we must... and see how we can make them work for us... alongside, of course, the things that already *do* work for us...

Kira
Then you know what you'll hear next? They'll say you've forgotten yourself... you think you're white and want to turn Africa to oyibo-land... And of course, this will be from critics who won't have any practical answers to any problems, because all they do is criticize....

Morowa
You just have to ignore those sorts... Look, we have to face it: are *our* ways, *our* systems and all that... as they stand now... are they working for us? Maybe a few are, but certainly not enough... some things need *serious* tweaking... And let me be perfectly honest with you, Kira... I know we're saying we have to help ourselves and this and that... but when I really sit and seriously think about the sheer scale of what needs to be done, my fear is: are we really up to it? It's not a small job oh... Do we Africans, at home and abroad or wherever... do we really have what it takes to sort Africa out?

Kira
Do we really have a choice? We just *have* to do it...

Morowa
I guess so, but I'm not hopeful... at all... We're in *so* much trouble... Dorle Cia was saying on her show the other day, that when it comes to Africa... it's like the horse has bolted...

Kira
As for that Dorle whatever... she should just keep herself quiet...

She thinks because she's got a talk show and she's married to a white man she knows everything about everything...

Morowa
Well, I'm black, married to a black man, but I can sort of see where she's coming from... Apart from what she said... it's like as a race, we're somehow not even programmed to make it...

Kira
Ah... don't say that, Moro...

Morowa
Of course I won't say this out loud... I'm not crazy... people will attack me... just like you've turned on Dorle Cia... They'll say I'm not wishing Africa well, I'm not patriotic and this and that... But that's just not true... I love Africa and I love being an African... I do and I always will... But it's like the challenges are *too* many... and even getting worse... Where do we start?

Kira
Anyone who says the answer to Africa is simple, is in denial... But we just have to try... do what we can to help sort things out... make our own contribution... however little... however humble... Our children and grandchildren should be able to see the evidence that at least we *tried*... Some time ago someone said to me, 'It must be really difficult being black'...

Morowa
Meaning what? Like being black is just the worst thing in the world... or what?

Kira
To be honest, I didn't sense any malice...

Morowa
Malice or no malice, you can't let a remark like that just go...

Kira
Oh no, of course I didn't... The fact is, there's nothing quite like 'black' *everything* ... and those who are black by birth, marriage, by association, or whatever, know that... Nothing really compares to black food... black company... black speech... black clothes... black humour... black swag... even black wahala... We're just special... if only we could get our act together...

Morowa
We need to get our act together for *ourselves*... because now it's like we're just entertaining the rest of the world... If we sort ourselves out, we wouldn't have to be explaining all this... it would be clear for *everyone* to see... and feel... and enjoy...

Kira
Look, all I know is this: there is no way Mama Africa and her children were made or meant to be permanently at the bottom everywhere, all the time... absolutely no way... Eventually, black people will do what they know they have to do, to assume their rightful place and make our Mama Africa proud... It *will* happen... it *has* to happen... it *must* happen...

Morowa
You know what you need to do for me? Give me some of your optimism and enthusiasm for Africa... you seem to have plenty...

Kira
Oh, I do... and I will never run out... And guess what? It's an eat as much as you like buffet, African style... so come fill your plate with as much optimism and enthusiasm as you can manage... call others to come and eat as well... and come back for more... as many times as you like...

Morowa
Ok... I will...

29 Wednesday 25 September

ON A DIFFERENT LEVEL

Morowa
I think death is doing a promotion oh... buy one, get one or two more free...

Kira
Oh... what's happened now? Who again?

Morowa
I'm really, really fed up... I told you my classmate died back home last week... Sonny's nephew, aged just 29, died in Oxford over the weekend... there's Mama Abena... now Sister Lola...

Kira
Oh no! I saw her just a couple of weeks ago at the supermarket... and she was telling me he wasn't a hundred percent, but he wasn't doing too badly... So what's happened to the bugger all of a sudden now?

Morowa
Hmmm... Kira... it's not the husband oh... Sister Lola *herself*...

Kira
What? What are you saying?

Morowa
I'm saying Sister Lola died... Sister Lola is dead...

Kira
Oh my God! Oh no! No!

Morowa
Can you just imagine?
(Cries)

Kira
Calm down, Moro... But what is this now, eh?

Morowa
You know even though I've left Joel's church, we've continued to pray together... I spoke to her just last Friday...

Kira
Oh... and she was looking so much better when I saw her... compared to that time when she came round to my place a few months ago... What happened?

Morowa
Her son said she collapsed at work yesterday... They rushed her to hospital, but she didn't make it... Sister Lola didn't make it...

Kira
Was she sick?

Morowa
Not that I know of... But the thing is, there's no way anyone could live with that her husband and not develop something... something fatal for that matter... Whatever may have been happening with her health, or in her life, that beast couldn't have helped matters... But you know what... *now* he'll see what life is really all about... because if he thinks anybody's going to have time for him like Lola did, he'd better think again... and think damn hard... He's going to suffer, I'm telling you... and he will well deserve it... As my granny would say: he will chew water and drink beef...

Kira
(Laughs)

Morowa

I'm serious... everything will soon be upside down for him... just wait and see... He really tormented that poor woman...

Kira

I wonder how he feels now... after all that meanness to her...

Morowa

That one... I don't think he'll be feeling anything oh... God, why didn't you take him instead and leave our Lola to live and get on with things? What is he living for anyway? He's pointless... like a snake... because what's a snake's function... apart from to cause grief? And that's all he does...

Kira

Poor Lola... I think she just turned fifty-four, right?

Morowa

That's all she was ... in July...

Kira

But she looked older... it's like she aged over the last couple of years...

Morowa

How wouldn't she age? She was unevenly yoked to this loser... he just dragged her down and behind... for years... Now look at what's happened... The son said his father was so distressed when they broke the news to him... apparently they had to sedate him... All one big act for sympathy, if you ask me... Bloody fool... he's probably worried that the post mortem may show that she was abused... *by him*... Poor Lola, she must've been exhausted... she's been the sole breadwinner for years now...

Kira

So you mean he wasn't working?

Morowa

He stopped... way before he even fell ill... Apparently he said he'd rather not work if it meant he had to pay child support... for the children he had with other women, if you please...

Kira

Well you see... this is why I'm a bit wary when it comes to QC... If you miscalculate with some men, this is how the story ends... in short, in a casket...

Morowa

This is not the first time you've sort of compared QC to Lola's husband... There's no way in creation that QC is in the same league as that ogre oh... not in any shape or form whatsoever... Did any of QC's girlfriends ever confront you? Did he ever lay a finger on you? Lola told me he only stopped beating her when he had the stroke... Apparently, he punched her in the eye one time, she ended up with a detached retina... she said she lost a couple of pregnancies in the early days... I suspect there was a whole catalogue of things... but it was only recently she started opening up to me... telling me some of these things... The thing is, I didn't want to ask too many questions too quickly, you know what I mean? At some point I was planning to ask her why she put up with all that... honestly... Now I guess we'll never know...

Kira

Most women in that position are just *so* beaten down... no self esteem... no nothing... they can't think straight...

Morowa

Well this is it... All I know is, he sapped the life and juice out of her... She said sometimes after a beating, or to avoid one in the first place, she would sleep in the car or in the garage... stuff like that... Can you imagine? And you want to compare him to QC... Please... I can't let you do that... And the thing is, Lola told me he started abusing her even *before* they got married...

Kira
Oh, the classic mistake... thinking that by some sort of magic, they'll suddenly change after marriage...

Morowa
Like that my cousin... His girlfriend... well, that's what she was at the time... she removed his mother's head-tie in a public place... stamped on it... and as if that wasn't enough, she made sure she scratched and pushed the woman's bald head when they were trying to bundle her away...

Kira
(Laughs)
I shouldn't laugh... But imagine the sight... But seriously, who does that?

Morowa
To the mother of the man you want to marry, for God's sake? But wouldn't any sober man have seen that as a clear red flag from the gods, to immediately halt... in fact *cancel* all plans? Not to talk of wedding plans... But what does the fool do? First of all, when we tried to make him see some sense... that this girl was not wife material... even the girl's family warned him... he backed her all the way, and disrespected so many of us in the family in the process... In fact he actually told *me* to my face to 'just get out' and to mind my own business... threatened me with police and all... Then, of course, he went ahead and married her...

Kira
He actually married her after all that?

Morowa
But you know who I'm talking about now... that my cousin with the wife with the gap teeth...

Kira
Oh... him?

Morowa
Look, those two... I think the road to hell is smoother and
sweeter than what they are on now... When he calls me to
complain about her, I just hold the phone and listen... I don't say
a word... I really don't know what he even wants me to say, or do
anyway... I just say to myself: 'This is just the beginning'... A
couple of years ago, he came back from work and she'd left a
note for him... she said she'd be gone for a while... She went and
stayed back home for about *six months*... just like that...

Kira
But what was he really expecting from a character like that?

Morowa
That head-tie incident was bad, no doubt about that... but to be
honest, when I first heard the story, I laughed good and proper...
because that my aunty... she's a nasty piece of work... I'll never
forget: one night my mother locked me out... in the rain... I was
in my early twenties or so... I went to this my aunty, and begged
her to take me in for the night... she refused point blank... she
told me to go back home... about 2 miles away... As I say, it
was pouring down... I was drenched... more or less shivering...
and it was late... In short, a night I will never forget...

Kira
Surely, she could've taken you in and asked questions later...

Morowa
Well, she didn't... You won't believe: it was her houseboy... in
some outhouse... a proper shack... he took pity on me and
sneaked me into his place that night...

Kira
No...

Morowa
Can you imagine? I was so frightened... but he was such a

gentleman... He just gave me a wrapper so I could take my wet clothes off... then he spread a mat for me... and then he just slept off... Of course *I* didn't sleep a wink...

Kira
Sleep? How could you sleep?

Morowa
One time when I went back home and asked after him... the houseboy... when they told me he had died, I cried like a baby...

Kira
Oh no....

Morowa
Anyway, I made contact with his wife, and started helping her with school fees for two of their children... from primary to secondary school... and in fact beyond that... and I'm still in touch with them... I made sure they somehow reaped the reward of their father's kindness to me that cold, rainy night...

Kira
OK, we accept that your cousin's wife is a problem... but who knows what that your aunty did to provoke her like that... to cause the head-tie incident? Because if she could treat *you*, her own niece, the way she did that night...

Morowa
Hmmm... But regardless... that my cousin's wife is something else... one really rough, tough cookie... I'm telling you... Some of the things he's told me she's done... he's full of regret now...

Kira
You see, that's why you have to make sure you look after yourself properly... life's too short to waste on the wrong

people... And wait a minute... that Joel... the man who claims he talks to God, sees visions and all that... How come he didn't get a revelation, or anything, about something as serious as Sister Lola actually *dying*... You mean God didn't send him at least a text or *something*?
(Hisses)

Morowa
Lola told me Joel said to her, that by the end of this year she'd be on a different level... travelling around as a disciple, or something like that...

Kira
Look at that... Well, she's on a different level alright... but somehow I don't think this is what she imagined oh...

Morowa
Who could've imagined anything like *this*? Anyway, as for Joel... you'll be pleased to know he's in trouble with a capital T... He's in serious hot waters... I didn't even want to tell you, because I know you'll gloat...

(They laugh)

Kira
Explain please... speak up...

Morowa
You won't believe this... Apparently he and one or two other so-called clergy... they've been getting church members, preferably elderly ones with no relatives, to will their property and houses to the church...

Kira
I don't understand...

Morowa
Very simple formula: you leave your house to the church in your will... Joel & Co sell the house... then they supposedly use the proceeds to further God's work...

Kira
Translation: they just share the money amongst themselves?

Morowa
Yeah... I told you it was simple... And they've been getting away with it for a good while... You know the oyibo people... some of them don't have relatives as such... so there wasn't too much trouble from their angle... no-one to raise any alarm as such... But of course with us... *we have too many relatives...*

Kira
Hungry ones too...

(They laugh)

Morowa
Anyway, as I understand it, one family was adamant, that there was no way their father would've excluded his grandchildren from his will, and left *absolutely everything* he had to the church.... Cut a long story short, apparently it turns out the poor man had been suffering from dementia or something like that... but somehow in that state, Joel got him to change his will...

Kira
What? But surely that's a crime...

Morowa
Of course... The matter is in the hands of the police now...

Kira
Good... high time and all...

Morowa

So they're doing a proper, official enquiry now... looking into all the properties, money and stuff that they got people to will to the church in the past...

Kira

It's disgusting, but I can't say I'm surprised...

Morowa

But as we've said, let's be fair... give credit where credit is due... It's not *all* pastors who are at it... there are some honest ones... In fact, apparently, it was one young pastor... he'd only been with the church a couple of months or so, when he started querying things... He started asking about accounts and where the money was going, even before the police got involved... Apparently Joel & Co allocated themselves all sorts of allowances... for clothing, food, travel, entertainment... you name it... and they thought this young pastor would just join them in their shenanigans, but he didn't... So initially they tried to keep him quiet... apparently they offered him a car and some stuff... but he refused... So of course they made life so difficult for him, he had to leave the church... he was more or less forced out... But as I understand it, he's now helping police with enquiries...

Kira

Good... I'm sure there must be some fake pastor network... where they just invite each other here, there and everywhere... so they can sit and laugh at all the people they're milking and fleecing in their so-called churches... You made a very narrow escape...

Morowa

But Joel still calls and texts me...

Kira

Joel won't stop just like that oh... he's a conman, through and through... he'll wear you right down if he has to... just as long as he eventually squeezes something out of you... I hope they actually convict him and his cronies... the whole lot of them... They forget they're not back home where any and everything goes... As for the havoc they're causing back home... if you drive around, nine out of every ten billboards are advertising for churches... People are holding church services in their kitchens, bathrooms, bedrooms, inside their cars, on motorcycles...

Morowa
I guess that's their interpretation of 'everywhere is holy ground'...

(They laugh)

Kira
The thing is, with our people, both here and back home: you can just wake up one morning, tell a few gullible folk that you had a vision overnight, in which the Lord told you to preach to them... you get them to come round to hear what God supposedly told you... and boom... you're a pastor... you're in business... It's as simple as that... Back home, Joel would probably be on first name terms with the police chiefs and judiciary... he'd have the money and trappings to be able to mix with the 'big' boys... he'd probably have them all on speed dial... they'd all be buddies... So who would go and arrest him? Who? It's a joke...

Morowa
Proper joke...

Kira
Hmmm... hmmm... You know what my problem is now? When the time comes, how are we going to face Lola's funeral? Her *funeral*... You mean she actually *died*... So that's the end of her? How?

Morowa
Our own Sister Lola... May God have mercy and pity on us all...

30 *Thursday 26 September*

THEY ALL NEED TO BE TOLD SOMEHOW

Featuring 'Liquid & Fluid', Morowa and Sonny's family friend.

Kira
You feel better today?

Morowa
I can't say I do, but... I was like a zombie at work today... Oh Lola... I just couldn't get her out of my mind... I can't cry any more... I'm exhausted...

Kira
It's just unbelievable, honestly... Yesterday night I was just going through the last couple of messages between us... about something I ordered from her... How could I have known that would be the last ever order I would place with her? I read the messages over and over, then I broke down completely... It took me a good while to pull myself together... Oh no... Anyway, you know what I was wondering? How much do you think we should put in her sympathy card?

Morowa
I dunno... Whatever the case, it can't be up to two thousand pounds...

Kira
What? *Two thousand pounds?* To put in the sympathy card? What are you talking about?

Morowa
Liquid & Fluid came to see me... in fact he just left... he wanted two thousand from me...

Kira
Two thousand? For what now?

Morowa
He says his grandfather died back home... aged 104.... and he doesn't have all the money he needs to go home for the funeral...

Kira
One hundred and four? Must he go, for God's sake?

Morowa
Of course that's what I asked him... According to him, everyone's looking to him to sort things out as he's abroad... He says he's got most of the money... he's just a bit short...

Kira
Just... a bit short... of two thousand pounds...
(Hisses)

Morowa
He was swearing to everything under the sun that he would pay me back as soon as he gets back from the funeral... He says he'll get it from his grandfather's estate...

Kira
Estate?

Morowa
Look, I'm pretty sure his grandfather probably didn't have two kola nuts to rub together, never mind an 'estate'...

(They laugh)

Morowa
Look, he and I know full well that if I make the mistake of giving him that money, I won't get it back without a serious fight...

Kira
That's if you get it back at all...

Morowa
The thing is, I know him... he'll just go missing... I won't be able to reach or find him... anywhere... he'll start dodging me... he won't take my calls... But look, there's absolutely no danger of all that happening, because I haven't got that kind of money to give *myself* at the moment, never mind anybody else...

Kira
So what's the idea anyway? You should have that kind of money spare, just lying around to give out... to people like *him*?

Morowa
As soon as he came through the door, he said he was starving... then started giving orders, you know him: he didn't want any chicken... but whatever I was giving him had to have plenty shito, this and that... First and foremost he came over an hour or so late... as usual... laughing... saying it's 'black man time'...

Kira
Our people think being late is funny; but it's not you know... it's just disrespectful... And a lot of times, because of that, we aren't taken seriously, and we miss out on things... all because we couldn't manage or bother to be on time...

Morowa
True... Anyway, when I offered him a drink, he said he just wanted water... he said he'd stopped drinking...

Kira
Oh... Really?

Morowa
So I gave him some food... next thing, he's telling me the food's

too small... that when he was drinking we called him 'Liquid &
Fluid'... and now he wants to eat, I won't give him enough...

Kira
What nonsense? Is he your child?

Morowa
I wonder...

(They laugh)

Morowa
Anyway, I put fifty pounds in an envelope and gave it to him...
He took the money out, counted it... then he screamed: "Ah...
Sister Moro... but you can do much better than this now"...

Kira
Imagine... the cheek...

Morowa
I told him: "Look, I've got a couple of funerals myself to deal
with now... and we all know what that means moneywise"... He
started muttering something to himself... Next thing I'm hearing:
'OK... let me have a beer then'...

Kira
But I thought you just said he'd stopped drinking...

Morowa
Wait now... I'm telling you as it happened... So of course I said
to him: "Didn't you just say you've stopped drinking?" Then he
says: "I said I want a *beer*... is that a drink?"

(They laugh)

Morowa
You should've seen him... he counted the money two or three

times in disbelief... he would look at the money, then look at me as if I'd let him down so badly... But that's his business... after all it's not a loan... he doesn't have to pay me back...

Kira
You even did well... to give him something... Did *he* bring anything for *you*?

Morowa
Like what?

Kira
Just a token... like a box of chocolates or something? Or even some gari or dried fish... something... anything...

Morowa
Are you kidding? Do people like him know how to give anybody anything? He just came with the usual outstretched fingers to receive and collect... I even had to give him a takeaway... I had to wrap some fish up for him... At a point, you should've seen the way he was hurrying me up so that Sonny wouldn't meet him...

Kira
So why didn't he want Sonny there? He's related to Sonny right, not you?

Morowa
They're not actually related... but they're from the same place... same hometown... The thing is, he knows Sonny can't stand him and his nonsense... I was his only hope of getting anything... In fact I told him to come as early as possible, because Sonny usually comes home late on Thursdays... he's not even back yet... He knows if Sonny had been around, he may not have even got the fifty pounds... I would've had to hide from Sonny to give him anything...

Kira
So what does he do for a living now anyway?

Morowa
Do I know? And I don't think I want to know any more... We've
tried to help him... many, many times ... but there's only so
much you can do for anybody... On a couple of occasions, years
ago, I arranged for him to see a music tutor I knew, cos you
know he's very talented... he can rival anybody on the piano and
a few other instruments as well... I'm sure that tutor would have
helped him... opened some doors for him... at the very least I'm
sure he would've pointed him in the right direction to use and
develop his talent... but he refused to keep the appointments...
He said he was going to go to university to study law or so... you
know our people with this university business... But it didn't
work out... Look, I've got my own problems...

Kira
And of course that his drinking wouldn't help matters...

Morowa
At all... he's always muddled up... And he's full of all sorts... he
talks anyhow... He thinks I've forgotten... some time ago he
came to us with a catalogue of woes... desperate for money as
usual... so we gave him what we could... Next thing, he's
badmouthing us all over the place... telling people not take any
notice of me and Sonny... that we're just show-offs... all we
have is book sense, nothing else... To quote him: we had very
poor cash flow...

(They laugh)

Kira
But he keeps coming back to the Bank of Moro & Sonny Ltd...

Morowa
All he'll be doing now, is going from place to place, making a nuisance of himself... trying to whip up sympathy, and in the process, needle as much money as he can out of people... just so that he can go and make a big show of a funeral back home... go and spend money that he just hasn't got... then come back with a million excuses and stories, but not a penny to repay the people he'd be owing...

Kira
I really don't get it... the amount of money our people are willing and prepared to spend on funerals... It's mind boggling...

Morowa
Your people don't spend money on funerals like we do... ours is a full theatre-style production, particularly back home... To start with, we don't bury straight away...

Kira
Why do they keep the bodies so long? Months and months? What's the point?

Morowa
Tradition, I guess... And before the final burial itself, it's ceremony after ceremony... there's the seven days ceremony... ten days... hundred days... whatever they can think of, really... and each one costs serious money for food, cloths, custom rites, this and that... It's just crazy...

Kira
And however long it takes, you have to pay for embalming and storage...

Morowa
Of course... that goes without saying...

Kira

My Muslim relatives don't waste any time; they usually bury
within two days tops... And even the Christian ones... usually
within a few weeks, it's all over...

Morowa

But I've been to many of your funerals... maybe they're not quite
as expensive as ours, but they're not cheap affairs either... top of
the range caskets, lavish repasts... the absolute works...

Kira

You're right... And it doesn't stop there... like your people,
there's the fortieth day ceremony... food and drink galore... then
they'll do the first year anniversary... then the fifth... tenth... and
so on and so on... and as you say, all 'lavish' affairs... Fair
enough, appreciating and remembering our loved ones who've
passed can't be a bad thing... In fact it's part of what makes us
African... we never mourn alone... that's one really good thing
about us... But our funerals just seem to be about money, more
money, the most money... taxing people really heavily... It's a
bit out of hand now, if you ask me... so unproductive... Our
people... they all need to be told somehow... to cut back a bit...

Morowa

So *you* want to go and tell our people that they should cut back
on the funeral spending? Good luck with that... Look, if you try
it, they'll say that you want to do things on the cheap, so that the
person won't be honoured and buried properly... And they'll
wonder: why is that? Because you must have had a hand in the
person's death, that's why...

(They laugh)

Kira
You can't win...

Morowa

Win? Your fate will be well and truly sealed, when before you know what's happening, one or two people come forward to say that they dreamt of you... and you know our people and their dreams... They'll come up with something like: in the dream you were holding a shining knife and fork in front of the dead person... and as far as they would be concerned, that could only mean one thing: you must've *eaten* the person... with the said cutlery, of course... Case closed...

(They laugh)

Morowa

By the time they're done with you... you'll actually find yourself confessing to the murder of people who died before you were even born...

(They laugh)

Kira

But seriously, you know what's starting to bother me about this death thing? In days gone by, if you asked after someone you hadn't seen for a while, they'd say: 'Oh, he lives in Kuwait or wherever now', or 'She's fine; I saw her just last week'... Now as we're getting older... you ask for someone... more and more there's this pause accompanied by this funny look... then next thing they're telling you: 'You didn't hear, eh? Hmmm... So-and-so passed last year'... or 'We buried him in January'... stuff like that...

Morowa

Hmmm... as you say... as we get older...

Kira

And I was thinking to myself the other day that: you would never think it at the time, but the last time you saw some people, was the last time you would ever see them... you will never get to see them, and they will never get to see you... ever again... It's a bit scary you know...

Morowa

You and your deep thinking... but you're absolutely right... Anyway, still on this morbid theme: I understand the plan is to take Mama Abena home...

Kira

They should hurry up... it's been quite a while already... But just as we were saying... taking her home ... more expenses... that's another good few thousand pounds to add to the tally... but I guess the family can afford it...

Morowa

Oh yes... they won't be going from place to place, trying to harass people for funds like Liquid & Fluid... And I suspect it was probably her last wish...

Kira

I hope they have a service here before they take her back...

Morowa

Oh I'm sure they will... and they'll definitely keep us posted... We *must* pay our last respects to her... Oh Mama Abena... May her special soul rest in peace...

Kira

And may our dear Lola rest in peace too...

Morowa

Hmmm... And even though we don't know him, may Liquid & Fluid's old grandfather rest in peace as well...

Kira

Amen.

31 *Thursday 3 October*

THERE'S A LOT TO THINK ABOUT

Kira
I've booked... Lapland here we come...

Morowa
Oh good... so which hotel did you book...

Kira
Our first choice was fully booked, so I booked the second one... it's even about a hundred pounds cheaper... but it's four star as well, with breakfast and transport to the Christmas markets...

Morowa
Oh, well done...

Kira
The hotel organises tours and hikes and treks and all that... in the snow...

Morowa
Hikes and treks... What's that got to do with us?

Kira
Let's be a bit adventurous...

Morowa
Look, I don't know about you, but where I come from, if you go climbing, hiking or anything like that... and you get into any difficulty, the question on everyone's lips will be: 'What were you looking for in the woods, mountains, or wherever?' And of course, you can whistle if you think anyone is going to risk their

life to go and rescue you... Not to talk of in the snow...

Kira
(Laughs)
That's part of our problem... black people... we're not
adventurous... we always think worst case scenario... Come on...
What could go wrong? And if it does come to the worst, those
people in Lapland will definitely have a rescue service...

Morowa
Look, you can go hiking in the snow, skiing, mountain climbing,
bungee jumping... whatever, if you must... Me... I'll go sight-
seeing and shopping, if that's OK with you?

(They laugh)

Morowa
So it's from the 27th to the 30th of December, right? Do you
know we haven't travelled anywhere together this year?

Kira
True... we've been very quiet... I think the bones are getting
rusty... but don't worry, we'll make up for it next year... We'll be
kicking off with Salma in February...

Morowa
Oh, I can't wait...

Kira
But you know I'm off to Freetown next month... and I need your
advice... I want to sell some of my land... What do you think?

Morowa
The land your parents left you?

Kira
No... It's those plots QC bullied me into buying some years

ago... Remember?

Morowa
OK... they're probably worth a whole lot now...

Kira
Well I hope so... The thing is, if I'm going to sell them, I can start advertising them even before I go...

Morowa
So what's QC saying?

Kira
What has he got to say? Apart from some conveyancing fee or so, he didn't contribute a penny towards anything... I paid for virtually everything...

Morowa
Oh...

Kira
As if you don't know... Don't forget, in those days he was in the business of giving my money away, not helping me save...
Look, we never got round to putting his name on the papers, thank God... so as far as I'm concerned, they're all mine... fair and square... Look, there's no argument about that oh...

Morowa
OK... well if that's the case... But do you really want to sell *all* of it? If I remember it was quite a lot of land...

Kira
About ten plots... But what's the point of holding on to them?

Morowa
So you mean you're not thinking of putting anything up back home? Not even something small?

Kira
I don't know, you know... Will I ever go home to stay that long,
that it warrants actually putting up a whole building? For now,
staying in the family home is OK for me... But if it does come to
the worst, I can just go and stay in hotels or guest houses...

Morowa
Look, with all the trouble we've had in Ghana, I should probably
be the last person to encourage anyone to go and start building
back home... but I still think, if you can afford it, it's nice to have
a place of your own... Because whether we like it or not, this is
not really home... There's a reason why a lot of us always feel
somewhat unsettled, no matter how long we've lived here...

Kira
True...

Morowa
There's always something or the other to remind us that we're
foreigners... guests... unwelcome ones as well sometimes... well
at least, that's the way *I* feel... And when you say 'whole
building'... you make it sound like a big thing... it doesn't have to
be you know...

Kira
But whichever way you look at it, building a house is quite a
serious project, Moro... particularly when you're not on the
ground to supervise... Putting relatives in charge is almost
always a disaster...

Morowa
You don't have to tell me... You know initially Sonny's brother
was the sort of project manager for us in Accra... The first
structure he put up was so bad... we just had to pull it all down
and start afresh... Then the land saga started...

Kira
What a mess...

Morowa
Total mess... thousands of pounds down the drain... just like
that... The doors wouldn't open properly... the windows were a
mess... but it was easier to climb into the house through the
dodgy windows rather than use the doors... Can you imagine?

(They laugh)

Morowa
Look, when we weighed everything up, we decided that it would
cost us less financially... and mentally... if between the two of us
we go to Accra whenever we can, to supervise things... And if
and when we settle our land issues... that's what we plan to do...

Kira
I hear there's some building companies... you pay them... they
build everything for you from scratch... and they just hand over
the keys of the completed building to you at the end... but they're
quite expensive...

Morowa
Well, that kind of service isn't going to be cheap... We have
them in Ghana too... But you know what, it may sound
expensive compared to building yourself... but in the long run,
when you look at everything involved... they're definitely some
advantages... For one, it's less stress... the finishing and little
touches are usually more professional... It's worth considering...

Kira
OK... I'm sure after two... maybe three armed robberies, which
you're going to have to help me plan and commit... I should have
enough to pay one of those companies...

(They laugh)

Morowa
There's no way QC will let it come to that...

Kira
Moro, I don't really want him involved in this project... I want to do it on my own... so please don't mention to him...

Morowa
OK... I get you... my lips are sealed... Look, I know there's a lot to think about if you want to build back home, but the bottom line is... warts and all... and believe me, there are plenty warts... there's no place like home... there isn't...

Kira
OK... if and when I finish, who'll be in the house when I'm away most of the time?

Morowa
That you have to think long and hard about... You could rent it out, maybe on an ad hoc basis, so it's free when you want to use it... there must be agencies that can help with stuff like that... Or you could get a caretaker... A lot of people put relatives in, but there's quite a few horror stories with those kind of arrangements, so you've got to be careful... very careful... As I say, that's something you have to really think properly about...

Kira
Hmmm... OK, thank you for your wise counsel, m'lady...

Morowa
You're welcome...

Kira
So I've got quite a lot of thinking to do... and I've got to think quick... What I think I'll do is sell some of the plots... hopefully

I'll get some good money from that... and I've got some savings... If I put those together, I should have enough to construct something you'll be happy with... because I know all *you* want is for me to get going, ASAP... put something up fast, so that you'll have somewhere to go and relax in my country...

Morowa
Oh Kira... why would you say, or even *think* that... even though it's the truth?

(They laugh)

Kira
You know no-one will believe that you've never been to Sierra Leone... at least I've been to Ghana a few times...

Morowa
It's a just a pure bad luck story... because the time we planned to go... in fact to both Sierra Leone and Ghana... tickets in hand and all... ebola showed up...

Kira
But that was a while ago... I think we need to plan again... Pray for me, who knows... maybe your wish will come true, and my house will be ready by the time we decide to go...

Morowa
If you decide to go ahead with the building, it shouldn't take too long, because as we were just saying, you don't need anything massive... just something portable...

Kira
I can't understand the mentality of some people... they work and live like slaves... depriving themselves... sacrificing their health and so many other things, just so they can build big mansions back home... And some never really get to enjoy them...

Morowa
Enjoy? Many even *die,* because they literally work themselves
to death to put the buildings up... It doesn't make any sense...
How much time do some of them actually spend back home in
those houses? Some manage to go home maybe once or twice a
year... if that... usually for just a few weeks at a time... So of
course the relatives move in... free accommodation...

Kira
Then invariably you have to send money for them, so it's like
you're paying them to stay in your house... And those ones...
most of them couldn't care less if the house isn't being
maintained... and even if they do care, *you* have to pay for the
maintenance anyway... whichever way you look at it or turn it,
you're always out of pocket... I'm sure having a house back
home is meant to give you some joy... but our people make sure
it's anything but a laughing matter...

Morowa
The thing is, sometimes the houses are too big and bogus to
maintain anyway...

Kira
Look, each to his own... If I do decide to go ahead, I'm thinking
something modest, but modern and functional... affordable and
manageable... Portable, as you say...

Morowa
But what more could you want? Ah, one other very important
thing: when I think of all the troubles we've had, you must
double and triple check absolutely *everything*... do very due
diligence, particularly with the paperwork and all the official
stuff... don't leave any stone whatsoever unturned...

Kira
I'm sure Ralston will be able to help me look into things like

that... he knows about those things... that's his area...

Morowa
Which Ralston? I don't think so oh... Ralston is an Englishman... I don't think Sierra Leone will be 'his area' oh...

(They laugh)

Morowa
Look, he can probably do the plumbing, electrics and that kind of thing... but I don't think he'll be able to deal with the system back home that easily... it's a different world to what he's used to... believe me... You'll need someone home grown... someone who really knows the lay of the land over there... If you joke, the next thing someone will be telling you to your face... and in fact with a very straight face as well... is that the land you know you bought in good faith... and with good, hard-earned money... actually is not yours... and they'll have some kind of paperwork to prove it... That's more or less what we've been going through for God knows how long now...

Kira
You're right... Well, it looks like, whatever the case, I won't be selling *all* the land then...

Morowa
No, I wouldn't advise you to do that... Who knows what projects you, or even the boys may want to do in the future, where those plots would come in handy? And we need to encourage our kids to look homewards... land could be a real incentive for them... a sweetener... Unless you have no option, hold on to your land, Kira... a lot of people have regretted selling theirs in the past...

Kira
Hmmm... OK...

32 *Friday 11 October*

BETWEEN NOW AND TOMORROW

Kira
What are you up to tomorrow?

Morowa
Nothing much... We're supposed to be going to some function in the evening, but our lawyer for the house in Ghana is in town... we'll be seeing him on Sunday... so tomorrow Sonny wants to sort out some paperwork and stuff for when we see him...

Kira
OK...

Morowa
As soon as I get up tomorrow I'm going to dye my hair... the greys are starting to come through fast now... and then after that, I'm just going to relax for the rest of the day... I'm not even going to cook...

Kira
Oh, that's a shame... I was thinking of maybe swinging by... but if you want to relax... you say you're not even going to cook...

Morowa
What do you mean? Come now... I've got soup in the freezer... Or if you want, I'll order pizza or something... I've got some Rosé wine I know you'll like... and I've got some piping hot, big woman gist for you...

Kira
You lie...

Morowa

No lie... I was going to call you later, but you'll get the full story when you come tomorrow... I'll give you a clue... check your phone when we finish talking... you won't believe your eyes...

Kira

OK... To be honest, I was hoping some banku and tilapia would be on the menu...

Morowa

Oh... don't be troublesome... I've told you I have soup... In fact a few... so you can take your pick...

Kira

Well... actually it was QC who was hoping for some...

Morowa

What? You're coming with QC?

Kira

I told him I'd check if you guys would be free...

Morowa

Look, we are free... very free... and even if I have to go and steal the banku and stuff between now and tomorrow... so be it...

(They laugh)

Kira

Oh you'll go and steal, eh? Like you stole my blue stuff... from my bag...

Morowa

You left me no choice... Why would you show them to me and then refuse to give me some? What kind of friend does that?

What did you want me to do? You wanted me to steal, so that's what I did... But you know what, they're really good oh...

Kira
I told you... I can't do without them...

Morowa
But you wanted *me* to do without them, right? Look, just be a good girl for once, and bring some more for me tomorrow... thank you...

Kira
What? You mean you've finished those ones already?

Morowa
Look, don't ask me any questions... just bring more...

(They laugh)

Morowa
So what time should we expect you guys?

Kira
Say between 3 and 4... Is that too early?

Morowa
That's s absolutely fine... I see QC is on point these days... I knew he wouldn't let me down...

Kira
I'm still giving him the corner eye... he thinks he's home and dry with me... I'm not done punishing him...

Morowa
Leave him alone...

Kira
He's being the perfect gentleman... But he can't deceive me...

I know him too well... I know what he can do with that innocent look of his... He's off to Japan next week... he says I should go with him...

Morowa
And?

Kira
Moro I've got work...

Morowa
Oh, don't give me that... you can take time off any time you want...

Kira
Within reason... But don't forget I've taken leave to go home next month... and I've taken time off for Lapland as well...

Morowa
Oh, OK...

Kira
But apart from that... look, let me handle QC the way I want to...

Morowa
OK, OK... calm down... Does he still drink whisky?

Kira
Will he ever stop?

(They laugh)

Morowa
Ah... Sonny will have an excuse to open one of his vintage bottles... he's got quite a good collection of really top-notch whiskies... he'll be so pleased to see QC... Oh, I can't wait for

tomorrow... it'll be like old times... we've really missed QC...
But I guess you've missed *so* much more... all round...

Kira
Meaning what?

Morowa
Meaning anything you like...

(They laugh)

Kira
Do you want me to bring anything?

Morowa
Apart from the blue stuff... and ah... I've just remembered that
my bowl... the wooden one I left at your place the last time...
Apart from that, just bring yourselves...

Kira
I should bring your bowl? After stealing my stuff... Look, just
forget about that bowl... you're not getting it back...

Morowa
Oh please now... it's part of a set...

Kira
Well, you should've thought of that before taking up robbery...

(They laugh)

Kira
Look, let me go call QC to confirm things... See you tomorrow...

33 *Monday 21 October*

IT'S COMPLEX STUFF

Featuring Morowa's childhood friend Hope and her children, and Sizani, another friend, and Kira's clients Makeda and Mukaya and their mother. Also featuring Leo, Sonny's friend.

Morowa
I just spoke to Hope... she says I should greet you...

Kira
As for Hope...

Morowa
Leave my friend alone oh... Look, seriously, I don't know what her problem is... She's actually gotten worse over the years with this her accent thing...

Kira
It's painful to listen to her... so fake...

Morowa
As far as she's concerned she's arrived... a role model, and everyone wants to talk and be like her... I've actually heard one or two wicked nuisances telling her they like the way she talks...

Kira
Trust our people to encourage you to make a fool of yourself...

(They laugh)

Morowa
Oh yes... And she's obsessed with social media and the

hundreds of 'likes' she claims she gets on there... According to her, she just needs to post a new picture of herself, and people go wild with the ticks and the comments...

(They laugh)

Kira
A grown woman... getting excited about social media 'likes' and 'ticks'... she really needs to get a life...

Morowa
She practically lives on social media... Anyway, you know what she called me for? Well, she started off by advising me to stop eating egusi... she says the egusi enzymes cause problems...

Kira
Egusi enzymes? Does Hope know what enzymes are?

Morowa
Apparently she and her daughter are now egusi intolerant...

Kira
Oh for God's sake...

(They laugh)

Morowa
Can you imagine? If I document some of the things Hope has piped up with over the years, I'll have a bestseller on my hands... no joke... But the main thing she called me for, was to tell me about some skin lightening gel that she thinks I should try...

Kira
What? Have you ever told her you want to be lighter?

Morowa
How could I? For what?

Kira

What damn cheek... I thought people had stopped this skin bleaching thing anyway...

Morowa

So did I... I know it's been banned in some places... but obviously it's still going on... thanks to people like Hope...

Kira

So you mean that mentality of lighter skin equals prettier and better, is still around?

Morowa

But what do you expect from someone like her? It's just a low class, slave mentality complex that some black just can't shake off... They've been well and truly conditioned... they just can't see beauty, or anything good as such, in a dark-skinned person... In their book, pretty and good can only be light, fair skinned... in short, as close to the white man as possible...

Kira

It's just pathetic... So does Hope really think people want to look like *her*, or what? She looks like one big sore... Anyway, as they say, beauty is in the eye of the beholder, because as for me, some of the most beautiful people I have met are dark skinned...

Morowa

And the crazy thing is: you needed to see her before she started bleaching herself... when we were going to school... she was a truly natural, dark and lovely beauty... and I'm not kidding...

Kira

You keep saying... but it's hard to picture her looking any different than she does now...

Morowa

I'm telling you, she looked really nice... she's destroyed her skin... and I guess now she's looking for some bleaching mates, to compare notes with...

Kira

So you... and I guess Debbie and Kukua as well... you should all go and use some cream that Hope of all people, got from God knows where... and go and damage that lovely skin you people have... People are just never satisfied... blacks want white skin and hair... whites want black bums and lips... What is it?

Morowa

Look, I wasn't in the mood for Hope this evening... at all... In fact, do you know some years ago she told me not to call her 'Hope' any more?

Kira

So what were you supposed to call her?

Morowa

She said I should call her 'Holly'...

Kira

(Laughs)
Oh for God's sake... So does she really think she actually rhymes with that name?

Morowa

That's more or less what I asked her... So she asked me what I meant by that... She was so annoyed with me; she didn't talk to me for a good while after that... One time she even told *me* that 'Morowa' is too African... she suggested 'Maureen'...

Kira

Imagine... *You* should have suggested that if she was looking for a name change, to try 'Hopeless'... I think that'll probably suit her much better...

(They laugh)

Kira

Even look at her children's names for God's sake... Penelope and
Bartholomew... If she could pronounce them properly, that
would be a big help... But that day we went on that outing and
she was calling them to get on the bus... 'Pay-nah-lor-pay... Bar-
tor-lor-moo...'

(They laugh)

Morowa

Stop exaggerating...

Kira

Ask Sizani... we thought she was singing... We just looked at
each other in shock, before we burst out laughing when we
realised what was going on... Do we see the oyibo people giving
their children our names? Even though we have such beautiful
names, they don't do it... But if we *must* choose their names,
must it be the ones we can't even pronounce properly?

Morowa

But you know the one thing about Hope... she's very pushful... or
pushy... depending on how you look at her... When she wants
something, she doesn't look sideways... doesn't care who's
looking at her... she just focuses straight ahead until she gets
what she set out for... She's started some charity back home for
disabled children...

Kira

In Accra?

Morowa

No, in her hometown, somewhere near Kumasi... and I think it's
a serious thing... She's more or less funded it herself... she's got
an office and all, and she's paying staff... Of course I don't think

she'll turn donations away... but if I understand things right, the bulk of the money is coming out of her pocket... She did actually tell me some time ago, that when she sold one of her houses, she would use most of the proceeds to fund a charity... and kudos to her... I think she's really doing just that...

Kira
Awww... if that's true, that's really good... and I take back all my comments...

(They laugh)

Kira
Ah... but talking about names... a couple of days ago at work, I interviewed this really nice woman from South Sudan... I thought of you because she said she was a teacher before she left her country... She and her two daughters were rescued from one of the migrant boats...

Morowa
Are you serious?

Kira
We see them all the time... we have to work closely with the migrant agencies, to assess and evaluate them... I fell in love with the daughters' names: 'Makeda and Mukaya...'

Morowa
Oh, those are pretty names... Sudanese?

Kira
That's what I thought, but apparently they're the names of ancient African queens... I thought to myself: I know all about ancient oyibo kings and queens: Queen Victoria, King Edward, Henry the 8th, Marie Antoinette, King Louis... all of them... But apart from Shaka Zulu and Mansa Musa... what other African

royalty do I really know about?

Morowa
That was the colonial curriculum... we had no choice...

Kira
But we do now... and you know what, I think I'm going to educate myself on African history... They say our kids don't know their history... But how are they supposed to know, when even *we* their parents don't know enough ourselves? How are we supposed to teach them? And it may not sound like much, but if every Christmas, birthday or celebration, as part of their presents, we made it a point of giving our kids books, films or some kind of literature on black people who've made their mark... black events and traditions... stuff like that... it's bound to make some difference to their understanding and awareness of themselves and their history and cultures and all that... They'll get to know about our peoples' contributions to science, politics, literature... positive, inspiring stuff for a change...

Morowa
True... A lot of our issues stem from the fact that we don't seem to know enough about *ourselves*... Apart from going online or to libraries for information, there are bound to be workshops we could probably attend as well...

Kira
And if there aren't any, what stops *us* from starting one? We can combine your teaching with my social work... do our research and learn as we teach... If we do things right, I'm sure people will be interested in what we may have to offer...

Morowa
You know what... I've known you a quarter of a century, and this is by far one of the best ideas you've ever had...

Kira

I shall take that as a compliment... others wouldn't...

(They laugh)

Kira

The Sudanese lady even offered to teach me Swahili when I'm ready... I'm not that good with languages, but I'd really love to learn that one...

Morowa

I understand it's such a beautiful language... But seriously, let's see how far we can get with the workshop idea... Who knows? That could just be the start of something serious, you know...

Kira

For me, the ultimate would be to get a platform, however small, to be able to dissuade people, particularly young ones, from leaving Africa... I've even thought of starting a blog or something...

Morowa

Well what's stopping you?

Kira

I don't want people to troll and abuse me online... But there must be a way of making Africans understand that at one time the grass may have been greener over here in the West, but things have changed...

Morowa

They really have... Now I don't think there's that much grass to start with... and whatever's there isn't that green any more... it's turned to a colour we can't even define...

(They laugh)

Kira

True... And the money these migrants use to get on those boats... you can't imagine... thousands and thousands of pounds and dollars... not to mention the energy...

Morowa

Well exactly... How do you cross the Sahara... virtually on foot?

Kira

Then go and cling onto those boats, with 'death' clearly written all over them... sometimes with children and all... Oh God...

Morowa

Maybe I'm missing something here... but I've always thought that surely the money they manage to assemble to get on those boats, or battle for visas and all that... if they channelled some of those resources into setting up businesses in Africa, wouldn't that be more beneficial... for everybody concerned? Or?

Kira

Well you would've thought so... But if you talk now, they'll say you and your family are enjoying the best of the West... eating sausage and bacon every day... with light and water, etc, etc... and you selfishly don't want them to come and enjoy as well... In fact some will even suggest an exchange programme... you go live and exist they way they do, and vice versa...

(They laugh)

Kira

Seriously, what I think we should all try to do, is to get Africa to a position where we're not lagging so far behind everywhere and everyone else in the world... If we can narrow that gap, that would be great for our collective psyche, our outlook, our wellbeing as Africans... everything would just perk up for us...

And I don't think we're even that far behind the rest of the world... we're just different...

Morowa

Maybe... But how is being 'different' benefitting us? Tell me...

Kira

Look, if we all come together in Africa, we could make that 'difference' work for us... We can develop standards that could be rolled out across the whole continent... so we'll all be singing from the same hymn sheet, and we'd be able to make a solid, *united* impact... any time, anywhere... We'd be able to face and measure up to the rest of the world, whilst maintaining, and in fact promoting, our 'difference', our Africanness...

Morowa

I think I get what you're saying... and if we could do that, it would be wonderful... But I don't mean to be a killjoy, but that's not going to be easy at all... How many of the fifty-four or so African countries are functioning properly on their own? Not to talk of coming together...

Kira

Moro, you and I don't have all the answers... nobody does... All we can do is look for a part to play, even if it's just a little one... For instance, if we can get our workshop going, we can encourage people like the Sudanese lady to tell their stories... If you hear what she says she went through, I defy you not to cry...

Morowa

Awww...

Kira

She said it was worse than she could've ever imagined... And to add some more spice to the story, she's pregnant now...

Morowa
Oh no...

Kira
She said she didn't know she was pregnant when they set off
from Sudan... Now the husband is stuck in Libya... they ran out
of money... they just didn't have enough to pay for the four of
them for the last leg of the journey... So she came with the two
girls... her hubby will have to hustle his way across later...

Morowa
What is all this? Well, call England what you may, but at least
she and her girls will be somewhat taken care of here... I don't
think other countries are so welcoming...

Kira
True... But you know what, maybe if more would-be migrants
listened to sober, articulate people like her... and there are many
like her... perhaps it might help to get the message across, that
Africans need to stay in Africa to help build Africa up to its full
potential... we all can't be away... Being abroad is not all it's
cracked up to be...

Morowa
More than enough of Africa's solid sons and daughters... and
their children... are already out of the continent, using their
brains and energy to build up other people's countries... It just
doesn't make sense...

Kira
I heard this discussion the other day... apparently, some people
were saying that a lot of Africans back home see diasporans as
people who've run away and more or less abandoned the
continent... So some were asking: how can we be away, and
expect the people back home to build Africa up for us to go back
and enjoy?

Morowa

Look, if most Africans abroad suddenly packed their bags and went back home, en masse... can you imagine what would happen? I'm no expert, but I suspect our countries would just collapse... they'd be totally overwhelmed...

Kira

Completely... Look, even when holidaymakers go home, usually over Christmas, you can actually feel the strain of overcrowding and pressure on the system... And that's just a few people going home for a few weeks...

Morowa

Exactly... So imagine thousands and thousands of people going home... for good... without proper planning or anything... Imagine the situation with housing, electricity, water, medical, etc, etc... it just wouldn't work... It would just be a disaster... big one... They'd end up begging people to go back to the diaspora...

Kira

In an ideal world, the cleverer ones among us would work out the logistics: things like the rate at which people should return to Africa... temporarily or permanently... based on what needs to be done, what areas need to be developed, and stuff like that... So many, many things would have to be considered...

Morowa

It's quite complex... And of course, everyone approaches Africa from slightly different angles and standpoints... Hmmm... the Sudanese woman wouldn't know the effect she's had on you...

Kira

Well, if things go according to plan, she might one day... I squeezed twenty pounds into her hand when she was leaving... I told her to keep quiet about it, because as you know, we're not

supposed to have any sort of private dealings with the clients...
But I just couldn't help putting myself in her shoes... I really felt
for her... an African sister... the desperation... the risks she took...

Morowa

Africa... with all the plenty God-given resources... the ones who
should be making her great, are prepared to risk everything...
their lives and even their children's lives, just to get away... It's
so sad...

Kira

The story of Africa... as you say, it's complex stuff...

Morowa

Very... And do you know, the ones who try to make things a
little less complex by trying to do things properly, in an orderly,
straightforward way... sometimes they struggle... big time... to
make any headway with our people...

Kira

Oh no, no... our people somehow seem to prefer the cowboys...
In fact, it's like they absolutely love them... strange but true...

Morowa

I've told you... our people are confused... Look at a case like
this: one of Sonny's schoolmates, Leo... He's an MP back
home... Sonny says from schooldays, he's always been a very
sober, decent person... He lives in the house his father left for
him... it's an old house, but very well maintained... But did some
of his people appreciate that? Of course not... they saw him as a
fool, obviously because he didn't steal to build his own... He
lives in his constituency, so he walks to the office instead of
using the official car... You know the kind of person who always
tries to do the right thing... and very humble... And because he's
honest... he doesn't steal... so he doesn't have extras to be

throwing about... making big donations and dashing people money anyhow... Anyway, he said some time ago, some of his constituents would tell him point blank that they regretted voting for him... that he was nothing but a liability... His straightforward ways were more or less getting on their nerves...

Kira
So that's not quite what they were quite looking for in an MP, or what?

Morowa
He showed us some of the letters and messages they sent him... What didn't they call him? One message started off... 'To Leo, your own MP stands for 'Master of Poverty'...

Kira
Well, look at that...

(They laugh)

Morowa
We're laughing, but it's not funny... Of course when it came to re-election time, he said it was more or less tug of war between those who valued his honesty and the way he did things, and those who didn't... But luckily and sensibly... and I think narrowly... he was re-elected... But I think now, slowly but surely, his people are beginning to appreciate the benefits of his way of doing things... his methods of accountability and transparency and all that... the things that help to make things work a bit better... for *everybody*...

Kira
Poor man... so it was as if by being straightforward and honest, he'd let everybody down... is that it? So the MPs and officials who *do* steal, and flaunt the things they've stolen in their faces... is that *really* what some of our people want?

Morowa

So it seems... and then they carry them shoulder high and worship them... They fight tooth and nail for them... Some even die for them, particularly during campaign and election times... That's apart from the regular dying from poverty and hardship...

Kira

So seriously, what can kind of people are we?

Morowa

I've told you: ignorance and confusion... that's our handicap... Most of our people don't understand the concept of making and holding our leaders accountable... In fact they've been conditioned to accept their abject poverty, hardship and misery, as just the way it is... their God-given portion to suffer and even die, whilst others enjoy and live large at their expense... What was Leo's crime? Nothing apart from just trying to do the right thing... that's all...

Kira

But for some crazy reason, a lot of the time, it's like the right thing sort of puzzles our people...

Morowa

Ah... that's the word right there that just sums Africa up... 'puzzle'... There must be a reason why God shaped Africa like a question mark... It's because we're a puzzle... jigsaw... and the pieces just never seem to quite fit...

(They laugh)

Kira

Look jigsaw or whatever... I just can't wait to go home... the countdown's begun... literally just days to go now... oh yes...

Morowa

I wish I was going too... I could really do with some sunshine...

34 *Wednesday 6 November*

OUR HEARTS ARE USUALLY IN THE RIGHT PLACE

Kira flew into Sierra Leone a few days ago on a planned trip.
She calls Moro back in the UK.

Kira
Moro... Can you hear me? What's happening? I've been trying
to get you since I got here...

Morowa
The reception's not too good here... I'm in hospital oh, Kira...

Kira
Did you say you're in *hospital?*

Morowa
Yes... I was admitted on Sunday morning...

Kira
Ah... for what?

Morowa
I started bleeding... heavily...

Kira
Your fibroids again?

Morowa
Well that's what I thought initially... but they say it's polyps...
But that's not the main issue... now they say I have an immune
deficiency disorder...

Kira
Eh? What's that, for God' sake?

Morowa
They did some blood tests... and that's what they came back
with... Bottom line, I've got to have a bone marrow transplant...

Kira
Transplant? What? That sounds quite serious... What's going
on? I leave you for just a few days and this is what I'm hearing
now? So how are you feeling?

Morowa
Not too bad actually... I feel OK...

Kira
So what caused all this now? Transplant? How long will that
take? How long will you be admitted for then?

Morowa
I'm not too sure... The consultant says in a couple of days they'll
be able to give me a better idea of everything and the plan for
me... so we're just waiting to hear what they say...

Kira
I can't believe this... How's everybody else? How's Sonny?

Morowa
He just stepped out before you called... I think he's gone to
smoke actually...

Kira
Oh no... he's started smoking again?

Morowa
I think he's just a bit stressed out with things at the moment...

Kira
I'm not surprised... Wasn't he supposed to be travelling to
Ghana next week?

Morowa
Yes... to go and sort out this our never ending land issue once
and for all... But with all this drama now, he's postponed it...
Actually, I told him to go, but he wouldn't...

Kira
Hmmm... Look, don't worry too much, you hear... God is in
control...

Morowa
Which god is that? Yours or mine?

Kira
All our gods... it sounds like we need all of them now...

(They laugh)

Kira
So this transplant thing... how does it work? What's the next
step?

Morowa
Well they say they're looking for a match for me on the bone
marrow donor register... In the meantime I'm having a whole lot
of tests done... to make sure I'm fit for the procedure... To be
honest, I'm still trying to get my head round everything... And I
don't want to check anything on the internet, so I don't read or
find out more than I can handle...

Kira
But how can this happen, just like that?

Morowa
That's life, my dear... You just never know what's just round the
corner... Anyway, how's the 'Athens of West Africa'?

Kira
Oh, fine... It's sunny, hot and hectic... noisy... and the traffic, just

crazy... but it's all good... It's always good to be home...

Morowa
Oh yes... always... When are you back anyway?

Kira
I've still got two weeks to go...

Morowa
But you've got quite a lot of running around to do for the land and house, right?

Kira
I do... and it's not easy... but I've got plenty help... You know I didn't really want QC too involved in this project... but it was hard to keep things from him... and to be fair, he's actually arranged quite a lot of contacts and stuff for me over here... He's spoken to one of his classmates... a surveyor... so I'll be meeting her tomorrow, and I'll be seeing an architect on Thursday... so I think it's so far so good...

Morowa
But make sure you find time to relax and have some fun in the sun... Because when you get back it'll be freezing...

Kira
Are you telling me? I know... it was pretty cold when I left... Well, my Thursday appointment is at a hotel by the beach... One of my good friends is coming this evening to take me for a meal at some resort on the peninsular... so it's definitely not all work and no play... But ooh... I think I could've done without this news you've just given me...

Morowa
Well... to be honest, it was a bit much to take in initially, but I'm OK... I'll be fine...

Kira

You say you're not in pain or anything?

Morowa

No... not really... just some slight discomfort in my arms where they put the drip in... They say as soon as they find a match I'll be good to start treatment... But one thing they did say, is that they may struggle to find a match for me, because there just aren't enough black bone marrow donors on the register...

Kira

Really?

Morowa

Black folks... our hearts are usually in the right place, but we often need a good push sometimes... Tell me why you and I... and in fact everyone we know... why aren't we all on this register?

Kira

As you say, we mean well, but a lot of times we don't follow things through... now look... But don't worry, they'll find a match... they will... As soon as I get back I'm going to register... and I'm going to encourage all my contacts to do the same...

Morowa

That'll be really good... Look, don't worry about me... I'm being very well looked after... You've got plenty stuff to do over there, so concentrate on that... Just make sure you bring me back one or two of those your print dresses... and those peppermint sweets... And I've got serious gist for you, you won't believe...

Kira

What gist is that now? What's up?

Morowa

Ah... not over the phone... Look, don't worry... me and my

sickness... we're not going anywhere... we're patiently waiting here to welcome you back...

(They laugh)

Morowa
Anyway, let me give you a clue... Rotimi...

Kira
Oh no... or should it be 'oh yes'? What's happened now?

Morowa
I say when you come back... Ah, and another thing... the way things are looking, I don't think I'll be able to make our Lapland trip oh... I was so looking forward to that... doing some nice Christmas shopping and all that...

Kira
Ah Moro... that's not really important now, you know... You just use all your energy to get better, please... you hear?

Morowa
Yes ma'am... I'll try... And you take care of yourself over there, OK?

Kira
Sure thing... I'll be fine... Greet Sonny for me...

35 *Monday 9 December*

LEFT WITH NO OTHER OPTION

Featuring Kojo, an acquaintance of Morowa's.

Kira
What's up? How did you know I was home anyway?

Morowa
You told me the boiler people were coming round... or?

Kira
You won't believe I'm still waiting... they said between 8 and 2... so I've got an hour or so to go before I can complain... They've wasted my whole day...

Morowa
But you know that's how it is with these kind of appointments... Anyway, this is just a quick one... Do you need dried or smoked fish? Because if you do, then I can get some from Kojo's wife for you... she says she's dealing in that now... and she delivers, so that makes life easy... She says she can come to me tomorrow...

Kira
Oh yes... great... I need some for Christmas for starters...

Morowa
OK, I'll send you the information...let me know what you want...

Kira
Which Kojo's wife is this anyway? Thanks to you, I must know at least a hundred Kojos and Kofis and Kwames...

Morowa

The short one who works for the council... near you....

Kira

Actually, I haven't seen him for a while, you know...

Morowa

How will you see him? I told you they suspended him...

Kira

You didn't tell me anything oh... Suspended... for what?

Morowa

I told you... two cases: embezzlement and sexual harassment...

Kira

No...

Morowa

He was cleared of all charges, thank God... As for the sexual harassment issue: *three* of his colleagues accused him... including a man...

Kira

What?

Morowa

You know his wife and Sonny's sister are very good friends... so that's how we got to hear about it all... I know racism is the last thing we like to resort to... *we* know that not every slight to black people is racist... there's so many other reasons sometimes... But sometimes we're left with no other option... Apparently, Kojo's never had a single issue or problem in the seven years or so that he's worked in that office.... that is until he applied for a senior management position...

Kira
Oh Kojo... very quiet man...

Morowa
Timid, if you ask me... The next time you see him, just look at the way he even holds a glass... like a mouse... so gentle.... Is that a man who could abuse three adults... including a man? Come on now...

Kira
So these three miserable supposedly abused musketeers... what are they trying to say? So they've been suffering in silence at his hands... all these years... those gentle hands, as you say... or he's just started this pattern of molesting all of a sudden... or what?

Morowa
Ah... his wife said the whole thing hit him very hard... I think he's going to sue them...

Kira
I think I would as well... But the thing is, whether you sue or not in this kind of situation, the damage has already been done...

Morowa
Of course... One of my colleagues used to say, these people have got all sorts of tricks to keep us 'down and out' in the workplace: 'down', as in they'll do everything they can to make sure you can't rise to anywhere near the top... and 'out', they just exclude you from things, outright...

Kira
Sometimes, it's like if they think you're pushing too hard career-wise... trying to progress, maybe a little too fast for their liking... they'll just frustrate you... in fact flatten you like they obviously tried to flatten poor Kojo... And sometimes, the more they realise you have to offer, the more they make sure they keep you down... Sometimes you can have whatever qualifications and

qualities you like... as far as they're concerned, that's your own business... you're not going to make any headway... They've got all sorts of underhand tactics... but just as we say about their leaders... the workplace bosses well know how to finesse their bad behaviour... so sometimes it's very hard... almost impossible to make a case against them... When they're ready they'll bring in their own people for you to train... At that point they humour you that you're good and competent enough... But next thing, the person you trained is your boss... So how does that work?

Morowa
I remember your own case with that Eastern European one...

Kira
That was classic... She'd only been working with us for a couple of months, and I was actually asked to show her the ropes... I was in the process of doing just that, when they made her my supervisor... And these same bosses had encouraged me to apply for the position... they'd more or less assured me that I'd get it...

Morowa
And what was the nonsense they ended up telling you about her language skills?

Kira
They say she had an edge because she could speak Ukrainian or Czech... or one of those kind of languages...

Morowa
Not French or Spanish or one of those main languages...

Kira
The thing is, absolutely nothing about another language featured in the job description or anything... if it had, I wouldn't have applied... All of a sudden, that was now the game changer... Look, even her *English* wasn't that great... But they looked me in the eye, with a straight face, and told me that nonsense...

Morowa
And of course, when you react to something like that, which
you're almost bound to because you're so upset and frustrated...
they turn that around and say you're aggressive, intimidating and
all that kind of crap... and in fact that's part of the reason why
you didn't get the job in the first place... It's soul destroying...

Kira
And just tiresome... Look, I may be sort of at the top of my
profession now, but it's been a bloody hard climb... In days gone
by, I used to argue and fight... but you get tired of explaining and
trying to prove yourself all the time... You actually get used to
seeing weak, fit for nothing candidates, always beating you for
jobs... and it's not just about jobs... you just get used to a whole
lot of wrong things... all over the place... in fact *everywhere*...
that are just down to pure racism and nothing else...

Morowa
And because they think we're all just generally slow, they insult
our intelligence all the time by telling us that racism and
prejudice doesn't really exist... it's all in our heads... And of
course, you have the miserable *blacks* who they recruit to
champion the 'racism doesn't exist' story... the ones who can
give the white man a good run for his money... sell out their
fellow blacks, to try to prove to the white man and to themselves
that they can match or even beat them at their own game...
because as far as they're concerned, they've made it in the white
world, and fellow blacks just haven't got what it takes....

Kira
But it has to be said though, there are some very fair and decent
white bosses... white people in general... in fact plenty of them...
and thank God... because let's not fool ourselves... without some
genuine ones helping us fight our corner, whatever forward steps
we've made as black people, would've been impossible...

Morowa
We know not all white people are racist, just like we know not
all black people are drugged, gun-toting gangsters... But look,
they keep saying things are improving on the racism front... All
I know is this: racism is alive and kicking... and its passport has
been stamped with: *'Indefinite leave to remain'*... so trust me, it's
here to stay... and in no rush to go anywhere any time soon...

Kira
Well, I hope to God you're wrong about that...

Morowa
You can hope all you want... but you know I'm right... Look,
just listen to the remarks some top, influential people make about
us when they're caught off guard... when their microphones are
left on by mistake and stuff like that... Then go online and see
what some people actually have to say and write about us... both
the high and mighty and the low lifes... in fact they seem to join
forces... they form a happy, united front when it comes to being
racist and attacking blacks in particular... And some don't even
want to be anonymous... just hateful... it's so frightening... I
wish someone could tell me what we did to some of these
people, to make them despise us the way they obviously do...

Kira
You know what... let's not upset ourselves... bottom line, Kojo
won this battle... We know it's a small victory... *very* small in the
grand scheme of things... but every little helps...

Morowa
True... Anyway, I told you this was a quick call... I'm expecting
my GP practice nurse... she's coming to have a look at that
oozing I was telling you about... I've sent you the fish list, so let
me know what you want... Ah, I see a car parking up... it's
probably the nurse... Later...

36 *Thursday 12 December*

THAT'S JUST THE WAY IT IS

Morowa is still recovering at home following her recent hospital admission.

Kira
Hiya... What's up? Did you vote?

Morowa
Oh yes... I told you I was going to... Sonny and I voted first thing this morning...

Kira
Oh brilliant... I'm happy you felt up to it...

Morowa
I had to push myself... They say black people don't vote, so we have to try...

Kira
I got to vote with about ten minutes to spare... I had this meeting at work that went on and on... from there I had to dash for my mammogram, before I eventually got to the polling booth... luckily it's just on the next street to mine...

Morowa
But this election... it looks like it's a foregone conclusion...

Kira
Hmmm... maybe... but whatever the case, we still have to vote...

Morowa

Oh no, I agree... and if *I* could manage to vote this time in my present condition, then most people don't have an excuse not to... But wait a minute... didn't you have a mammogram just a few weeks ago?

Kira

I did, but they said the images weren't clear, or something like that...

Morowa

What does that even mean?

Kira

Do I know for these people?

Morowa

So when will you get the results?

Kira

They say in the New Year...

Morowa

OK... hmmm...

Kira

Look, I refuse to worry from now till then... all through Christmas and New Year... No... When I get the results I'll take things from there... You know what, I can't even believe Christmas is just round the corner... So what's happening this year?

Morowa

Honestly, after these past couple of months, just being alive is more than enough for me... The girls say they'll do all the food shopping and cooking... so what's my problem? I'm just decorating my tree... I'm a bit late this year... it's usually up and twinkling by now...

Kira
You know I prefer the natural trees... but I saw this video somewhere on social media... this woman got bit by some insect or something, that apparently came with the tree from some tropical place... She nearly died, so that just put me right off...

Morowa
Really? That's a bit scary oh... But maybe it's fake news... you know social media...

Kira
Well... true or lie... I thought, let me just manage my small artificial tree this year...

Morowa
You'll never guess what I found amongst my decorations... Remember those Christmas stockings Lola gave us some years ago... the personalised ones?

Kira
Oh my God... mine's green and you've got the red one, right?

Morowa
That's right... To think Lola's gone... just like that...

Kira
Unbelievable... Hmmm...

Morowa
I'll call her son... I don't want to talk to that her husband at all... but I'll probably call him as well... just out of respect for Lola... to find out how they're doing, particularly at this time of year... I vividly remember last Christmas, I gave her a lift home after our church social evening... We sat in my car for a good while...

in fact, I remember, she was a bit tipsy... we chatted and laughed... I can almost hear her laughing now... Now this Christmas she's gone... just like that... hmmm... Anyway... So are you working over Christmas?

Kira
Well I'm on call on Christmas Day, so I won't be able to really relax... or drink much, because if there's an emergency or something, I'll have to go in...

Morowa
You'll make up for it on Boxing Day... Or will you still be on call?

Kira
No-oh...

Morowa
Well come over to us now...

Kira
What? You want Nish to kill me? You know I always go to her on Boxing Day...

Morowa
I'm just kidding...

Kira
I'll be going with QC this year... she's really excited about that...

Morowa
QC's the man... he's right back where he rightfully belongs...

(They laugh)

Kira
He's actually travelling next week... but he'll be back in time for Christmas...

Morowa

He's always away though... Where's he off to now?

Kira

Australia and the Far East... He says he'll slow down next year... apparently there's this big oil project he's involved in now...

Morowa

You know what, I'm just so happy for you both... honestly... I really am... So what are the Two Rs saying about Mum and Dad?

Kira

Well, I was going to issue an 'official statement' to them... tell them that me and their dad are trying to work things out... But QC says we don't owe them an explanation as such... He says they're big men now... obviously they know what's going on...

Morowa

I think I agree with him... Explain what? Why?

Kira

What's new? You always agree with QC... The thing is Richie's not too fussed... but some time ago Ralston was saying, that individually, me and his father are good... but we're not good together as a couple...

Morowa

Oh... So what does he mean by that? Who asked him anyway?

Kira

My boys were the ones who kept me going when QC was away, so I can't just dismiss them...

Morowa

Of course not... but they're not boys any more... and it's not about *them* or what *they* want...

Kira
But this is a bit different... it's their father...

Morowa
Of course, but you have to put yourself first for a change, Kira...
After looking after them so selflessly, don't you think you're
entitled to some fun and happiness and peace now?

Kira
I guess so...

Morowa
No, you need to stop guessing... Look, if *you* want QC around
you, then that's all that should matter... You wouldn't be
tolerating him now if he wasn't doing right by you, would you?
You gave Ralston and Richie *everything*... It's time for *you*
now... And as for that Ralston... I'm going to phone him and
deal with him... 'You and his father are not good together'...
What nonsense...

Kira
(Laughs)
Leave my son alone... He's says he's going to Cape Verde for
Christmas... with Tarina and some friends...

Morowa
Oh, so Tarina's back on the scene? Those two, eh...

Kira
I don't think they can do without each other...

Morowa
So they've resolved the sickle cell issue?

Kira
That wasn't really the main reason they broke up... but anyway

we've talked about that... at length actually... and he was telling me that apart from the techniques that can probably help them, if and when the time comes that they may want to start a family... they'll look into other options like adoption, or surrogacy and stuff like that...

Morowa
Aha... good...

Kira
He actually reminded me a bit of his father... QC used to say, you don't marry just to have children...

Morowa
But come oh... do you see? Ralston is sorting his own life out... overcoming whatever obstacles to be with Tarina... Why can't he let you do the same? So left to him, you should be over here, languishing in the cold, on your own this Christmas, whilst they go and sun themselves in Cape Verde? He's being selfish... that's all... You're wasting time... when you tell him you're pregnant and he's going to have a baby brother or sister, he'll come to his senses...

Kira
What? I think you're just desperate to see a baby born with a beard and moustache, or something like that...

(They laugh)

Morowa
How? What do you mean?

Kira
So what do you think QC and I are likely to come up with at this time of our lives, for God's sake? Look, let's leave babies and all that to Ralston, Tarina & Co now...

Morowa
You don't know what's happening... go on the internet... women in their seventies and eighties are having babies...

Kira
I refuse to even imagine... Look, for one, what will the poor mite drink? I didn't have much milk when I was breastfeeding the boys all those years ago... not to talk of now...

Morowa
Is that your problem? Don't worry about that... Trust me... after the baby sucks blood a couple of times, the milk will start to flow eventually... that's what happens...

Kira
Ehn? Says who, Moro?

Morowa
Ask anybody...

Kira
Ask 'anybody'? Ask them *what*? Exactly what question am I supposed to ask? Please God, help my sister Moro... she's gone from bad to worse... and well on the way to critical now...

(They laugh)

Morowa
Look, you may not realise it yourself, but you seem so much more relaxed nowadays... sort of at peace... I'm telling you... And it's down to you and QC sorting yourselves out... seriously...

Kira
If you say so...

Morowa
I *know* so...

Kira
Anyway, enough about me and my blood-sucking baby... I'm
just so happy you're on the mend and clearly getting back to
your old feisty self... and in time for Christmas as well...

Morowa
I'm still a bit shaky, but I'm getting there... You know, when I
was in hospital, with my life really hanging in the balance, I had
so much time to think about many things... in fact everything...
At one time I really thought the game was up for me...

Kira
Which game was that? And who was playing with you anyway?

(They laugh)

Morowa
Seriously... You know when they were struggling to find a
match for my transplant?

Kira
Oh, that was rough... Let me tell you... one time I came to visit
you, Sonny was sitting in the hospital corridor, more or less
talking to himself... I sat down right next to him for a good few
minutes before he realised it was me...

Morowa
You're joking...

Kira
I'm telling you... I must remember to tease him about that...

(They laugh)

Morowa

By the way, thanks for registering... as a bone marrow donor...

Kira

It was the least I could do... And the thing is, there's nothing to really worry about... it's quite a straightforward process... more or less pain-free... I wouldn't hesitate to do it again... I've sent the information and details on how to register to everybody I know... even at work...

Morowa

Thank you... And Kukua and Debbie say they're going to try to start a campaign on social media to encourage black people to become donors...

Kira

That's a very good idea... All hands are on deck... everybody just wants you to get firmly back on your feet... we want the old you back... an upgraded version if possible, if you know what I mean...

(They laugh)

Morowa

Have no fear... I'm well on the way back... new and improved...

Kira

Me and you... we need to be in top form... we've got plenty to do...

Morowa

And see... and talk about...

Kira

Oh yes... there's plenty stuff in the pipeline... For starters, as soon as you're up to it, we're going for a belated birthday treat...

Morowa
Look, when they scheduled my transplant therapy to start on my birthday, I didn't know what to think...

Kira
But all went well, so what better birthday present could you have asked for, eh? And you'll be pleased to know I've found a few places we need to go check out, where we can probably start running our black history workshop from...

Morowa
Oh really? That's good...

Kira
Actually, QC has access to a few premises he says we could use, but I'm not too keen...

Morowa
Why? They're no good?

Kira
Why did I open my big mouth and tell you this? Moro, let's keep business and pleasure separate, if you know what I mean... I don't want QC's charity in this case...

Morowa
How is that charity? So if Sonny does something for us, which of course he will have to if and when we get going... and for free, of course... will there be a problem with that?

Kira
Sonny is your *husband*...

Morowa
And QC is your what, for God's sake? Or am I missing something here?

Kira

Look, I'm not seeing him as my husband... well not just yet anyway... It's like we've just met, sort of... just going out... seeing each other... boyfriend girlfriend style... and I'm enjoying things just the way they are now... thank you...

Morowa

OK, I hear you... Anyway, talking about charity... you sent me something about some special project?

Kira

Oh yes... Makwanoo... that's a charity with a twist... Someone sent it to me, and I thought: 'Ah... Moro will like this... it's like you... it's 'different'...

Morowa

So how am I different?

Kira

(Laughs)

Ask me... Look, just check it out and you'll see exactly what I mean... It's something else we could look into next year...

Morowa

If we get the time... cos I think next year's going to be quite busy for us... I'll have a look at the website anyway... You know everything just seems to be in the right place and heading in the right direction for me now... A brush with death makes you appreciate life and the things that really matter... I'm so content now and just looking forward to the future...

Kira

That's all we want for ourselves... and each other... for things to be in the right place, so we can actually look forward to a few good tomorrows...

Morowa

One thing I know I have to do, is stop worrying so much...
particularly about the girls... I've realised you can't rush or push
anything... Sonny keeps telling me they know what they're doing
and that they'll be just fine...

Kira

Hold it right there... if you say the Two Rs, as you call them, are
not '*boys*', how can Kukua and Debbie be '*girl*s'?

Morowa

OK... you got me there... you've scored your point...

(They laugh)

Kira

But seriously, the thing is, if you try rushing or pushing these
young folk, they may push you right back... And don't forget,
they're younger, so they've got much more strength and
stamina... so you're likely to end up worse off if any pushing
goes on... Look, all we can do is pray for our children... pray
that they make the right decisions, meet the right people and live
good, happy lives...

Morowa

Amen... And by God's grace, they all will... Hmmm... Look at
Rotimi, who I was ready to throw on the scrapheap...

Kira

And set alight, if you'd had the chance...

(They laugh)

Morowa

Look, I must confess, I've done an about face turn... I told you
the role he played the day I was taken into hospital... Without
him that day, I don't know what we would've done... Ah... I'll

never forget... And when I was actually admitted, he came to visit me a good few times, and I got to know him a bit better... He told me so much about himself... He's so funny... He says he never ceases to be amused by the shock on people's faces when they hear his name, talk to him, crack jokes and all in Yoruba... and then realise he can't speak Yoruba that well...

Kira

He can't? Really? I always thought that Nigerians make that extra effort to make their children speak their language... particularly the Yorubas... some of their children born here speak the language so well... very impressive...

Morowa

The thing is: his father is Yoruba... but his mother is half Igbo, half Hausa...

Kira

Oh... he's a proper son of the Nigerian soil...

Morowa

That's what I told him... And he was born here in the UK... but from the age of 2, he went to live with his Hausa grandparents in northern Nigeria, so he speaks Hausa fluently... He came back to join his parents over here when he was about 12...

Kira

OK... The thing is, a lot of us tend to identify with just one group, but in reality we have blood and family links from all over... My grandmother Ashia was half Gambian, half Burkina... my father's granny came from Nova Scotia... We're all mixed up... or should I say rather, we're all connected...

Morowa

We are... Look, I won't say this out loud, or to anybody else; but I'm a bit ashamed of myself... the way I judged the poor boy... I didn't know *anything* as such about him, apart from the fact that

he's a Nigerian... The thing is, I didn't *want* to know anything...
I didn't give him a chance... I just put the barriers right up...
May God forgive me...

Kira
I have to say, the first time I saw Rotimi, I was a bit confused
too... I thought to myself: is this the chap Moro says has bad
luck and wahala, etc, etc, written all over him? Where's the
page, where's the writing? I wasn't expecting what I saw...
Here was this very charming young man... so well-groomed...
And even the beard... it was just some stubble... but really nice...
he could easily be a male model... but you made it sound like he
had some forest on his face... I remember you saying you
weren't even sure whether he had any teeth... Oh Moro...

(They laugh)

Morowa
Forget all that... I've asked for forgiveness... Debbie says he
treats her so well... all the time... And apparently he can cook...
maybe because his granny raised him... She's says he's so
caring... and I can't lie... when I got to know him a bit better,
that's the impression I got too... he really is a nice young man...

Kira
To be honest, I even prefer him to Liam...

Morowa
Oh definitely... let's face it... that Liam was a bit on the cocky
side... a bit too sure of himself...

Kira
Well exactly... So I take it Rotimi's not 419 any more?

Morowa
419? That number rings a bell, but... remind me... what's that

again? You know I'm no good with figures... words yes... but I struggle with figures...

(They laugh)

Morowa
Look, me and my son, Rotimi... nothing is going to come between us... there's no looking back... we're moving forward...

Kira
Your *'son'*? So he can call you 'mummy' now?

(They laugh)

Kira
See? So Kukua was right after all... he *is* a nice fellow... Talking about Nigerians and numbers... the thing about them is, there's a lot of them...

Morowa
Oh yes... plenty... The thing is, Nigeria is a big, big place... it's the most populous country in Africa... I think their population is over 200 million ... or something like that...

Kira
That's a serious number... My country could fit into that about ten times...

Morowa
Easily... If I'm not mistaken, the country that comes next to it in terms of population, is Ethiopia... and it's population is only about *half* of that... so you're bound to find a Nigerian in almost every African situation... you can't escape them... They're everywhere... good and bad...

Kira
But of course, it's the *bad* stories and the *dodgy* ones that the media are more interested in, so those are the ones we hear about

all the time... Someone was arguing one time that Nigeria doesn't have more criminals, or corruption, or anything else for that matter, than any other country per se... It's just that they're such a massive country with so many people... So if you have to make a comparison, pro rata, between them and most other countries about *anything*... they're bound to have more... more dodgy people, more crooks and criminals... but by the same token, they'll also have more top scientists, big-time business-men and people like that...

Morowa
That must be right... But look, bottom line... a lot of people just have this very negative image and perception of Nigerians... even fear, to be honest...

Kira
True... we tend to have some kind of tolerance and understanding for other people; but because of their image, we always think the worst when it come to Nigerians... reluctant to give them the benefit of the doubt, if there's any issue... If you think about it though, you just have to feel sorry for the millions and millions of ordinary, regular, decent Nigerians out there, who've all been painted with the same brush... always treated with suspicion, and fear, and stuff like that... It must be horrible...

Morowa
But that's just the way it is... Look, Nigeria's supposed to be the giant of not just *West* Africa...but the *whole* of Africa... so if *they* can't sort themselves and their image out... then please...

Kira
The sad reality is, Nigerians, like *all* Africans, are victims of dodgy leadership... that's what it all boils down to... And as we say, everything about them seems a bit exaggerated... sort of out of proportion... because of their sheer size...

Morowa
Look, you know what, I don't want to know about those plenty,
plenty Nigerians and their problems now... I just know about
one... just one... my dear Rotimi...

(They laugh)

Morowa
Apparently he told Debbie that he could see that I was very wary
of him...

Kira
Oh, poor chap...

Morowa
But he told her would win me over... if it was the last thing he
did...

Kira
And he obviously has...

Morowa
He has oh... Look, as I say, we're putting the past way behind
us... just like you and QC... Let's all just move forward and
enjoy life and each other...

Kira
I've told you, it's slowly, slowly with QC...

Morowa
You can keep taking things as slowly, slowly as you like...
QC told me that even though technically you're not divorced, he
wants you two to sort of 'remarry'... renew your vows... as soon
as possible... Look, don't waste time... just do it...

Kira
You know what, I must put a full stop to this free for all
communication between you and QC... I'm going to tell him to
block you... and I think I should do the same...

Morowa
That's right... that's gratitude for you... So you and QC now want to gang up on me and throw me to the wolves? I see... After everything I've done... put myself at personal risk and all... just to ensure a happy outcome for you both... Instead of asking me to be the flower-girl for the renewal or 're-wedding' or whatever, this is what I get... Thank you very much...

(They laugh)

Morowa
Oh, and Kukua has good news too... all being well, she'll be opening the cake shop, hopefully at the end of January... She's calling it KK... Kukua's Kakes... Look, she can do the 'vow renewal' cake for you guys...

(They laugh)

Kukua
She'll do well... she's really talented... Look at that cake she did for Omar...

Morowa
That was just a small one... If you see the one she did for her friend, Lisa, not too long ago... six tiers... out of this world... She got so many orders after people saw that cake...

Kira
The only thing I'll advise her, is to run her shop as professionally as possible... We black folks always whinge about not supporting each other in business... and it's not that some of us just don't want to...

Morowa
I know you don't have too much time for black businesses...

Kira
It's not that... our people need to step up their game... they really

do... Sometimes we have some very good products, ideas, concepts, what have you... but professionalism and discipline... that's where we fall short... all the time... Sometimes the business won't be open on time... poor customer service... tacky layout and stuff... Sometimes they look at you funny when you enter the premises... They give you that look that only black people know how to give...

Morowa
Oh yes... The look that makes you genuinely forget what you went into the shop for in the first place...

(They laugh)

Morowa
Sometimes they won't let you inspect the stuff properly... it's like the moment you touch anything, you can't put it down again; you have to buy it... And if you dare point out one or two of these things to them, or make any constructive criticism that they may not quite like, that could be it... you're now their enemy...

Kira
Look, I will not patronise black people just for the sake of it... If things are up to scratch, up to a standard... why won't we proudly support and happily recommend to others?

Morowa
But there are some good black businesses out there...

Kira
Of course there are... in fact there are some *excellent* ones... but it's like they're few and far between... like you have to go out of your way to find them... The point is this: there's so much competition from everybody else out there, and we're a minority... so we just can't afford not to measure up... because it's not about attracting just *black* people to our businesses... we need *everybody*...

Morowa
Well this is it... Anyway, you know Kukua's quite fussy... she likes things just right... She will insist on the highest of standards when it comes to her products and staff and setup... everything... I can tell you that for free... She's already got an accountant and a couple of professional bakers... I haven't been to the premises yet... but Sonny and Debbie say it's superb...

Kira
Well as long as she sets and maintains a high standard... coupled with that talent she's got... she can't go wrong...

Morowa
She's worked too hard and invested a whole lot to get this far... she's got too much to lose... For the past six months or so, I don't think she's had a free weekend... she supplies about ten or twelve cafés and restaurants with cakes and stuff... every week...

Kira
You said so... that's a serious commitment, you know...

Morowa
Oh yes... and that's alongside her regular job... She said to me, 'Mum, I'm starting small, but I'm thinking big'... She says she wants to build a brand... hopefully expand...

Kira
Good girl... she's thinking long term... another thing we black people don't seem to be able to do when it comes to business... With us, it's like one generation and the business is completely over... kaput...

Morowa
A generation? Do they even last that long? Some of the businesses are doomed right from the word 'go', because we don't set them up properly or seriously in the first place... For starters, instead of getting the right staff, we think we're being

clever and cutting costs by employing friends and relatives...
usually clueless ones... So of course, if you're not careful, before
you know it, they run the business into the ground in no time...
So it's all over before it even had the chance to start properly...

Kira
Then what really gets me is: when everything collapses, we start
looking round... all baffled and confused... as if we just can't
believe how or why things went wrong... As you say, we don't
seem to understand that we have to put sentiment aside and
employ the *right* people... we have to maintain standards... keep
proper accounts... re-invest... All these things are vital for the
success of a business... but it's like we see them as optional...

Morowa
No, I agree with you wholeheartedly, we really need to wake and
shape up... But if anybody can do it, it's Kukua...

Kira
And it really is high time some of these our young people do
some *serious* business... I don't know about your people, but
when we were growing up, we were actively discouraged from
doing business... it was sort of looked down on...

Morowa
Similar story... the emphasis was always on education... books,
books, books... read, read, read... And we've done that... no
harm... but now I think it's time for some money, money, money
for a change... And to change things for ourselves as a people...
to help ourselves... we need as much money as possible...

Kira
True... you can't do much with an empty purse... But then again,
money isn't everything...

Morowa
And pray tell, how would *you* know?

Kira
What?

Morowa
Only people who've had money can say that, one way or the other... It's only poor people who come up with that line all the time... obviously to console themselves...

(They laugh)

Morowa
Anyway, Kukua wants Sonny and I to have a meal with her and her accountant... I've met him once... he appears quite nice... She talks about him all the time, but she says it's strictly business...

Kira
But let me guess... Aunty Moro, the matchmaker, sees a possible future here...

Morowa
(Laughs)
When I asked a few questions about him, I got a good mouthful from her... she put me straight: she told me not every man she meets is a potential boyfriend... and that I can forget about her having any serious relationship or anything like that, until her business is up, running and booming...

Kira
Well, you've been cautioned...

(They laugh)

Morowa
And last but not least... I have the final proof now that you just don't check your emails...
(Sings)
Three is the magic number... I'm in the last three...

Kira

Last three... of what?

Morowa

The competition you forced me to enter...

Kira

You've won? I knew it! I told you!

Morowa

Calm down, you're not listening... I said I'm in the last three... They sent me an email... I forwarded it on to you... They say they'll make the final decision on Christmas Eve...

Kira

Look, even the third prize is a few thousand dollars... and that's worst case scenario now... But you know what, there's no way you came third... you didn't come second either, I'm telling you... I don't know about you, but my bags are already packed... Safari here we come!

Morowa

But wait oh... Sonny may want to go with me as my plus one...

Kira

Well he can't... he cannot... tell him oh... If he insists on going, I'll kill him...

(They laugh)

Kira

I will oh... Does Sonny know what I went through to get you... get *us*... to this point with this play? Where was he when all sorts was going down? From begging, to bribery, to death threats... No... I'm very sorry, but he can't go...

(They laugh)

Kira
(Coughs)

Morowa
This is the first time you've coughed today, you know... The other day, it was like you couldn't stop...

Kira
I think the mere suggestion just now, that I may not go on the safari, must've brought it back on... triggered this reaction...

(They laugh)

Kira
Then again, maybe I have the Chinese flu...

Morowa
Which one is that now?

Kira
I read on the internet that apparently there's some wild flu over there... in Beijing or some place... I've forgotten the name now...

Morowa
Look, there's *always* a story with those Chinese people... What's our business with them, anyway?

Kira
I wonder... All I know is, roll right up 2020... we've got plenty things to do in the new year... Next year is going to be special; I can feel it... Look, even the safari is winking at us now...

(They laugh)

Kira
Seriously, well done for the play... you did well... But do you know you never sent me the final draft before you sent it off?

Morowa
Of course I did... I've just told you; you don't check your email...
In between being wined, dined and God knows what else by
Sir QC Esquire... have you got time to read anything?

(They laugh)

Morowa
Oh, before I forget, you know what I was thinking? About
Lapland... as I won't be able to go... maybe you could go with
someone else?

Kira
Someone else? Who will I find to go with at this eleventh hour?
But guess what? I've got more good news... I was going to wait
for them to confirm things before telling you... but as you've
brought it up... For once I think we're going to reap the benefits
of using the same travel agent for God knows how many years
now... I had a word with them... fingers crossed, we probably
won't lose anything as such... they say they'll credit our money
from this trip towards our next flight or holiday... just minus
some small admin fee of course...

Morowa
Are you serious?

Kira
As I said, it's not fully confirmed, but I think we can relax on
that front...

Morowa
Well that's our Valentine trip sorted... Hmmm... I hope I'll be
well enough to go...

Kira
Oh, by then you'll be in top form... don't worry... And even
Lapland isn't going anywhere... we'll get there eventually...

37   *Monday 23 December*

LOVE AND LEAVE YOU FOR NOW

Morowa
(Sings)
Jingle bells... jingle bells... jingle all the way...

Kira
You sound happy... tell me you've won the competition...

Morowa
But I told you... they say they'll announce the winner on the 24th... tomorrow... I really don't know how I'm going break it to you, and console you if I don't win...

(They laugh)

Kira
I can't believe Christmas is here... again...

Morowa
True... As I can't go food shopping and all that this year, I don't know how Debbie and Kukua managed to rope Sonny in... but he's gone to meet them to finalise things...

Kira
'Finalise'? You mean 'pay for'...

(They laugh)

Kira
Have you seasoned your turkey? I know you season yours for at least four or five days...

Morowa
Not this year... Kukua's sorting that out... I told you she and

Debbie are doing the cooking this Christmas... for a change...

Kira
Lucky you...

Morowa
To be honest, I'm feeling much, much better... but I dare not say that too loudly... because, between me and you, if I stop complaining, I know them... they'll just say 'good... all is well'... and they'll just come and fling the turkey and everything else on me, and I won't see them till Christmas Day... dinner time, to be precise...

(They laugh)

Kira
Actually, me and QC *might* swing by some time tomorrow... *might*... Will you be in?

Morowa
Where am I going?

Kira
I've got your Christmas presents... and QC got you guys something from Australia...

Morowa
Australia? Really? What is it? Tell me...

Kira
Look, at you... like a child... you can't wait... But seriously, it's fully wrapped... he refused to tell me what it is... he said it's not mine... Look, if I'm coming, which soup do you want? I've got potato or cassava leaves? Take your pick...

Morowa
Did I hear you say 'soups'?

Kira

No... you heard me say 'soup'... singular... it's either or... potato or cassava leaves? Which one do you want?

Morowa

And what about your famous homemade mulled wine?

Kira

You know what, I just didn't get round to making any this year... I'm knackered...

Morowa

OK... so let me get this straight: there's no mulled wine, but you want to bring just *one* soup? Who does that? Look, you know I'm recovering, I'm not well... so please don't upset me... You'd better bring both soups if you know what's good for you...

(They laugh)

Kira

Look, it's not definite definite that I'll be coming...

Morowa

No, it is definite definite... believe me... You're definitely coming tomorrow... and you'll definitely be coming with *all* the things we've just discussed: presents from Australia, a variety of soups, etc... Don't try me oh...

(They laugh)

Kira

Me and my big mouth... So apart from waiting for your folks to come back, what are you doing for the rest of the day?

Morowa

Nothing much... I was listening to some reggae Christmas music... in fact I was dancing away when the phone rang... Now,

I think I'm just going to put my feet up, with some port and mince pies, of course... watch some telly and just chill... What else? What are *you* up to?

Kira

Me? I've got quite a few things to sort out... Ralston says he'll be coming with my present at some point... he's off to Cape Verde tomorrow... he says when I see the present I'll scream...

Morowa

Oh-oh... What could *that* be?

Kira

I've been racking my brain... You never can tell with Ralston... Anyway, you know something? If I really know what's good for me, I think I'd better love and leave you for now... lots to do...

Morowa

Oh... before you go, you must hear this... this one is an all round Christmas cracker... Ralston says you'll scream? Trust me... this will make you start screaming before he comes... Remember that hotel where we stayed for that our girls' weekend away in...

(Morowa's other phone rings.)

Morowa

Oh, who is this now? Oh, it's Debbie... let me just answer her quickly... Don't go yet oh, Kira...

(Kira hears Morowa's side of the conversation:
Yes Debbie... I'm fine, but I'm just on the other phone... You say what? How? So what happened? I don't understand... So where are you people now? OK, I'll meet you there... I'll have to call a cab... there's no way I can drive... So what is this now? Ah!)

Kira

Moro, what is it? What's going on? Are you OK?

And that's where we must leave Morowa and Kira... for now...
I hope you've enjoyed their company.

"If you don't like someone's story, write your own."
Chinua Achebe

CHARACTERS *(1)*

Aunty Lois, Morowa's elderly friend
Aunty Mahira, Kira's aunt, her mother's sister
Bartholomew and Penelope, Hope's children
Bev, attends Morowa's church
Bolu, Nish's husband
Brianna, QC's former mistress
Carol, Trevor and 'Granny Five', Morowa's former neighbours
Caspar Danso, Morowa's childhood acquaintance
Celine, Morowa's friend
Debbie, Morowa's daughter
Deji, Mama Razia's nephew
Dorle Cia, television talk show personality
Efa, Sonny's sister
Elmy, Milly's son, Rocco's brother
Faisal, Kira's brother
Gavin, an acquaintance of Morowa and Kira's
Goliath and Gulliver Jenkins, twins Kira came across at work
Grandma Ashia, Kira's grandmother
Greg, Mama Abena's nephew
Hauwa, Mama Razia's niece
Hope, Morowa's childhood friend
James, an acquaintance of Kira's
Joel, Morowa's pastor
Justice Otto Dighton, a judge
Kojo, an acquaintance of Morowa and Kira's
Kukua, Morowa's niece and adopted daughter
Leo, Sonny's friend
Liam, Debbie's former boyfriend
'Liquid & Fluid', a family friend of Morowa's
Lisa, Kukua's friend
Lola, a friend of Morowa and Kira's
Makeda and Mukaya, clients Kira came across at work
Mama Abena, Morowa's elderly friend
Mama Razia, Bolu's mother
Mr Yeboah, Kira's teacher
Mrs Osei, attends Morowa's church

CHARACTERS *(2)*

Nish (Nausha), Kira's younger sister
Omar, Nish's son
Pa Die-Go, Kira's after school lesson teacher
Pa Magwa, Morowa's grand-uncle
PC Cole, Mama Razia's neighbour
Pearlette, attends Morowa's church
QC, Kira's husband
Racquel, Kira's friend
Ralston, Kira's older son
Richie, Kira's younger son
Rocco, Elmy's brother, Milly's son
Rotimi, Debbie's boyfriend
Salma, Kira's older sister
Sizani, Morowa's friend
Sonny, Morowa's husband
Susannah, Pa Die-Go's assistant
Tarina, Ralston's girlfriend
Travis Gulliver, Morowa's student
Wusi, Morowa's younger sister
Yaa, Morowa's, older brother

MISCELLANEOUS AFRICAN WORDS

Ankara, a type of fabric
Ashoebi, uniform attire, usually African fabric, worn at special occasions
Banku, fermented corn and cassava dough
Egusi, ground melon seeds
Gari, dried and grated cassava
Jollof rice, popular West African dish
Kelewele, seasoned and spiced fried plantains
Kenkey, fermented corn meal
Kente, traditional fabric
Oyibo, foreign, mainly European
Shito, hot pepper
Waakye, rice dish
Wahala, trouble, problem(s)